THE POISONED CROWN

BY MAURICE DRUON

The Accursed Kings

The Iron King

The Strangled Queen

The Poisoned Crown

The Royal Succession

The She-Wolf

The Lily and the Lion

The King Without a Kingdom

THE POISONED CROWN

Book Three of The Accursed Kings

MAURICE DRUON

Translated from French by
Humphrey Hare

HarperCollins*Publishers*

HarperCollins*Publishers*
77–85 Fulham Palace Road,
Hammersmith, London W6 8JB

www.harpercollins.co.uk

First published in French as *Les Poisons de la Couronne*
First published in Great Britain by Rupert Hart-Davis 1957
Pan edition 1970
Arrow edition 1988

Published by HarperCollins*Publishers* 2013
1

A catalogue record for this book
is available from the British Library

ISBN: 978-0-00-749130-8

This novel is entirely a work of fiction.
The names, characters and incidents portrayed in it,
while at times based on historical figures, are the
work of the author's imagination.

Printed and bound in Great Britain by
Clays Ltd, St Ives plc

MIX
Paper from
responsible sources
FSC® C007454

FSC is a non-profit international organization established
to promote the responsible management of the world's forests.
Products carrying the FSC label are independently certified
to assure consumers that they come from forests that are managed
to meet the social, economic and ecological needs
of present and future generations.

Find out more about HarperCollins and the environment at
www.harpercollins.co.uk/green

'History is a novel that has been lived'
E. & J. de Goncourt

'It is terrifying to think how much research is needed to determine the truth of even the most unimportant fact'
Stendhal

Foreword

GEORGE R.R. MARTIN

Over the years, more than one reviewer has described my fantasy series, *A Song of Ice and Fire*, as historical fiction about history that never happened, flavoured with a dash of sorcery and spiced with dragons. I take that as a compliment. I have always regarded historical fiction and fantasy as sisters under the skin, two genres separated at birth. My own series draws on both traditions . . . and while I undoubtedly drew much of my inspiration from Tolkien, Vance, Howard, and the other fantasists who came before me, *A Game of Thrones* and its sequels were also influenced by the works of great historical novelists like Thomas B. Costain, Mika Waltari, Howard Pyle . . . and Maurice Druon, the amazing French writer who gave us the *The Accursed Kings*, seven splendid novels that chronicle the downfall of the Capetian kings and the beginnings of the Hundred Years War.

Druon's novels have not been easy to find, especially in English translation (and the seventh and final volume was never translated into English at all). The series has *twice* been made into a television series in France, and both versions are available on DVD . . . but only in French, undubbed, and without English subtitles. Very frustrating for English-speaking Druon fans like me.

The Accursed Kings has it all. Iron kings and strangled queens, battles and betrayals, lies and lust, deception, family rivalries, the curse of the Templars, babies switched at birth, she-wolves, sin, and swords, the doom of a great dynasty . . . and all of it (well, most of it) straight from the pages of history. And believe me, the Starks and the Lannisters have nothing on the Capets and Plantagenets.

Whether you're a history buff or a fantasy fan, Druon's epic will keep you turning pages. This was the original game of thrones. If you like *A Song of Ice and Fire*, you will love *The Accursed Kings*.

George R.R. Martin

Author's Acknowledgements

I am most grateful to Georges Kessel, Edmonde Charles-Roux, Christiane Grémillon, and Pierre de Lacretelle for the assistance they have given me with the material of this book; to Huguette Roman for her help in compiling it; and to the *Bibliothèque Nationale* in Paris and the Municipal Library of Florence for indispensable aid in research.

Contents

The Characters in this Book xiii

Family Tree xvi

The Poisoned Crown xix

Prologue xxi

Part One: France Awaits a Queen

1 Farewell to Naples 3

2 The Storm 11

3 The Hôtel-Dieu 18

4 Portents of Disaster 27

5 The King Receives the Oriflamme 35

6 The Muddy Army 43

7 The Philtre 63

8 A Country Wedding 76

Part Two: After Flanders, Artois

1 The Insurgents 95
2 The Countess of Poitiers 101
3 The Second Couple in the Kingdom 114
4 A Servant's Friendship 125
5 The Fork and the Prie-dieu 140
6 Arbitration 150

Part Three: The Time of the Comet

1 The New Master of Neauphle 167
2 Dame Eliabel's Reception 176
3 The Midnight Marriage 185
4 The Comet 198
5 The Cardinal's Spell 204
6 'I Assume Control of Artois' 217
7 In the King's Absence 230
8 The Monk is Dead 237
9 Mourning Comes to Vincennes 251
10 Tolomei Prays for the King 260
11 Who is to be Regent? 267

Historical Notes 279

The Characters in this Book

THE KING OF FRANCE AND NAVARRE:

LOUIS X, called THE HUTIN, great-grandson of Saint Louis, son of Philip IV, the Fair, and of Jeanne of Navarre, widower of Marguerite of Burgundy, aged 26.

HIS SECOND WIFE:

CLÉMENCE OF HUNGARY, a descendant of a brother of Saint Louis, granddaughter of Charles II of Anjou-Sicily and of Marie of Hungary, daughter of Charles Martel and sister of Charobert, King of Hungary, niece of King Robert of Naples, aged 22.

HIS BROTHERS:

MONSEIGNEUR PHILIPPE, Count of Poitiers, Count Palatine of Burgundy, Lord of Salins, Peer of the Kingdom, future Philip V, aged 22.

MONSEIGNEUR CHARLES, Count de la Marche, future Charles IV, aged 21.

THE VALOIS BRANCH:

MONSEIGNEUR CHARLES, brother of Philip the Fair, Count of Valois, Titular Emperor of Constantinople, Count of Romagna, Peer of the Kingdom, the King's uncle, aged 45.

PHILIPPE OF VALOIS, son of the above, future Philip VI, aged 22.

THE EVREUX BRANCH:

MONSEIGNEUR LOUIS, brother of Philip the Fair, Count of Evreux, the King's uncle, aged about 42.

THE ARTOIS BRANCH, DESCENDANTS OF A BROTHER OF SAINT LOUIS:

ROBERT III OF ARTOIS, Seigneur of Conches, Count of Beaumont-le-Roger, aged 28.

THE COUNTESS MAHAUT OF ARTOIS, his aunt, widow of the Count Palatine Othon IV of Burgundy, Peer of the Kingdom, aged about 41.

JEANNE OF BURGUNDY, daughter of Mahaut and wife of the Count Philippe of Poitiers, the King's brother, aged about 22.

THE GREAT OFFICERS OF THE CROWN:

ETIENNE DE MORNAY, a Canon, Chancellor of the Kingdom.

GAUCHER DE CHÂTILLON, the Constable.

MATHIEU DE TRYE, Grand Chamberlain to Louis X.

HUGUES DE BOUVILLE, late Grand Chamberlain to Philip the Fair, Envoy Extraordinary to the King of Naples.

MILES DES NOYERS, a Justiciar, Councillor to Parliament, Knight Banneret to the Count of Poitiers.

THE HIRSON FAMILY:

THIERRY, a Canon, Provost of Ayré, Chancellor to the Countess Mahaut.

DENIS, his brother, Treasurer to the Countess Mahaut.

BEATRICE, their niece, Lady-in-Waiting to the Countess Mahaut.

THE LOMBARDS:

SPINELLO TOLOMEI, a Siennese banker established in Paris.

GUCCIO BAGLIONI, his nephew, aged about 19.

THE CRESSAY FAMILY:

DAME ELIABEL, widow of the Lord of Cressay, aged about 41.

PIERRE and JEAN, her sons, aged 21 and 23.

MARIE, her daughter, aged 17.

THE TEMPLARS:

JEAN DE LONGWY, nephew of the last Grand Master.

EVERARD, clerk, an ex-Knight Templar.

AND THESE:

QUEEN MARIE OF HUNGARY, widow of Charles II of Anjou-Sicily, called The Lame, and mother of King Robert of Naples, grandmother of Clémence of Hungary, aged about 70.

CARDINAL JACQUES DUÈZE, Cardinal of the Curia. The future Pope John XXII, aged about 70.

EUDELINE, Louis X's first mistress.

THE REBELLIOUS ARTOIS BARONS:

CAUMONT, FIENNES, GUIGNY, JOURNY, KENTY, KIEREZ, LIQUES, LONGVILLERS, LOOS, NÉDONCHEL, SOUASTRE, SAINT-VENANT, AND VARENNES.

All the above names have their place in history.

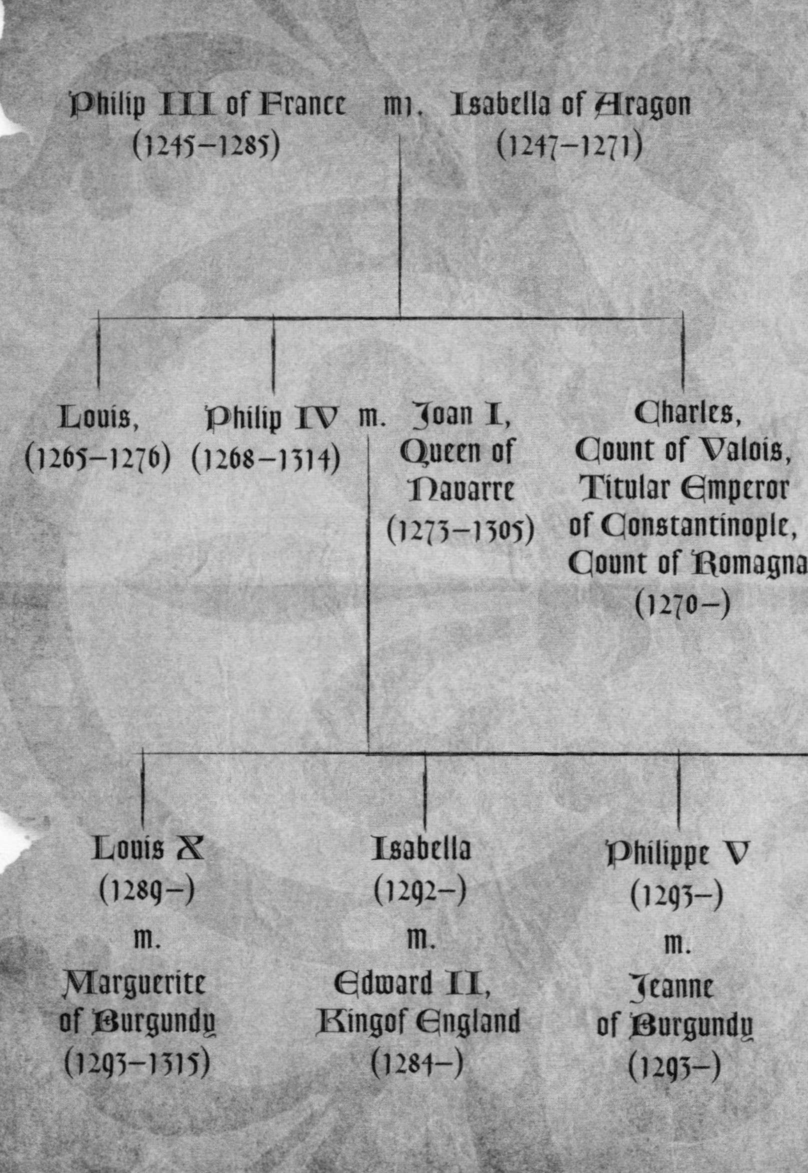
Philip III of France
(1245–1285)
m1.
Isabella of Aragon
(1247–1271)
Louis,
(1265–1276)
Philip IV
(1268–1314)
m.
Joan I,
Queen of
Navarre
(1273–1305)
Charles,
Count of Valois,
Titular Emperor
of Constantinople,
Count of Romagna
(1270–)
Louis X
(1289–)
m.
Marguerite
of Burgundy
(1293–1315)
Isabella
(1292–)
m.
Edward II,
Kingof England
(1284–)
Philippe V
(1293–)
m.
Jeanne
of Burgundy
(1293–)

m2. Marie of Brabant
(1254–1321)

Louis Capet,
Count of Evereux
(1276–)

Blanche
(1278–1305)

Margaret
of France
(1282–)

Charles IV
(1294–)
m.
Blanche
of Burgundy
(1296–)

The House of Capet 1315

The Poisoned Crown

Standing at one of the windows in the huge Castelnuovo, which had a view over the port and bay of Naples, the old Queen Mother, Marie of Hungary, watched a ship weighing anchor. Making sure that no one could see her, she wiped a tear from the corner of a lashless eyelid with a roughened finger.

'Now I can die,' she murmured . . .

For her dearly loved Clémence, a princess of twenty-two without territorial inheritance, rich only in her reputation for beauty and virtue, she had recently obtained the most important of alliances, the most imposing of marriages. Clémence was leaving to become Queen of France. Thus she, who was the most deprived by fate of all the princesses of Anjou, who had waited the longest for a match, was now to receive the finest of kingdoms and to reign as suzerain over all her relations. It clearly illustrated the teaching of the Gospel.

Prologue

PHILIP THE FAIR HAD been dead six months. To the government of that remarkable monarch France owed the benefits of a long period of peace, the abandonment of disastrous overseas adventures, the organization of a powerful network of alliances and suzerainties, notable increases of territory by union rather than conquest, a definite economic expansion and a relative stability of currency, the non-interference of the Church in temporal affairs, the control of wealth and large private interests, the expression of the voice of the people in the councils of power, the security of the individual, and the organization of State administration.

His contemporaries were naturally not always very conscious of these ameliorations. Progress has never meant perfection. Some years were less prosperous than others, there were periods of crisis and revolution; the needs of the people were far from being satisfied. The Iron King had methods of making himself obeyed which were not to everyone's taste; and he was more concerned with the grandeur of his Kingdom than with the individual happiness of his subjects.

Nevertheless, when he died, France was the foremost, wealthiest, and most powerful of all the nations of the western world.

It took his successors thirty years of perseverance to destroy his work, and, inordinate ambition alternating upon the throne with extreme incompetence, to open the country to invasion, deliver society over to anarchy, and reduce the population to the lowest condition of misery and despair.

In the long succession of vain imbeciles who, from Louis X, The Hutin, to Jean the Good inclusive, were to wear the crown, there was to be but one exception: Philippe V, the Long, second son of Philip the Fair, who returned to the methods and principles of his father – even though his passion for reigning led him to commit crimes and invent dynastic laws which led directly to the Hundred Years War.

The processes of decay were therefore to continue during a third of a century, but it must be admitted that a great part of the destruction was completed during the first six months.

Institutions were not sufficiently stable to be able to function without the personal intervention of the sovereign.

The feeble, nervous, and incompetent Louis X, overwhelmed from the very first day by the magnitude of his task, resigned the cares of power to his uncle, Charles of Valois, who was, it appears, a good soldier though a detestable politician, who spent his whole life searching for a throne and had now, at last, found an outlet for his turbulent blundering.

The middle-class ministers, who had been the backbone of

the preceding reign, had been imprisoned, and the skeleton of the most remarkable of them all, Enguerrand de Marigny, once Rector-General of the Kingdom, was bleaching on the forks of the gibbet of Montfaucon.

Reaction was triumphant; the Barons' Leagues were sowing disorder in the provinces and subverting the royal authority. The great Lords, Charles of Valois at their head, minted their own currency which they circulated throughout the country to their own personal profit. The Administration, no longer held in check, became corrupt, and the Treasury was empty.

A disastrous harvest, followed by an exceptionally hard winter, caused famine. The death-rate was rising.

During this time Louis X had been mainly preoccupied with repairing his domestic honour and endeavouring to efface, if it were possible, the scandal of the Tower of Nesle.

For lack of a Pope, whom the Conclave seemed unable to elect, and who was required for the purpose of pronouncing an annulment, the young King of France, so that he might remarry, had had his wife, Marguerite of Burgundy, strangled in the prison of Château-Gaillard.

Thus he became free to marry the beautiful Neapolitan Princess who had been found for him, and with whom he was making preparations to share the felicities of a long reign.*

---

* The end of Philip the Fair's reign and the beginning of Louis X's are dealt with in the two first volumes of *The Accursed Kings*: *The Iron King* and *The Strangled Queen*.

PART ONE

FRANCE AWAITS A QUEEN

I

Farewell to Naples

STANDING AT ONE OF the windows in the huge Castelnuovo, which had a view over the port and bay of Naples, the old Queen Mother, Marie of Hungary, watched a ship weighing anchor. Making sure that no one could see her, she wiped a tear from the corner of a lashless eyelid with a roughened finger.

'Now I can die,' she murmured.

She had lived a full life. Daughter of a king, wife of a king, mother and grandmother of kings, she had settled one branch of her descendants upon the throne of central Italy, and obtained for the other, by war and intrigue, the Kingdom of Hungary, which she looked upon as her personal heritage. Her younger sons were princes or sovereign dukes. Two of her daughters were queens, one of Majorca, the other of Aragon. Her fecundity had been a means to power for the Anjou-Sicily family, a cadet branch of the Capet tree, which was now beginning to spread across all Europe, threatening to become as great as its trunk.

If Marie of Hungary had already lost six of her children she had at least the consolation of knowing that they had died as piously as she had brought them up; indeed, one of them, who had renounced his dynastic rights to enter the Church, was shortly to be canonized. As if the Kingdoms of this world were too narrow for this expanding family, the old Queen had dispatched her progeny to the Kingdom of Heaven. She was the mother of a Saint.[1*]

At over seventy she had but one duty left to fulfil and that was to assure the future of one of her granddaughters, Clémence, the orphan. This had now been achieved.

Because Clémence was the daughter of her eldest son, Charles Martel, for whom she had so persistently laid claim to the throne of Hungary, because the child had been orphaned at two years of age, because she herself had assumed entire responsibility for her education, and because finally this task was the last of her life, Marie of Hungary had held the girl in particular affection, in so far as a capacity for affection existed in that old heart, subordinated as it was to force, duty, and power.

The great ship, which was weighing anchor in the harbour upon this brilliantly sunny day of the first of June 1315, represented to the eyes of the Queen Mother of Naples both the triumph of her policy and the melancholy of things achieved.

For her dearly loved Clémence, a princess of twenty-two without territorial inheritance, rich only in her reputation

* The numbers in the text refer to historical notes at the end of the book.

for beauty and virtue, she had recently obtained the most important of alliances, the most imposing of marriages. Clémence was leaving to become Queen of France. Thus she, who was the most deprived by fate of all the princesses of Anjou, who had waited the longest for a match, was now to receive the finest of kingdoms and to reign as suzerain over all her relations. It clearly illustrated the teaching of the Gospel.

It was, of course, true that the young King of France, Louis X, was reputed to be neither particularly handsome of face nor pleasant of character.

'But what does that matter? My husband, upon whom God have mercy, was excessively lame, but I succeeded, without much difficulty, in reconciling myself to the fact,' thought Marie of Hungary. 'Moreover, one does not become a queen in order to find happiness.'

People wondered, in covert whispers, that Queen Marguerite should have died in her prison so opportunely, just when King Louis, for the lack of a Pope, was unable to obtain an annulment of his marriage. But need one listen to scandal? Marie of Hungary was little inclined to waste pity upon a woman, particularly upon a Queen, who had betrayed her marriage vows and provided from such an exalted position so reprehensible an example. She saw nothing for surprise in the fact that God's punishment should so naturally have fallen upon the scandalous Marguerite.

'My beautiful Clémence will restore virtue to a place of honour in the Court of Paris,' she told herself.

In a gesture of farewell she made the sign of the Cross upon the window with her grey hand; then, her crown resting upon her silver hair, her chin jerking with a tic, her walk stiff but still firm, she retired to her chapel to thank the Lord for having helped her to the accomplishment of her long royal mission and to offer up to God the deep unhappiness of all women who have come to the end of their earthly task.

In the meantime, the *San Giovanni*, the great ship with a round hull entirely painted in white and gold and flying from her mast and yards the pennants of Anjou, Hungary, and France, was beginning to tack away from the shore. The captain and his crew had sworn upon the Bible to defend their passengers against storm, Barbary pirates, and all the perils of the sea. The statue of Saint John the Baptist, the patron of the ship, shone in the sun upon the prow. In the fore- and after-castles, half as high as the masts, a hundred men-at-arms, look-outs, archers, and slingers were at their posts to repel the attacks of pirates. The holds were overflowing with provisions, and the sand of the ballast had been filled with amphorae containing oil, flagons of wine, and fresh eggs. The giant iron-bound chests, holding the silk robes, the jewels, the gold plate, and all the princess's wedding presents, were stacked against the bulkhead of the saloon, a vast compartment between the mainmast and the poop where, among oriental carpets, the gentlemen and equerries were to be lodged.

The Neapolitans crowded upon the quays to watch the departure of what appeared to them a ship of good omen. Women held up their children at arms' length. Through the loud murmur rising from the crowd were to be heard shouts, uttered with the noisy good nature with which the populace of Naples has always treated its idols:

'Guardi com' è bella!'
'Addio, Donna Clemenza! Sia felice!'
'Dio la benedica, nostra principessa!'
*'Non si dimentichi di noi!'**

For Donna Clemenza personified a sort of legend to the Neapolitans. They remembered her father, the handsome Carlo Martelo, the friend of poets and in particular of the divine Dante, a learned prince, as good a musician as he was valiant in arms, who travelled the peninsula, followed by two hundred French, Provençal, and Italian gentlemen, all dressed, as he was himself, half in scarlet and half in green, their horses caparisoned in silver and gold. It was said of him that he was a true son of Venus, for he possessed 'the five gifts that incite to love and which are health, beauty, wealth, leisure, and youth'. They had looked forward to his becoming king; but he had died of the plague at twenty-four and his wife, a princess of Hapsburg, had expired upon hearing the news, an event which had struck the popular imagination.

Naples had transferred its affection to Clémence who, as she grew up, had developed a likeness to her father. The royal orphan was adored in the poor quarters of the town to which she went to distribute charity; she was invariably affected by distress. Her face inspired the painters of the school of Giotto in their representations of the Virgin and the saints in their

* 'Look how beautiful she is!'
'Goodbye, Madam Clémence! Be happy!'
'May God bless our princess!'
'Don't forget us!'

frescoes; and to this day travellers who visit the churches of Campania and Apulia may admire upon the walls of the sanctuaries the golden hair, the clear gentle eyes, the grace of the slightly curving neck, the long slender hands, without knowing that it is the portrait of the beautiful Clémence of Hungary.

Upon the crenellated deck which covered the after-castle, some thirty feet above the waves, the fiancée of the King of France gazed for the last time upon the land of her childhood, upon the old Castell'Ovo in which she had been born, upon Castelnuovo where she had grown up, upon the swarming crowd who threw her kisses, upon the whole lively, wonderful, dusty scene.

'Thank you, Madam my Grandmother,' she thought, her eyes raised to the window from which the figure of Marie of Hungary had just disappeared. 'I shall doubtless never see you again. Thank you for all you have done for me. Having reached the age of twenty-two, I was in despair at not having yet found a husband; I thought that I should never find one and that I should have to enter a convent. It was you who were right to counsel patience. And now I am to be queen of that great kingdom which is watered by four rivers, and lapped by three seas. My cousin the King of England, my aunt of Majorca, my kinsman of Bohemia, my sister the Crown Princess of Vienna, and even my uncle Robert, who reigns here and whose subject I was till today, will become my vassals for the lands they have in France, or the links they have with that crown. But will it not be too heavy for me?'

She was experiencing at one and the same time joy and

exaltation, fear of the unknown and that peculiar disquiet which comes upon the spirit at an irrevocable change of destiny, even when it surpasses every dream.

'Your people are showing how much they love you, Madam,' said a fat man standing beside her. 'But I wager that the people of France will soon love you as much, and merely upon seeing you will welcome you as demonstratively as these are bidding you farewell.'

'Oh, you will always be my friend, Messire de Bouville,' Clémence replied warmly.

She felt the need of spreading her happiness around her and of thanking everyone.

The Comte de Bouville, once chamberlain to Philip the Fair and King Louis X's envoy, had come to Naples on a first visit during the winter to ask for her hand; he had returned two weeks ago to fetch the Princess and conduct her to Paris now that the marriage could be celebrated.

'And you too, Signor Baglioni, you are also my friend,' she added, turning towards the young Tuscan who acted as secretary to Bouville and controlled the expedition's finances, which had been lent by the Italian banks in Paris. The young man acknowledged the compliment with a bow.

Indeed, everyone was happy that morning. Fat Bouville, sweating a little in the June heat and throwing his black-and-white locks back behind his ears, felt confident and proud at having succeeded so well in his mission and at conducting so splendid a wife to his king.

Guccio Baglioni was dreaming of the fair Marie de Cressay, his secret fiancée, for whom he was taking home a whole chest of silks and embroideries. He was uncertain whether he had been right to ask for the Neauphle-le-Vieux branch of the bank from his uncle. Should he content himself with so small an establishment?

'But it's only a start; I shall easily be able to change it for another post, and besides I shall spend most of my time in Paris.' Assured of the protection of his new sovereign, he set no limits to his ambition; he already saw Marie as lady-in-waiting to the Queen, and himself becoming Grand Pantler or Grand Treasurer within a few months. Enguerrand de Marigny had started with no greater advantages. Of course he had come to a pretty bad end. But then he was no Lombard.

His hand on his dagger, his chin held high, Guccio looked at Naples deployed before him, as if he were about to buy it.

Ten galleys escorted the ship to the open sea; then the Neapolitans watched this white sea-fortress fade into the distance.

2

The Storm

A FEW DAYS LATER THE *San Giovanni* was no more than a half-dismasted, tortured hulk, running before the squalls, tossed in huge seas, while the captain endeavoured to keep her afloat and make what he conceived to be the coast of France, though doubtful whether he would ever succeed in bringing his passengers safely into port.

The ship had been caught on the latitude of Corsica by one of those brief but devastating storms which, on occasion, ravage the Mediterranean. Six anchors had been lost in an endeavour to hold the ship to the wind off the coast of Elba, and she had barely escaped being wrecked upon the island's rocky shore. They had managed to sail upon their course, but in a tremendous sea. A day, a night, and another day had been spent amid the hell of waters. Several sailors had been injured in taking in what remained of the sails. The crow's nest had gone overboard with all the weight of stones destined for Barbary pirates. The saloon hatch had had to be forced open with axes in order to free the Neapolitan gentlemen imprisoned by the fall of the mainmast. The Princess's chests of dresses, jewels, and plate, all her wedding presents, had been washed away. The surgeon-barber's sick bay in the forecastle was crowded. The chaplain was even unable to celebrate the *aride*[2] Mass because ciborium, chalice, books, and ornaments had been swept overboard by a wave. Clutching the rigging, crucifix in hand, he listened to the confessions of those who thought they were soon to die.

The magnetized needle was now utterly useless, since it bobbed wildly upon the residue of water left in the container in which it floated. The captain, an excitable Latin, had torn his robe open to the waist as a sign of despair and was heard to cry, between a couple of orders: 'Lord, come to my help!' Nevertheless, he seemed to know his business well enough and to be doing his best to extricate them from their difficulties; he had had the oars shipped. They were so long and heavy that seven men were needed to work each one of them. And he had summoned a dozen sailors to control the helm, six on each side.

Nevertheless, Bouville had been furious with him at the beginning of the storm.

'Well, Master Mariner, is this the kind of shaking you give a Princess engaged to the King my master?' the ex-Grand Chamberlain had cried. 'Your ship must be badly loaded to roll like this. You know nothing of navigation or how to make use of favourable currents. If you do not quickly do better, I shall upon arrival have you haled before the justices of the King of France and you'll learn seamanship on a galley's bench.'

But his anger had quickly evaporated, since for the next eight hours he had been sick upon the oriental carpets, in company, moreover, with the majority of the suite. His head rolling upon his shoulders, his face pale, his hair, coat, and hose drenched, the unhappy man prepared to give up the ghost every time a wave lifted the ship, groaning between a couple of hiccups that he would never see his family again and that, during the whole of his life, he had not committed sufficient sins to deserve this intensity of suffering.

Guccio, on the other hand, showed remarkable courage. Clear of head and light of foot, he had taken the precaution of carefully lashing his money-chest and, during moments of relative calm, ran through the spray in search of drinking-water for the Princess, or sprayed scent about her in order to overcome the stench of her seasick companions.

There are certain sorts of men, particularly very young ones, who instinctively behave in the manner expected of them. If they are looked upon with contempt, there is every likelihood of their behaving in a contemptible way. On the other hand, if they feel that people esteem them and have confidence in them, they can surpass themselves and, though as frightened as the next man, can conduct themselves like heroes. Guccio Baglioni was to some extent of this breed. Because Princess Clémence had a way of behaving towards people, whether rich or poor, nobleman or commoner, which maintained their self-respect, because she also used the young man with particular courtesy, since he had been to some extent the harbinger of her good fortune, Guccio, in her company, felt himself to be a knight and behaved with more spirit than any of her gentlemen.

He was a Tuscan and therefore capable of daring all in order to shine in female eyes. And yet, at the same time, he remained body and soul a banker and gambled with fate as one gambles on the exchange.

'Danger presents the best opportunity of becoming intimate with the great,' he said to himself. 'If we've got to founder and perish our fate will certainly not be changed by lapsing into lamentation like poor Bouville. But, if we escape I shall have acquired the esteem of the Queen of France.' To be able to think thus at such a moment was in itself evidence of considerable courage.

But Guccio, that summer, believed himself invincible; he was in love and assured of being loved in return. His head stuffed with heroic tales – for dreams, plans, and ambitions were still chaotically mingled in the boy's mind – Guccio knew that those engaged in adventure always came out safely in the end if a beautiful damsel is awaiting them in a castle! His was at the Manor of Cressay.

He therefore assured the Princess Clémence, against all the evidence, that the weather was improving, asserted that the ship was sound when it was in fact being strained to the limit, and drew comparisons with the much more terrifying storm, or so he pretended it had been, that he had experienced the previous year when crossing the Channel and from which he had issued safely.

'I was on my way to Queen Isabella of England with a message from Monseigneur Robert of Artois.'

Princess Clémence was also behaving in exemplary fashion. Lodged in the stern cabin, a state apartment arranged for royal passengers in the stern-castle, she was endeavouring to calm her ladies who, like a flock of frightened sheep, moaned at every wave.

Clémence had uttered no single word of regret when she was told that her chests of dresses and jewels had gone overboard.

'I would have given twice as much,' she merely said, 'if it could have saved the poor sailors from being injured by the mast.'

She was less afraid of the storm than of the augury she saw in it.

This marriage was more than I deserved,' she thought; 'I have been too happy in the thought of it and have sinned from pride; God will shipwreck me because I do not deserve to become a queen.'

Upon the third morning, when the ship was in a temporary lull, though the sea gave no sign of abating nor the sun of appearing, fat Bouville, his feet bare, dishevelled, wearing only a shirt, was discovered kneeling on the deck with his arms crossed.

'What on earth are you doing there, Messire?' asked Princess Clémence.

'I'm doing what Monsieur Saint Louis did, Madam, when he was nearly drowned off Cyprus. He promised to give a silver ship weighing five marcs[3] to Monsieur Saint Nicolas de Warangeville, if God would bring him safely back to France. It was Messire de Joinville who told me the story.'

'I join you in your vow, Bouville,' replied Clémence, 'and since our ship is under the protection of Saint John the Baptist, I promise, if we survive and I am mercifully permitted to give the King of France a son, to call him John.'

She at once knelt down and began praying.

Towards midday the violence of the sea began to decline and everyone became more hopeful. Then the sun burst through the clouds; land was sighted. The captain joyfully recognized the coast of Provence and, as they drew nearer, the *calanques* of Cassis. He was extremely proud of having kept to his course.

'You will land us here upon the coast at once, I presume, Master Mariner,' cried Bouville.

'I must take you to Marseilles, Messire,' replied the captain, 'and we are not far from it. In any case I no longer have sufficient anchors to lie off those cliffs.'

A little before evening the *San Giovanni*, under oars, was lying off the port of Marseilles. A boat was sent off to warn the city authorities to lower the heavy chain which protected the entrance to the harbour between the Malbert tower and Fort Saint-Nicolas. The Governor, the sheriff, and magistrates (Marseilles was at that time an Angevin city) came off in a strong *mistral* to welcome the niece of their suzerain lord, the King of Naples.

Upon the quay labourers from the salt-pans, fishermen, makers of oars and rigging, caulkers, money-changers, merchants from the ghetto, clerks from the Genoese and Siennese banks, gaped in astonishment at the huge ship, now a sail-less, dismasted wreck, as the sailors danced and embraced each other on the deck, crying that a miracle had occurred.

The Neapolitan gentlemen and the ladies of the suite endeavoured to put some order in their dress.

Brave Bouville, who had lost a stone during the voyage and whose clothes now hung loose upon him, continually assured those about him that it had been his idea to make a vow and that it was this which had prevented their being shipwrecked, that everyone, in fact, owed their life to him.

'Messire Hugues,' Guccio replied with an ironic gleam in his eye, 'there never has been a storm, from what I hear, in which someone has not made a vow similar to yours. How then do you explain the fact that so many ships manage to go to the bottom all the same?'

'It must be because they have a miscreant like you on board!' replied the ex-Chamberlain with a smile.

Guccio was the first to jump ashore. He leaped lightly from the shrouds in order to prove how vigorous he was. There was a rending cry. After several days upon a pitching deck, Guccio had miscalculated the earth's stability; his foot had slipped and he had fallen into the sea. He barely escaped being crushed between the stone quay and the ship's hull. The sea around him at once turned red; in his fall he had torn himself on an iron hook. He was pulled out in a half-fainting condition, bleeding, his thigh cut to the bone. He was immediately taken to the Hôtel-Dieu.

3

The Hôtel-Dieu

THE HUGE WARD FOR men was like a cathedral nave. At the end of it was an altar where four masses, vespers, and evensong were celebrated every day. The privileged patients occupied little cells, called 'rooms of consideration', which lined the walls; the rest were lying two in a bed and head to foot. The monks, in long brown habits, were continuously passing up and down the centre aisle, either to sing the office, to attend to the sick or serve the meals. Religious exercises were intimately related to medical treatment; the groans of the sufferers were mingled with verses of the psalms; the odour of incense could not overcome the atrocious smell of fever and gangrene; death was a public spectacle. Inscriptions, painted in high gothic letters upon the walls, prepared the patient for death rather than recovery.[4]

For three weeks Guccio had lain there in a cell, gasping for breath in the appalling heat of summer, which always has a tendency to make illness more exhausting and hospitals more disagreeable. He looked sadly at the rays of the sun which entered by the windows pierced high in the wall and threw large golden patches upon this assembly of human desolation. He could make no movement without groaning; the balms and elixirs of the nursing brothers burnt him like so many flames, and every dressing was a time of torture. No one seemed to be able to tell him whether the bone was affected; but he felt sure that the wound was more than a flesh-wound, since he nearly fainted whenever they touched his thigh or the small of his back. The doctors and surgeons assured him that he was in no mortal danger, that at his age one recovered from anything, and that God had performed many another miracle, as He had for that caulker's boy who had come in the other day, carrying his intestines in his hands, and who had left after a short time even gayer than before. Guccio despaired none the less. He had been there three weeks already and there seemed no reason to suppose he would not be there for another three, or even three months, or that he would not be lame and crippled for ever.

He saw himself condemned for the rest of his life to crouching huddled behind a money-changer's counter in Marseilles because he could not make the journey to Paris. If, that was, he died from no other disease. Every morning he saw one or two corpses carried out. They had already turned a horrible black colour, since there were always, as in every Mediterranean port, a few cases of plague about. And all this because he had wished to show off by jumping on to the quay before his companions. And when he had just escaped shipwreck too!

He was furious at fate and his own stupidity. He sent for

the letter-writer almost every day and dictated to him long letters for Marie de Cressay which he sent by the couriers of the Lombard banks to the branch at Neauphle, so that the chief clerk might give them secretly to the girl.

With all the emphasis and richness of image which Italians use in speaking of love, Guccio sent the most passionate declarations. He assured her he only wished to get well for her sake, for the happiness of seeing her again, looking upon her, and cherishing her day by day for ever. He besought her to be faithful to the pact they had sworn, and promised her enduring happiness. 'You dominate my whole heart, as no one else will ever do, and if you should fail me, my life too would fail.'

Now that he was confined through his own stupidity to a bed in the Hôtel-Dieu, he was presumptuous enough to begin to doubt everyone and everything and to fear that the girl he loved was no longer waiting for him. Marie would grow tired of an absent lover, would fall for some young provincial squire, a huntsman and champion in tournaments.

'My good luck,' he said to himself, 'was to have been the first to love her. But now it is a year and soon will be eighteen months since we kissed each other for the first time. She will reconsider the matter. My uncle warned me. What am I in the sight of a daughter of a noble house? A Lombard, that is to say a little more than a Jew, a little less than a Christian, and most certainly not a man of rank.'

As he contemplated his wasted, motionless legs, wondering whether he would ever be able to stand upon them again, he described in his letters to Marie de Cressay the wonderful life he would give her. He had become the friend and protégé of the new Queen of France. To read his letters one might have thought that it was he alone who had negotiated the King's marriage. He told of *his* embassy to Naples, the storm, and how he had behaved in it, relating the courage of the crew. He attributed his accident to a chivalrous design; he had leapt forward to assist Princess Clémence and to save her from falling into the sea, when she was on the point of leaving the ship, which was, even in harbour, still tossed by waves.

Guccio had also written to his uncle Spinello Tolomei describing his misfortune, begging that the Neauphle branch be kept for him and asking for a credit with their Marseilles correspondent.

He had a number of visitors who distracted his mind a little and gave him a chance of complaining in company, which is more satisfying than complaining to oneself. The representative of the Tolomei Bank was assiduous in his attentions and arranged for better food than that supplied by the hospital brothers.

One afternoon Guccio had had the pleasure of seeing his friend Signor Boccaccio di Cellino, senior traveller of the Bardi company, who happened to be passing through Marseilles. Guccio had been able to unburden himself to him as much as he pleased.

'Think of all I'll miss,' Guccio said. 'I shall not be able to attend Donna Clemenza's wedding, where I would have taken my place among the great lords. Having done so much to bring it about, it really is bad luck not being able to be there! And I shall also miss the coronation at Rheims. It's really quite intolerable. And I've had no reply from my darling Marie.'

Boccaccio did his best to console him. Neauphle was not a suburb of Marseilles, and Guccio's letters were not carried by royal couriers. They had to go by the usual Lombard stages, Avignon, Lyons, Troyes, and Paris; the couriers did not leave every day.

'Boccacino, my dear friend,' cried Guccio, 'since you're going to Paris, I beseech you, if you have the time, go to Neauphle and see Marie. Tell her all I've said! Find out if my letters have reached her safely; try and discover whether she still loves me. Don't hide the truth from me, even if it's unpalatable. Don't you think, Boccacino, that I might travel in a litter?'

'What, so that your wound can reopen, worms get into it, and that you may die of fever in some filthy inn upon the road? What an idea! Are you mad? Really, Guccio, you're twenty now, after all.'

'Not yet!'

'All the more reason for staying where you are; what's a month here or there at your age?'

'If it happened to be the operative month, my whole life might be ruined.'

Princess Clémence sent one of her gentlemen every day to ask news of the invalid. Fat Bouville came three times himself to sit beside the young Italian's bed. Bouville was overwhelmed with work and anxiety. He was doing his best to get the future Queen's attendants properly fitted out before setting forth on the road to Paris. Exhausted by the voyage, some of the company had had to retire to bed. No one had any clothes but the soaked and spoiled garments they had been wearing when they disembarked. The gentlemen and ladies of the suite were placing orders with tailors and dressmakers without worrying about payment. The whole of the Princess's trousseau, which had been lost at sea, was to be made again; silver, china, trunks, all the necessities of the road, which at the period formed the normal equipment for a royal personage's journey, had to be bought again. Bouville had sent to Paris for funds; Paris had replied that Naples should be approached, since the loss had taken place during that part of the journey which was in the territorial waters of the Crown of Sicily. The Lombards had had to be brought into play. Tolomei had remitted the demands to the Bardis, the usual money-lenders of King Robert of Naples; which explained Signor Boccaccio's short stay in Marseilles, since he was on his way to arrange matters. In these chaotic circumstances Bouville much missed Guccio's assistance, and when the ex-Chamberlain came to visit him, it was more to complain of his own lot and to ask the young man's advice than to bring him comfort. Bouville had a way of looking at Guccio which seemed to imply: 'Really, how could you do this to me!'

'When are you leaving?' Guccio asked him, looking forward to the moment with despair.

'Oh, my poor friend, not before the middle of July.'

'Perhaps by then I shall be well.'

'I hope so. Do your best; your being well again would be a great help to me.'

But the middle of July came without Guccio being up on his feet, far from it indeed. The day before her departure, Clémence of Hungary insisted upon saying goodbye to the sick man herself. Guccio was already much envied by his companions in the hospital for the number of visitors who came to see him, the solicitude with which he was surrounded, and the ease with which his demands were satisfied. He became an almost legendary and heroic figure when the fiancée of the King of France, accompanied by two ladies-in-waiting and six Neapolitan gentlemen, strode in through the doors of the great ward of the Hôtel-Dieu. The brothers, who were singing vespers, looked at each other in astonishment, and their voices turned a little hoarse. The beautiful Princess knelt down, like the most humble of the faithful, and then, when the prayers were over, advanced down between the beds, through the long expanse of suffering, followed by a hundred pairs of astonished eyes.

'Oh, poor people,' she murmured.

She immediately ordered her following to give alms in her name to every patient, and that two hundred pounds should be given to the foundation.

'But, Madam,' Bouville, who was walking beside her, whispered, 'we haven't enough money to pay with.'

'What does that matter? It's better than buying chased drinking-cups or silks for dresses. I feel ashamed of such vanities; I even feel ashamed of my own health when I see so much misery.'

She brought Guccio a little reliquary which enclosed a minute piece of Saint John's robe 'with a visible stain of the Baptist's blood' which she had bought at a great price from a Jew who specialized in this particular business. The reliquary was suspended from a little gold chain which Guccio immediately hung round his neck.

'Oh, dear Signor Guccio,' said Princess Clémence. 'I am so

sorry to see you lying here. You have twice made a long journey so as to be, with Messire de Bouville, the messenger of good tidings; you were of great assistance to me at sea, and now you will not be present at the celebration of my wedding!'

The ward felt as hot as an oven. Outside a thunderstorm threatened. The Princess took a handkerchief from her bag and wiped away the sweat which shone upon the invalid's face with so natural and gentle a gesture that Guccio's eyes filled with tears.

'But how did this happen to you?' Clémence went on. 'I saw nothing at the time and, indeed, do not yet know what occurred.'

'I . . . I thought, Madam, that you were about to disembark, and as the ship was still rolling, I . . . I leapt forward wishing to give you my arm for support. It was growing dark and the light was bad and, there it is, my foot slipped.'

From then on he had to believe in the half-lie himself. He would so like it to have happened like that! And, after all, the sudden whim which had made him want to jump ashore first . . .

'Dear Signor Guccio,' said Clémence, much moved. 'I do hope you get well quickly. And come and tell me of it at the Court of France; my door will always be open to you as a friend.'

They gazed into each other's eyes but with perfect innocence, because she was the daughter of a King and he the son of a Lombard. Had the circumstances of their birth been different, this man and this woman might have fallen in love.

They were never to see each other again, and yet their destinies were to be more strangely and tragically linked than any two destinies have ever been.

4

Portents of Disaster

THE FINE WEATHER WAS short-lived. The tempests, gales, rain, and hailstorms which that summer devastated the west of Europe, and which Princess Clémence had already suffered on her voyage, began again the day after the cavalcade's departure. After staging first at Aix-en-Provence and then at the Château d'Orgon, they arrived at Avignon in pouring rain. The painted leather hood of the litter in which the Princess was carried poured water like a cathedral gargoyle. Were the fine new clothes to be spoilt so quickly, the trunks flooded with rain, and the silver-embroidered saddles of the Neapolitan gentlemen destroyed before they had even been admired by the people of France? Messire de Bouville had caught cold, which did not make things easier. Could one imagine anything more absurd than to catch cold in the middle of July? The poor man was coughing, spitting, and snivelling in the most horrible way. As he grew older, his health was becoming more delicate, unless it were that the

Rhône valley and the neighbourhood of Avignon were peculiarly unlucky for him.

Hardly had the cavalcade installed itself in one of the palaces of the papal town than Monseigneur Jacques Duèze,[5] Cardinal of the Curia, came to greet Clémence of Hungary with a large number of clergy in his train. This old and alchemistical prelate, who had been a candidate for the triple tiara for the last fifteen months, still preserved, in spite of his seventy years, his strangely youthful walk. He danced among the puddles beneath the pouring rain which had put out the torches his people carried before him.

Cardinal Duèze was the official candidate of the family of Anjou-Sicily. That Clémence should be marrying the King of France was clearly an advantage to him and strengthened his position. He counted upon the new Queen to support him in Paris, and thus to win over to him the votes he lacked among his French colleagues.

Agile as a deer, he dashed up the stairs, compelling the pages who were carrying his train to break into a run behind him. He was accompanied by Cardinal Orsini and the two Colonna Cardinals, who were equally devoted to the Neapolitan interest. They had some difficulty in keeping up with him.

Though his handkerchief was to his nose and his speech hoarse, Messire de Bouville resumed some of his ambassadorial dignity to receive these empurpled dignitaries.

'Well, Monseigneur,' he said to the Cardinal, treating him as an old acquaintance, 'I see that it is easier to meet you when one is accompanying the niece of the King of Naples than when one comes to you on the orders of the King of

France. It is no longer necessary to gallop across country in search of you.'

Bouville was in a position to permit himself such amiable teasing; the Cardinal had cost the French Treasury four thousand pounds.*

'The fact is, Monseigneur,' the Cardinal replied, 'that Madame Marie of Hungary and her son, King Robert, have consistently done me the honour of giving me their pious confidence and the union of their family to the throne of France, by means of this fair Princess of high repute, is an answer to my prayers.'

Bouville heard once more that strange voice which was at once rapid, broken, smothered, and almost extinct, seeming to issue from some throat other than the Cardinal's and to be directed at some third person. At the moment, what he had to say was addressed to Clémence, whom the Cardinal never quitted with his eyes.

'Moreover, Messire Comte, circumstances have somewhat changed,' he went on, 'and we no longer perceive the shade of Monseigneur de Marigny behind you, and he held power for a long time and seemed always ready to practise defenestration. Is it true that he was proved to be so dishonest in his accountancy that your young King, of whose charity of soul we are all aware, was unable to save him from just punishment?'

'You know that Messire de Marigny was my friend,' replied Bouville courageously. 'He began as a page in my household.

---

* For the first encounter between Bouville and Cardinal Duèze see *The Strangled Queen*.

I think that his agents, rather than himself, were dishonest. It was a grief to me to see a friend of so old a standing come to disaster through stubborn pride and a desire to control everything himself. I warned him . . .'

But Cardinal Duèze had not yet reached the end of his perfidious courtesies.

'You see, Messire,' he went on, 'that there really was no need to press so hastily for your master's annulment, about which you came to speak to me. Providence often comes to our rescue, provided one is prepared to assist it with a firm hand.'

He never took his eyes off the Princess. Bouville hastened to change the subject and to lead the prelate aside.

'Well, Monseigneur, how goes the Conclave?' he asked.

'It's still in the same state, that is to say nothing has supervened. Monseigneur d'Auch, our revered Cardinal Camerlingo, has not succeeded, or does not wish to succeed, for reasons known only to himself, to bring us into assembly. Some of us are at Carpentras, others at Orange, we ourselves are here, and the Caetani are at Vienne.'

Thereupon, he launched into a subtle but, nevertheless, ferocious indictment of Cardinal Francesco Caetani, the nephew of Boniface VIII and his most violent adversary.

'It is so delightful to watch him display so much courage today in the defence of his uncle's memory; nevertheless, we are unable to forget that, when your friend Nogaret came to Anagni with his cavalry to besiege Boniface, Monseigneur Francesco abandoned his devoted relation, to whom he owed his hat, and, dressed as a footman, took flight. He seems born to felony as others are to the priesthood,' said Duèze.

His eyes, alight with senile anger, seemed to shine from the depths of his withered, sunken face. To listen to him, one would have thought that Cardinal Caetani was capable of the most heinous crimes; the devil was clearly in him.

'And, as you know, Satan may appear anywhere; and surely nothing could be more grateful to him than to establish himself within the College of Cardinals.'

And, what's more, to speak of the devil at that period was not merely a conversational image; his name was not mentioned lightly, since it might be a prelude to a ban of heresy, to torture and the scaffold.

'I am well aware,' Duèze added, 'that the throne of Saint Peter cannot remain indefinitely vacant, and that this is bad for the whole world. But what can I do? I have offered myself, however little I may desire to accept so heavy a task; I have offered to accept the burden since it appears that agreement can be achieved only upon myself. If God, in selecting me, wishes to raise the least worthy to the highest place, I submit to the will of God. What more can I do, Messire de Bouville?'

After which he presented Princess Clémence with a superb copy, richly illuminated, of his *Elixir des Philosophes*, a treatise on hermetic philosophy which had considerable renown among the specialists of the subject and of which it was extremely doubtful that the Princess would understand a single word. For Cardinal Duèze, a master of intrigue, possessed a universal mind, was versed in medicine, alchemy, and in all the humane sciences. His works were to stand for another two centuries.

He departed, followed by his prelates, vicars, and pages; he was already living a Pope's life and would deny, to the limits of his strength, election to anyone else.

When, the following morning, Madame of Hungary's cavalcade took the road for Valence, the Princess asked Bouville, 'What did the Cardinal mean yesterday when he spoke of assisting Providence to accomplish our desires?'

'I don't know, Madam, I don't very well remember,' replied Bouville, embarrassed. 'I think he was talking of Messire de Marigny, but I didn't very well understand.'

'It seemed to me that he was speaking rather of my future husband's annulment, which was impossible of realization. Of what did Madame Marguerite of Burgundy die?'

'Of a chill she caught in her prison, and of remorse for her sins without doubt.'

And Bouville blew his nose to conceal his disquiet; he knew only too well the rumours which were current about the sudden death of the King's first wife and had no wish to speak of them.

Clémence accepted Bouville's explanation, but it did not set her mind at rest.

'I owe my future happiness,' Clémence said to herself, 'to the death of another.'

She felt herself to be inexplicably allied to this queen whom she was to succeed and whose sins caused her as much horror as the punishment inspired her with pity.

Is not true charity, so rarely felt by those who inculcate it, precisely the emotion which impels the individual, however unreasonably, to identify himself with the crime of the criminal as well as with the responsibility of the judge?

'Her sins led to her death, and her death to my becoming

queen,' Clémence thought. She saw it as a sort of judgement upon herself and felt that she was surrounded with portents of disaster.

The storm, the accident to the young Lombard, and the rain which was becoming calamitous, were all signs of ill omen.

For the weather grew no better. The villages they passed through had an appearance of desolation. After a winter of famine, the harvest had promised well and the peasants had regained courage; a few days of *mistral* and terrible storms had shattered their expectations. And now apparently inexhaustible rain was rotting their crops.

The Durance, the Drôme, and the Isère were in flood and the Rhône, along whose banks they were journeying, was dangerously swollen. From time to time they had to stop to free the road of a fallen tree.

For Clémence, the contrast between Campania, where the sky was always blue and the people smiling, the orchards laden with golden fruit, and this ravaged valley, haunted by a wasted populace and depressed villages, half-depopulated by famine, was depressing.

'And the farther north we go, doubtless the worse it will become. I have come to a hard land.'

She wished to relieve all the misery she saw, and constantly halted her litter to distribute charity to anyone who seemed in need. Bouville was compelled to reason with her.

'If you give at this rate, Madam, we shall not have enough left to reach Paris.' It was when she arrived at Vienne, the home of her sister Beatrice, who was married to the ruling

Prince of Dauphiné, that she learnt that King Louis X had just left to make war upon the Flemings.

'Dear Lord,' she murmured, 'am I to be widowed before even setting eyes upon my husband? Have I arrived in France merely to witness disaster?'

5

The King Receives the Oriflamme

Enguerrand de Marigny, during the course of his trial, had been accused by Charles of Valois of having sold himself to the Flemings in negotiating with them a peace treaty which was contrary to the interests of the Kingdom.

And now, when Marigny had but barely been hanged in the chains of Montfaucon, the Count of Flanders had broken the treaty. To do so he had employed the simplest means: he had refused, though summoned, to come to Paris to render homage to the new King. At the same time he ceased to pay the indemnities and reaffirmed his claim to the territories of Lille and Douai.

Upon receiving this news, King Louis X fell into an appalling rage. He was subject to fits of fury which had won for him the nickname of 'Le Hutin' and which terrified his entourage, not only for themselves but for him, since at these moments he bordered upon dementia.

His rage, upon hearing of the Flemings' rebellion,

surpassed in violence anything that he had manifested before.

For many hours, as he prowled about his study like a wild beast in a trap, his hair in disorder, his neck empurpled, breaking ornaments, kicking chairs over, he incessantly shouted meaningless words, while his cries were interrupted only by fits of coughing which bent him double, half suffocating him.

'The indemnity!' he cried. 'And the weather! Oh, they'll pay for the weather too! Gibbets, that's what I need, gibbets! Who's refused to pay the indemnity? On his knees! I'll have the Count of Flanders on his knees! And I'll put my foot on his head! Bruges? I'll set fire to it! I'll burn it down!'

His tirade was a confused mixture of the names of the rebellious towns, the delay of Clémence of Hungary's arrival and promises of punishment. But the word that came most often to his lips was that of 'indemnity'. For Louis X had but a few days before decreed the raising of an extra tax to cover the expenses of the previous year's military campaign.

Without daring to say so openly people were beginning to regret Marigny and his methods of dealing with this form of rebellion; for instance, his reply to the Abbé Simon of Pisa, who informed him that the Flemings were becoming inflamed: 'Their ardour in no way astonishes me, Brother Simon; it's the effect of hot blood. Our lords are also hotheaded and in love with war. Yet the Kingdom of France is not to be dismembered by mere words; deeds are necessary.' People wanted the same tone to be adopted; unfortunately the man who could have spoken thus was no longer of this world.

Encouraged by his uncle Valois, whose bellicose ardour

had in no way been diminished by the exercise of power, on the contrary rather, and who never ceased wishing to give proof of his capacity as a great commander, The Hutin began to dream of valour. He would mobilize the greatest army that had ever been seen in France, fall like a mountain eagle on the rebellious Flemings, carve a few thousand of them to pieces, ransom the rest, bring them to their knees in a week and, where Philip the Fair had never completely succeeded, show the whole world what he was capable of. Already he saw himself returning, preceded by triumphant standards, his coffers filled with plunder and with the indemnities imposed upon the towns, having at once surpassed his father's reputation and effaced the misfortune of his first marriage, for a war at least was necessary to make people forget his marital disaster. Then, amid a popular ovation, he would gallop home, a conquering prince and a hero of war, to meet his new wife and lead her to the altar and to coronation.

Clearly the young man was a fool and one might have pitied him, because there is always something pathetic about folly, if he were not the ruler of France and its population of fifteen millions.

On June 23rd he summoned the Court of Peers, stuttered violently at them, declared the Count of Flanders to be a felon, and resolved to mobilize the army before Courtrai on August 1st.

This concentration-point was not a particularly good choice. It seems that there are places where disaster has a habit of striking, and Courtrai, to people of that period, sounded very much as the name Sedan does to modern ears. Unless it was that Louis X and his Uncle Charles decided presumptuously upon Courtrai precisely so as to exorcize the memory of the disaster of 1302, one of the few battles lost in the reign of Philip the Fair, at which several thousand knights, charging like madmen in the absence of the king, had foundered in the ditches only to get themselves cut to pieces by the knives of the Fleming weavers; a carnage in which no prisoners were taken.

To maintain the formidable army which was to bring him glory, Louis X needed money; Valois, therefore, had recourse to the expediencies which Marigny had previously employed, while people openly wondered whether it had really been necessary to condemn the old Rector of the Kingdom to death merely so as to reapply his methods less efficiently.

Every serf who could pay for his franchise was freed; the Jews were recalled, on payment of a crushing tax for the right to reside and trade; a new levy was raised on the Lombards who, from then on, looked upon the new reign with less favourable eyes. Two urgently demanded contributions within less than a year was rather more than they expected to be subjected to.[6]

The Government wished to tax the clergy; but the latter, arguing that the Holy See was vacant and that no decision could be made without a pope, refused; then, in negotiation, the bishops consented to help provided no precedent were created, and profited by the opportunity to get certain concessions, exonerations, and immunities which ultimately were to cost the Treasury more than the funds obtained.

The mobilization of the army took place without difficulty, and was even conducted with a certain enthusiasm by the barons who, pretty bored at home, were delighted with the idea of donning their breastplates and setting off on an adventure.

There was less enthusiasm among the people.

'Isn't it enough,' they said, 'that we should be half-starved without having to give our men and our money to the King's war?'

But the people were assured that every ill derived from the Flemings; the hope of loot and free days of rape and pillage were dangled before the soldiers; for many it was a way of easing the monotony of daily labour and the anxiety of finding enough to eat; no one wished to show himself a coward, and if there were recalcitrants, the sergeants of the King or of the great lords were numerous enough to maintain discipline by decorating the trees bordering the roads with a hanging or two. According to Philip the Fair's Order in Council, which was still in force, no healthy man could, in theory, be exempted if he were more than eighteen and less than sixty, unless he bought himself out with a money contribution or exercised an indispensable trade.

At that time mobilization was a matter of purely local organization. The knights were sworn men, and it was incumbent upon them to raise a force among their vassals, subjects or serfs. The knight, and even the squire, never went alone to war. They were accompanied by pages, sutlers, and footmen. They owned their own horses and arms and those of their men. The ordinary knight without a banneret held approximately the rank of a lieutenant; once his men were assembled and equipped, he reported to the knight of a superior grade, that is to say his immediate suzerain.

The knights with pennons were approximately equivalent to captains, the knights banneret to colonels, and the knights with double banners approximated to generals who commanded the whole tactical force raised from the jurisdiction of their barony or their county.

During the battle itself all the knights would upon occasion, leaving their footmen to one side, rally for the charge, often with the splendid results we know so well.

The 'banner' of Count Philippe of Poitiers, the King's brother, must have rallied something in the nature of an army corps, since it assembled all the troops from Poitou, together with those of the county of Burgundy of which Philippe was Count Palatine by marriage; moreover, ten knights banneret were administratively attached to it, among whom were the Count of Evreux, the King's uncle, Count Jean de Beaumont, Miles des Noyers, Anseau de Joinville, son of the great Joinville, and even Gaucher de Châtillon who, even though Constable of France, that is to say Commander-in-Chief of the armies, had the troops from his fief incorporated into the enormous unit.

Philip the Fair had had good reason for confiding to his second son, before he even reached the age of twenty-two, so important a military command, and for concentrating under his authority, as if to reinforce it, the men in whom he placed the greatest confidence.

Under the 'banner' of Count Charles of Valois marched the troops from Maine, Anjou, and Valois, among whom was the old Chevalier d'Aunay, the father of Marguerite and Blanche of Burgundy's two dead lovers.

The cities were laid under contribution no less than the

country. For this Flanders army, Paris had to furnish four hundred horsemen and two thousand footmen, whose maintenance was guaranteed by the merchants of the Cité, fortnight by fortnight, which showed that in the King's opinion the war would not last long. The horses and wagons for the supply train were requisitioned from the monasteries.

On July 24th, 1315, after some delay, as was always the case, Louis X received, at Saint-Denis, from the hands of the Abbot Egidus de Chambly, who was its *ex-officio* guardian, the Oriflamme of France, a long band of red silk embroidered with golden flames (from which its name derived), ending in a swallow-tail and attached to a staff of gilded brass. Beside the Oriflamme, which was venerated as might have been a relic, the two King's banners were carried, one blue with fleurs-de-lys and the other with the white cross.

The huge army set itself in motion with all the contingents that had arrived from the west, the south, and the south-east, the knights from Languedoc, troops from Normandy and Brittany. At Saint-Quentin it was joined by the 'banners' of the duchy of Burgundy and those of Champagne, Artois, and Picardy.

That particular day was a rare one of sunshine in an appalling summer. The sun shone upon a thousand lances, on breastplates, and chain-mail, on brightly painted shields. The knights showed off to each other the latest fashions in armour, a new form of helm or bassinet giving greater protection to the face while affording a wider field of vision, or some larger form of *ailette* which, placed upon the shoulder, gave greater protection against the blows of maces or made sword-thrusts glance off.

Several miles behind the soldiers followed the train of four-wheeled wagons which carried food, forges, supplies of bolts for crossbows, and a variety of traders who were authorized to follow in the army's wake, as well as whores by the cartful under the control of the brothel-masters. The whole procession advanced in an extraordinary atmosphere which smacked at once of the heroic and the fairground.

The next day rain began to fall once more, soaking, unceasing, flooding the roads, opening ruts, trickling down steel helmets, dripping from breastplates, plastering the horses' coats. Every man weighed five pounds the heavier.

And it was rain, continuous rain, throughout the following day.

The army of Flanders never reached Courtrai. It stopped at Bonduis, near Lille, before the swollen river Lys, which barred its advance, flooded the fields, swamped the roads, and soaked the clay soil. As it was no longer possible to advance, the army encamped there in pouring rain.

6

The Muddy Army

INSIDE THE VAST ROYAL TENT, embroidered with fleurs-de-lys, but where the mud was as elsewhere ankle-deep, Louis X, in company with his brother the Count de la Marche, his uncle Count Charles of Valois, and his chancellor, Etienne de Mornay, listened to the Constable Gaucher de Châtillon reporting on the situation. The report was not a happy one.

Châtillon, Count of Porcien and Lord of Crèvecoeur, had been Constable since 1286, that is to say from the very beginning of Philip the Fair's reign. He had seen the disaster of Courtrai, the victory of Mons-en-Pevèle, and many other battles on this threatened northern frontier. He was in Flanders for the sixth time in his life. He was now sixty-five years of age. He was a tall good-looking man, with a determined jaw; neither years nor fatigue seemed to have affected him; he seemed slow because he was reflective. His physical strength and his courage in battle earned him respect as much as his strategical abilities. He had seen too much of war to be enamoured of it any longer, and now merely regarded it as a political necessity. He neither minced his words nor hid his meaning behind vainglorious phrases.

'Sire,' he said, 'food supplies are no longer reaching the army, the wagons are stuck in the mud fifteen miles away, and they're breaking the traces trying to get them out. The men are hungry and beginning to grumble angrily; the companies who still have food are having to defend their reserves against those who have nothing left; the archers of Champagne came to blows with those of Perche a little while ago, and there is a danger that your troops will fight among themselves before ever they come face to face with the enemy. I shall have to hang some of them, which is not a thing I like doing. But erecting gibbets does not fill stomachs. We've already got more sick than the surgeon-barbers can attend to; it will soon be the chaplains who'll have most work to do. There has been no sign of a break in the weather in the last four days. Two days more and we shall have a famine on our hands, and no one will be able to stop the men deserting in search of food. All the supplies have gone mouldy, rotten, or rusty.'

He pulled off the steel camail which covered his head and shoulders and smoothed his hair. The King walked to and fro, nervous, anxious, and alarmed. From outside the tent came the sound of cries and the cracking of whips.

'Stop that row,' cried The Hutin, 'one can't hear oneself think!'

An equerry raised the flap of the tent. The rain was still falling in torrents. Thirty horses, sinking in the mud to their knees, were harnessed to a huge wine-cart which they were unable to draw.

'Where are you taking that wine?' the King asked the wagoners who were floundering in the clay.

'To Monseigneur the Count of Artois, Sire,' one of them replied.

The Hutin looked at them for a moment with his huge pale eyes, shook his head and turned away without another word.

'As I was saying, Sire,' Gaucher continued, 'we may still have some wine to drink today, but don't count on it for tomorrow. Oh, I should have given you more insistent counsel. I was of the opinion that we should have stopped earlier, establishing ourselves on high ground rather than advancing into this morass. Both my cousin of Valois[7] and yourself insisted that we should advance and I feared to be taken for a coward and that my age would be blamed if I stopped the army moving forward. I was wrong.'

Charles of Valois was about to reply when the King asked, 'And the Flemings?'

'They're opposite us, on the other side of the river, in as great numbers as we and no more happy, I should think, though they are nearer their supplies, and are maintained by the people of their towns and villages. If the flood waters should diminish tomorrow, they'll be better prepared to attack us than we shall be to fall on them.'

Charles of Valois shrugged his shoulders.

'Come now, Gaucher, the rain's depressed your spirits,' he said. 'You're not going to make me believe that a good cavalry charge won't account for that rabble of weavers.

They've only got to see our lines of breastplates and our forest of lances to be off like a flock of sparrows.'

The Count was superb in his surcoat of gold-embroidered silk which he wore over his coat of mail and in spite of the mud that covered him; indeed, he looked more kingly than the King himself.

'You make it quite clear, Charles,' the Constable replied, 'that you were not at Courtrai thirteen years ago. You were then fighting in Italy, not for France but for the Pope. But I've seen that rabble, as you call it, destroy our knights when they acted too precipitately.'

'That was doubtless because I was not there,' said Valois with his own peculiar conceit. 'This time I am.'

The Chancellor de Mornay whispered into the ear of the young Count de la Marche, 'It won't be long before the sparks are flying between your uncle and the Constable; whenever they're together one can set fire to the tinder without having to strike a light.'

'Rain, rain!' cried Louis X angrily. 'Is everything always to be against me?'

Uncertain health, a clever but overbearing father whose authority had crushed him, an unfaithful wife who had scoffed at him, an empty treasury, impatient vassals always ready to rebel, a famine in the first winter of his reign, a storm which threatened the life of his second wife – beneath what disastrous conjunction of the planets, which the astrologers had not dared reveal to him, must he have been born, that he should meet with adversity in every decision, every enterprise, and end by being conquered, not even nobly in battle, but by the water and mud in which he had engulfed his army.

At this moment there was announced a delegation of the barons of Champagne, with the Chevalier Etienne de Saint-Phalle at their head, desiring an immediate revision of the Charter of Privileges which had been accorded them in the month of May; they threatened to leave the army if they did not receive satisfaction.

'They've chosen a good day!' cried the King.

Three hundred yards away, Sire Jean de Longwy, in his own tent, was conversing with a singular personage who was dressed half as a monk and half as a soldier.

'The news you bring me from Spain is good, Brother Everard,' said Jean de Longwy, 'and I am glad to hear that our brothers of Castille and Aragon have resumed their Commanderies. They are better off than we, who must continue to act in silence.'

Jean de Longwy, short of stature and heavy-jowled, was the nephew of the Grand Master of the Templars, Jacques de Molay, of whom he considered himself the heir and successor. He had vowed to avenge the blood of his uncle and to re-habilitate his memory. The premature death of Philip the Fair, which fulfilled the famous triple curse, had not quenched his hate; he had transferred it to the Iron King's heirs, Louis X, Philippe of Poiters, and Charles de la Marche. Longwy caused the Crown all the trouble he could; he was one of the leaders of the baronial leagues; and at the same time he was busily and secretly reconstructing the order of the Knights Templar, by means of a network of agents who maintained contact between the fugitive brothers.

'I long for the King of France's defeat,' he went on, 'and

I am only present with the army in the hope of seeing him killed by a sword-thrust, and his brothers too.'

Thin, ungainly, his dark eyes set close together, Everard, a former Knight Templar, whose foot was deformed by the tortures he had undergone, replied, 'I hope your prayers are answered, Messire Jean, if possible by God, and if not by the devil.'

The clandestine Grand Master[8] suddenly raised the tent-flap to make sure that no one was spying on them, and dispatched on some duty two grooms who were doing no more than shelter from the rain beneath the pent-roof of the tent. Then, turning back to Everard, he said, 'We have nothing to hope for from the Crown of France. Only a new Pope could re-establish the Order, and restore to us our Commanderies here and overseas. Ah, what a wonderful day that would be, Brother Everard!'

For a moment or two both men dreamed. The destruction of the Order dated only from eight years before, its condemnation from still less, and it was barely more than a year since Jacques de Molay had died at the stake. All their memories were fresh, their hopes alive. Longwy and Everard could see themselves donning once more the long white cloaks with their black crosses, the golden spurs, exercising the ancient privileges and indulging once again in great commercial activities.

'Very well, Brother Everard,' Longwy went on, 'you will now go to Bar-sur-Aube, where the Count de Bar's chaplain, who is well disposed towards us, will give you a position as a clerk so that you need no longer live in concealment. Then you will go to Avignon, from where I am informed that

Cardinal Duèze, who was a creature of Clement V's, has once again a considerable chance of being elected. This we must prevent at all costs. Find Cardinal Caetani – if he is not at Avignon, he will not be far away – who is nephew of the unfortunate Pope Boniface and is also resolved to avenge the memory of his uncle.'

'I guarantee he'll receive me well, when he hears that I have already assisted his vengeance by helping to send Nogaret out feet first. You're creating a league of nephews!'

'That's exactly it, Everard. So see Caetani and tell him that our brothers in Spain and England, and all those in France in whose name I speak, have chosen and desired him in their hearts as Pope and are ready to support him, not only with prayers, but by every means in their power. Put yourself under his orders for whatever he may require of you. And, while you're there, see also Brother Jean du Pré who's in those parts at the moment and may be of great help to you. And don't fail to learn during the journey if there be any of our old Brothers in the neighbourhood. Try to organize them into little companies, and get them to take the oath you know. That's all, Brother; this safe-conduct, which names you Chaplain-Brother of my "banner", will help you to leave the camp without being asked awkward questions.'

He handed the ex-Templar a document and the latter slipped it under the leather jerkin which covered his rough serge robe down to the thighs; then the two men embraced. Everard put on his steel helmet and left, his back bent, his walk limping beneath the rain.

* * *

The Count of Poitiers's troops were the only ones who still had anything to eat. When the wagons had begun to stick in the mud, the Count of Poitiers had ordered the food to be portioned out and carried by the foot-soldiers. At first they had complained; today they blessed their commander. A strict guard maintained discipline, since the Count of Poitiers loathed disorder; and since he also appreciated his comforts, a hundred men had been put to digging drains, while his tent had been placed on a foundation of logs and faggots upon which one might live more or less in the dry. The tent, almost as large and rich as the King's, consisted of several different rooms separated by tapestries.

Sitting amid the leaders of his 'banner' on a camp-stool, his sword, his shield, and his helmet within reach, Philippe of Poitiers asked one of the bachelors[9] of his staff, who acted as his secretary and aide-de-camp, 'Adam Heron, have you read, as I asked you, the book by this Florentine – what does he call himself?'

'Messire Dante dei Alighieri.'

'That's it, the man who treats my family so badly? He is under the special protection, so I'm told, of Charles Martel of Hungary, the father of this Princess Clémence who's arriving shortly to be our Queen. I should like to know what his poem says.'

'I've read it, Monseigneur,' Adam Heron replied. 'This Messire Dante imagines at the beginning of his Comedy that, at the age of thirty-five, he loses his way in a dark forest where the road is barred by terrifying animals, from which Messire Dante realizes that he has strayed from the world of the living.'

The barons surrounding the Count of Poitiers at first looked at each other in surprise. The King's brother never ceased to astonish them. Here they were in the middle of a warlike camp and in considerable chaos, and he suddenly had no concern other than talking of poetry, as if he were by his own fireside in his Paris house. But the Count of Evreux, who knew his nephew well and who, since he had been under his command, admired him more every day, had understood at once. 'Philippe is trying to take their minds off this trying inaction,' he said to himself, 'and instead of allowing them to fret and fume, he is leading them to dream while waiting to lead them into battle.'

For already Anseau de Joinville, Goyon de Bourçay, Jean de Beaumont, Pierre de Garancière, Jean de Clermont, sitting about on chests, were listening with bright eyes as the bachelor Adam Heron told them Dante's story. These rough men, often so brutal in their way of life, were charmed by the mysterious and the supernatural. Legends enchanted them; their minds were always ready to accept the marvellous. It was a strange spectacle to see this steel-clad company passionately following the Italian poet's masterly allegories, longing to know who this Beatrice was who inspired so great a love, trembling at the memory of Francesca da Rimini and of Paolo Malatesta, and suddenly guffawing because Boniface VIII, in company with some other Popes, was to be found in the eighteenth circle of the inferno, in the pit reserved for cheats and simoniacs.

'The poet's found a good way of avenging himself upon his enemies and relieving his own feelings,' said Philippe of Poitiers, laughing. 'And where has he put my relations?'

'In purgatory, Monseigneur,' replied the bachelor who, at the general demand, had gone to fetch the book which was copied out on thick parchment.

'Very well then, read us what he has written, or rather translate it for those of us who don't understand Italian.'

'I hardly dare, Monseigneur.'

'Yes, go on, don't be afraid. I must know what people who don't like us think of us.'

'Messire Dante pretends that he meets a shade who groans loudly. He questions the shade upon the source of his pain and this is the answer he gets.'

And Adam Heron began to translate the following passage from Canto XX:

I was root
Of that ill plant, whose shade such poison sheds
O'er all the Christian land, that seldom thence
Good fruit is gather'd. Vengeance soon should come,
Had Ghent and Douay, Lille and Bruges power;
And vengeance I of heav'n's great Judge implore.

'Well, that seems prophetic enough and is completely in accord with our present circumstances,' said the Count of Poitiers. 'Clearly the poet is perfectly aware of our troubles in Flanders. Go on.'

Hugh Capet was I hight: from me descend
The Philips and the Louis, of whom France
Newly is govern'd; born of one, who ply'd
The slaughterer's trade at Paris. When the race
Of ancient kings had vanish'd (all save one

Wrapt up in sable weeds) within my gripe
I found the reins of empire.

'This is completely false,' the Count of Poitiers interrupted, uncrossing his long legs. 'It's a wicked lie that has been spread abroad in recent times to our prejudice. Hugues le Grand was descended from the Dukes of France.'[10]

As the reading proceeded, he commented calmly, sometimes with irony, on the ferocious attacks the Italian poet, who was already famous in his own country, made upon the French princes. Dante accused Charles of Anjou, the brother of Saint Louis, not only of having assassinated the legitimate heir to the throne of Naples, but also of having poisoned Saint Thomas Aquinas.

'Our cousins of Anjou are well peppered,' said the Count of Poitiers in a low voice.

But the French prince whom Dante attacked with the greatest violence, for whom he reserved his worst curses, was another Charles, who had gone to ravage Florence and had pierced it in the stomach, the poet wrote, 'with the lance with which he fought Judas'.

'Ah, that's my Uncle Charles of Valois he's talking of there!' Poitiers cried. 'That's why he's so vindictive. My uncle seems to have made us a lot of friends in Italy.'[11]

Those present looked at each other, not quite knowing what attitude to adopt. But they saw that Philippe of Poitiers was smiling, rubbing his face with his long white hand. They therefore dared to laugh. Monseigneur of Valois was little liked in the Count of Poitiers's circle.

* * *

The encampment of Count Robert of Artois gave a totally different impression from that of the Count of Poitiers. Here, in spite of the rain, was a constant coming and going, a confusion so universal that it seemed deliberate.

The Count of Artois had let to the merchants accompanying the army stands close to his own tent, which could be recognized from afar by its red cloth and the banners surmounting it. Whoever wanted to buy a new baldrick, replace a buckle on his helm, acquire new iron elbow-pieces or have a coat of chain-mail repaired had to come there. It was as if a fair were going on before Messire Robert's door; and he had arranged for the prostitutes to be in his neighbourhood too, so that every amenity might be under his control and he could make his friends free of them.

As for the archers, crossbowmen, grooms, servants, and camp followers, they had been kept at a distance and were taking shelter as best they could in the houses of the peasants who had been turned out, or in huts made of branches, or even under the wagons.

They were not talking of poetry inside the great red tent. A cask of wine was constantly on tap, goblets circulated in the hubbub, dice rolled on the lids of the great chests; they played on credit, and more than one knight had already lost more than his ransom would have cost him.

One fact was particularly to be remarked: while Robert had under his command the troops from his County of Beaumont-le-Roger, a great number of knights from Artois, who were part of the 'banner' of the Countess Mahaut, were permanently in his camp where they had, militarily speaking, no business to be.

With his back to the central tent-pole, Count Robert of Artois dominated the whole turbulent scene with his colossal height. Wearing a scarlet surcoat upon which fell his lion-like mane, he was amusing himself by playing with a whole array of weapons. Nevertheless, there was a crack in the giant's spirit, and it was not without intent that he wished to distract himself with drink and noise.

'Battles in Flanders have never done my family any good,' he confided to the lords about him. 'My father, Count Philippe, whom many of you knew well and served faithfully . . .'

'Yes, we knew him! He was a pious and a brave man!' the barons of Artois replied.

'Well, my father received a mortal wound at the Battle of Furnes. And my grandfather, Count Robert . . .'

'Oh, he was a brave man and a good suzerain! He respected our good old customs! One never asked justice of him in vain!'

'He was killed four years later at Courtrai. Two never go without a third. Perhaps tomorrow, Messeigneurs, you'll be burying me.'

There are two kinds of superstitious people: those who never mention disaster, and those who speak of it so as to defy it and put it to flight. Robert of Artois was of the second sort.

'Caumont, pour me out another goblet of wine; let's drink to my last day!' he cried.

'No, we won't do that! Our bodies will be your rampart,' the barons cried. 'Who but you defends our rights?'

They looked upon him as their natural suzerain, and

his strength and vitality had made of him a sort of idol.

'Yet see, my good lords, how one is rewarded for so much blood spilt in the service of the Kingdom,' he went on. 'Because my grandfather was killed after my father, yes, for that reason alone, King Philip took the opportunity of doing me out of my inheritance and of giving Artois to my aunt Mahaut who treats you so well, with all her ill-omened Hirsons, the chancellor, the treasurer, and all the rest, who crush you with taxes and deny you your rights.'

'If we go into battle tomorrow, and a Hirson happens to be within arm's reach of me, I can promise him a blow or two which will not necessarily have been given him by the Flemings,' declared a fellow with huge red eyebrows who called himself the Sire de Souastre.

Rather drunk though he might be, Robert of Artois's brain remained clear. So much wine dispensed, so many girls on offer, so much money spent, all had a reason. He was working to gratify his vengeance and advance his own affairs.

'My noble lords, my noble lords, the King's war must come first. We are his loyal subjects and he is, at this moment, I assure you, entirely sympathetic towards your just complaints,' he said. 'But when the war is over, then, Messeigneurs, I advise you not to disarm. To be on a war-footing with your vassals mobilized is a good opportunity, go back to Artois and chase Mahaut's agents from the whole countryside, flog their backsides in the marketplaces of the towns. And I will support you in the King's Council Chamber, and will reopen once again the lawsuit in which I was the victim of a travesty of justice; and I guarantee that you shall have your old customs back, as in the times of my father.'

'That's what we'll do, Messire Robert, that's what we'll do!'

Souastre opened his arms wide.

'Let us swear,' he cried, 'not to disperse before our demands have been granted, and our good Lord Robert has been given back to us as our Count.'

'We swear it!' the barons replied.

They embraced each other and many more bumpers were poured out; then torches were lit as night was drawing on. Robert of Artois felt a happy thrill of excitement running through his huge body. The league of Artois, which he had secretly founded and led for many months, was gaining strength.

At this moment an equerry came into the tent and said, 'Monseigneur Robert, the commanders of "banners" are required immediately in the King's tent!'

The torches spread an acrid smoke which mingled with the strong smell of leather, sweat, and wet iron. Most of the great lords, sitting in a circle about the King, had neither washed nor shaved for the last six days. Normally they would never have spent so long without going to the baths. But dirt was part of war.

The Constable Gaucher de Châtillon had just repeated for the commanders of 'banners' his report upon the disastrous situation of the army.

'Messeigneurs, you have heard the Constable. I desire your counsel,' said Louis X.

Putting his blue silk surcoat across his knees, Valois began speaking in his haranguing voice.

'I have already told you, Sire, my Nephew, and now repeat

it before everyone: we can no longer remain in this place where everything is going to rack and ruin, the men's morale and the horses' condition. Inaction is doing us as much damage as the weather.'

He interrupted his speech because the King had turned round to speak to his chamberlain, Mathieu de Trye; but it was only to ask for a sweet, which was handed him. He was always in need of something to chew.

'Go on, Uncle, I pray you.'

'We must move at dawn tomorrow,' Valois went on, 'find a ford by which to cross the river upstream, and fall upon the Flemings so as to defeat them before evening.'

'With hungry men and unfed horses?' said the Constable.

'Victory will fill their stomachs. They can hold out for another day; but the day after tomorrow will be too late.'

'I tell you, Charles, that you'll either be drowned or cut to pieces. I see no alternative but to withdraw the army to high ground towards Tournai or Saint-Amand, so that the rations can reach us and the flood water have a chance to drain away.'

It often happens that as we mention lightning the skies thunder, or that someone enters the door at the very moment we are speaking ill of them. Coincidence seems malicious in the way it challenges our words.

At the very moment the Constable was counselling them to let the flood water drain away, the roof of the tent caved in over Monseigneur of Valois, who was soused. Robert of Artois, who was sitting in a corner smelling strongly of wine, began laughing and the King followed his example, which made Charles of Valois lose his temper.

'We all know, Gaucher,' he cried, rising to his feet, 'that you are paid a hundred pounds a day while the King is with the army and that you have no wish to bring the war to an end.'

Wounded to the quick, the Constable replied, 'It is my duty to remind you that even the King cannot decide to attack the enemy without the advice and orders of the Constable. And in the present circumstances I shall not give these orders. That being the case, the King can always change his Constable.'

An extremely painful silence ensued. The matter was a grave one. Would Louis X, to please Valois, dismiss the head of his armies, as he had dismissed Marigny, Raoul de Presles, and all Philip the Fair's other ministers? The results of that policy had not been altogether happy.

'Brother,' said Philippe of Poitiers in his calm voice, 'I entirely agree with the counsel Gaucher has given you. The troops are in no condition to fight till they have had a good week in which to recuperate.'

'That is also my advice,' said Count Louis of Evreux.

'And so we are never to punish the Flemings!' cried Charles de la Marche, the King's second brother, who always shared his uncle Valois's opinions.

Everyone began to speak at once. Retreat or defeat, that was their choice, the Constable affirmed. Valois replied that he saw no advantage in retreating fifteen miles merely that the army should continue to rot. The Count of Champagne announced that his troops, having been raised only for a fortnight, would return home if no attack were launched; and Duke Eudes of Burgundy, brother of the assassinated

Marguerite, took advantage of the argument to show how little eager he was to serve his ex-brother-in-law.

The King remained hesitant, uncertain with which party to side. The whole expedition had been conceived as a rapid campaign. Both the condition of the Treasury and his personal prestige depended upon quick results. He saw the chances of a lightning war diminishing. To follow the path of wisdom and good sense, to regroup elsewhere and wait, was to postpone both his marriage and his coronation. Whereas to expect to be able to cross a river in flood and charge through the mud at a gallop . . .

It was at this moment that Robert of Artois rose to his feet and, an impressive sight in his massive scarlet and steel, strode into the centre of the meeting.

'Sire, my Cousin,' he said, 'I understand your concern. You have not enough money to maintain this huge army in idleness. Moreover, you have a new wife awaiting you, and we are all impatient to see her made Queen, as we are to see you crowned. My advice is not to persist. It is not the enemy that forces us to turn back; it's in the rain I see the will of God before which everyone, however great he may be, must bow. Who can tell, Cousin, whether God has not wished to warn you not to fight before you have been anointed with holy oil? You will gain as much prestige from a fine coronation as from a rash battle. Therefore, renounce for the moment your intention of whipping these wretched Flemings, and if the terror with which you have inspired them is not in itself sufficient, let us come back with as great a force next spring.'

This unexpected advice, coming from a man whose

courage in battle could not be doubted, received the support of part of the meeting. No one understood then that Robert was pursuing ends of his own, and that his desire of raising Artois was closer to his heart than the interests of the Kingdom.

Louis X, impulsive but not particularly prompt to act, was always ready to give up in despair when events did not turn out as he wished. He seized the lifeline Artois offered him.

'You have spoken wisely, Cousin,' he said. 'Heaven has given us a warning. Let the army withdraw, since it cannot advance. But I swear to God,' he added, raising his voice and thinking thus to preserve his grandeur, 'I swear to God that if I am still living next year, I shall invade these Flemings and will make no armistice with them short of unconditional surrender.'

From that moment he had no concern but to break camp as quickly as possible, and his sole preoccupations were with his marriage and his coronation.

The Count of Poitiers and the Constable had considerable difficulty in persuading him to take certain indispensable precautions, such as maintaining garrisons along the Flanders frontier.

The Hutin was in such a hurry to be gone, as were most of the commanders of 'banners', that the following morning, since they lacked wagons and could not extract all their gear from the mud, they set fire to their tents, their furnishings, and equipment.

Leaving behind it a huge conflagration, the foundering army arrived before Tournai that evening; the terrified inhabitants closed the gates of the town, and no one insisted that they should open them. The King had to find asylum in a monastery.

Two days later, on August 7th, he was at Soissons, where he signed a number of Orders in Council which put an end to this distinguished campaign. He charged his uncle Valois with making the final preparations for his coronation, and sent his brother Philippe to Paris to fetch the sword and the crown. Everyone would gather between Rheims and Troyes to meet Clémence of Hungary.

Though he had dreamed of meeting his fiancée as a hero of chivalry, Louis's only concern now was that the distressing expedition be forgotten, an expedition which was already known as 'The Muddy Army'.

7
The Philtre

AT DAWN A MULE-BORNE litter, escorted by two armed servants, entered the great porch of the Artois house in the Rue Mauconseil. Beatrice d'Hirson, niece of the Chancellor of Artois and lady-in-waiting to the Countess Mahaut, alighted from it. No one would have thought that this handsome dark-haired girl had travelled nearly a hundred miles since the day before. Her dress was hardly creased; her face with its high cheekbones was as smooth and fresh as if she had just awakened from sleep. Besides, she had slept part of the way under comfortable rugs, to the swinging of the litter. Beatrice d'Hirson, and it was rare in a woman of that period, had no fear of travelling by night; she saw in the dark like a cat and knew that she was under the protection of the devil. Long-legged and high-breasted, walking with steps that seemed slow because they were long and regular, she went straight to the Countess Mahaut, whom she found at breakfast.

'It is done, Madam,' said Beatrice, handing the Countess a little horn box.

'Well, and how is my daughter Jeanne?'

'The Countess of Poitiers is as well as can be expected, Madam; her life at Dourdan is not too harsh and her gentle disposition has won over her gaolers. Her complexion is clear and she has not grown too thin; she is sustained by hope and by your concern for her.'[12]

'What of her hair?' the Countess asked.

'It has only a year's growth, Madam, and is not yet as long as a man's; but it seems to be growing thicker than it was before.'

'But is she presentable?'

'With a veil about her face, most certainly. And she can wear false plaits to hide her neck and ears.'

'You can't keep false hair on in bed,' said Mahaut.

She finished up her bacon-and-pea stew in great spoonfuls and then, to cleanse her palate, drank a full goblet of red Poligny wine. Then she opened the horn box and looked at the grey powder it contained.

'How much did this cost me?'

'Seventy pounds.'

'Damn it, these witches make one pay heavily for their art.'

'They run a big risk.'

'How many of the seventy pounds have you kept for yourself?' said the Countess, looking her lady-in-waiting straight in the eye.

Beatrice did not turn her eyes away and, still smiling ironically, replied in her slow voice, 'Hardly any, Madam.

Merely enough to buy this scarlet dress which you had promised me but failed to give me.'

Countess Mahaut could not help laughing; the girl knew how to handle her.

'You must be hungry, have some of this duck pâté,' she said, helping herself to a huge slice.

Then, reverting to the horn box, she added, 'I believe in the value of poisons for getting rid of enemies, but not much in philtres for the winning over of adversaries. It's your idea, not mine.'

'And yet I assure you, Madam, that you must believe in them,' Beatrice replied, showing more animation than usual, for everything which had to do with magic excited her strongly. 'This philtre is peculiarly effective; it is not made from a sheep's brain, but from herbs only and was prepared in my presence. I went to Dourdan, as I asked your permission to do, and drew a little blood from Madame Jeanne's right arm. Then I took the blood to Dame Isabelle de Férienne, who mixed it with vervain, campion, and lovage; and Dame de Férienne pronounced the spell; she put the mixture on a new brick and burnt it with ashwood to obtain the powder I have brought you. Now it only remains to put the powder in a drink, make the Count of Poitiers swallow it, and in a little while you will see him in love with his wife once again and so violently that nothing will be able to destroy it. Is he still coming to see you this morning?'

'I'm awaiting him now. He came home from the army last night, and I have asked him to call on me.'

'In that case I shall mix the philtre with hippocras so that you may give it to him to drink. Hippocras, which is well spiced and dark in colour, will conceal the powder well. But I counsel you, Madam, to go back to bed and pretend to be indisposed so as to have a pretext for not drinking yourself. It would hardly do if you drank the concoction and found yourself in love with Madam your daughter,' said Beatrice, laughing.

'Receiving him in bed and pretending that I am unwell is an excellent idea,' replied the Countess of Artois. 'One can say things more straightly.'

She therefore went back to bed, had the table cleared, and sent for her Chancellor, Thierry d'Hirson, and for her cousin, Henri de Sulli, who lived in her house and to whom she was much attached these days, so as to work with them upon matters affecting her county.

A little later the Count of Poitiers was announced. He came in sombrely dressed as usual, his heron's legs covered with soft leather boots, and his head, beneath the hood he was wearing, somewhat inclined to one side upon his long body.

'Ah, Son-in-law,' cried Mahaut, as if she had seen her Saviour appear to her, 'how delighted I am to see you! Do you know what I'm busy doing? I was having the inventory of my possessions read over to me so that I might make my will. I have spent one of the worst nights of my life, with the agony of death in my entrails; and I was much afraid of passing over without having opened my thoughts to you, for, despite all that has happened, I love you with a mother's heart.'

To insure against the sin of lying as she was about to do, she secretly touched the relic of Saint Druon[13] which she always wore upon a golden chain between her breasts.

Henri de Sulli turned away in order not to burst out laughing, for he had spent a great part of the night with his cousin and well knew that what she had had in her entrails was not all that agonizing; the Countess Mahaut was not made for widowhood, that was all there was to it; she had the needs and appetites of an ogress, as much in bed as at the dining-table.

Moreover, Mahaut, comfortably propped among her brocaded cushions, her cheeks broad and high in colour, her shoulders wide, her arms plump, gave every appearance of being in the most robust health. All that she needed was to be bled perhaps of a pint or two of blood.

'Well, she's up to some game,' thought Philippe of Poitiers. 'Both physically and mentally she is extraordinarily like Robert of Artois, so much so that one might think they were brother and sister rather than nephew and aunt. I am sure she is going to speak to me of him.'

He was not wrong. Mahaut immediately began complaining about her wicked nephew, his manoeuvres and intrigues, the league of the barons of Artois whom he had roused against her. For Mahaut as for Robert, everything that happened in the world was reduced to terms of the county over which they had been fighting for thirteen years; their thoughts, their plotting, their friendships, their alliances, even their love affairs were all determined in one way or another by this tussle; one joined a certain political party because the other belonged to the opposite one; Robert supported a royal Order in Council only because Mahaut disapproved of it; Mahaut was immediately hostile to Clémence of Hungary because Robert had supported Charles in the negotiations for the marriage. Their hate, which excluded every possible basis for agreement, every possible compromise, seemed to extend beyond the object in dispute, till one might well have wondered if there did not perhaps exist a sort of perverse passion between the giant and the giantess of which they were unaware, one which might better have been appeased by incest than by war.

'Every bad turn he does me brings nearer the hour of my death,' said Mahaut. 'I know that my vassals, assembled by Robert, have taken an oath against me. This is what has upset me and caused my present condition.'

For she was now beginning to persuade even herself that she had spent a bad night.

'They have sworn to kill me, Monseigneur,' said Thierry d'Hirson.

Philippe of Poitiers turned towards the Canon-Chancellor and saw that it was he, and not Mahaut, who was really ill, from sheer fright.

'I was about to go to the army, to put some kind of order into my "banner",' Mahaut went on; 'as you see, I have had my war dress prepared.'

She indicated an imposing lay figure in a corner of the room which was draped with a long coat of chain-mail and a silk surcoat embroidered with the arms of Artois; beside it lay helm and gauntlets.

'And then I heard of the end of this glorious campaign which has cost the Kingdom so much in money and more in honour. Indeed, one may say that your poor brother is not covering himself with glory, and that everything he undertakes goes agley. In truth, and I am merely saying what

I believe, you would have made a much better king than he, and it's a great pity for us all, Son-in-law, that you were born the second. Your father, upon whom God have mercy, often deplored it.'

Since the prosecution at Pontoise, the Count of Poitiers had not seen his mother-in-law except at public ceremonies and occasions such as the funeral of Philip the Fair, or the sessions of the Chamber of Peers, never in private. The scandal in which her daughter had been concerned had necessarily rebounded upon Mahaut. Philippe of Poitiers, throughout all this time, had treated her with coldness. As a way of reopening relations, the flattery was gross, but Mahaut was prepared to lay on compliments with a trowel. She invited her son-in-law to sit beside her bed. D'Hirson and Sulli retired towards the door.

'No, my good friends, don't go away; you know that I have no secrets from you,' she said.

At the same time she made them a sign to leave the room.

For at that period great lords and important personages rarely received visitors alone. Their rooms and apartments were constantly full of relations, friends, vassals, and clients. Private conversations therefore were apt to take place in the view of all; from which came the necessity for allusion, the half-word, and confidence in the people about one. When the two principal personages began to speak in lowered voices, or retired into the embrasure of a window, everyone in the room might wonder whether it was not his own fate which was being discussed. Conversations behind closed doors took on an aspect of conspiracy. And this was precisely the aspect Mahaut wished to give to her conversation with the Count of Poitiers, if it were only to compromise him a little and therefore make him the easier to involve in her game.

As soon as they were alone, she asked, 'What are your feelings towards my daughter Jeanne?'

As he hesitated to reply, she launched out into her speech for the defence. Certainly Jeanne of Burgundy had been wrong, even very wrong, in not warning her husband of the intrigues of the alcove which dishonoured the royal family, and in becoming an accomplice – voluntarily, involuntarily, who could say? – of the scandal. But she herself had not actually sinned with her body, nor had she betrayed her marriage; everyone knew that; and King Philip himself, incensed as he was, had been convinced of it, since he had put Jeanne under certain restraints but had never said that her confinement was to be for life.

'I know, I was at the council of Pontoise,' said the Count of Poitiers, to whom the memory was still painful.

'And how could Jeanne have betrayed you, Philippe? She loves you. She loves only you. You need only remember her cries, as she was being taken away in the black-draped cart: "Tell Monseigneur Philippe that I am innocent". My mother's heart still bleeds to have witnessed it. And for all the fifteen months that she had been at Dourdan, I know it from her confessor, she has never said a word against you, nothing but words of love and prayers to God that she may recapture your heart. I assure you that you have in her a wife more faithful, more devoted to your will than many another, and that she has been harshly punished.'

She threw all the blame on Marguerite of Burgundy and

with all the less qualms because Marguerite was not a member of her family and was now dead. Marguerite was the shameless one; it was Marguerite who had led Blanche, the poor innocent child, astray, who had made use of Jeanne and taken advantage of her friendship. Besides, there were even excuses for Marguerite herself. The mere hope of being Queen was not all-sufficient, and what woman could have been happy with the husband she had been given! Finally, Mahaut held Louis X primarily responsible for his own betrayal and misfortunes.

'It appears that your brother lacks a certain virility.'

'On the contrary, I have been assured that he is perfectly normal in that respect, possibly somewhat over-excitable and violent, but certainly not impotent,' replied the Count of Poitiers.

'Clearly, unlike myself, you have not heard the confidences of women,' replied Mahaut.

She sat up, massive among her pillows, looked her son-in-law straight in the eye, and said, 'Philippe, let's put our cards on the table. Do you think that the heiress to the throne, little Jeanne of Navarre, is Louis's child or the child of Marguerite's lover?'

Philippe of Poitiers momentarily passed his hand across his chin.

'My uncle Valois asserts that she is a bastard,' he replied, 'and Louis himself, by keeping her at a distance as he does, would seem to confirm the fact. Others, such as my uncle of Evreux and the Duke of Burgundy, believe her to be legitimate.'

'If some mishap occurred to Louis, whose health is weak,

as everything goes to show, you are for the moment the second in line of succession. But if little Jeanne of Navarre is declared to be a bastard, as *we believe* she is, you become the first, and you will become King. You would make a good king, Philippe.'

'Unless the new wife who is coming from Naples gives my brother an heir in the near future.'

'If he is capable of procreating one, which is doubtful. And if God should allow him the time to do so.'

At that moment Beatrice d'Hirson came in, bringing a tray laden with a jug of hippocras, silver-gilt goblets, and comfits, which was a proper refreshment to offer a visitor. Mahaut made an impatient gesture. What an unsuitable moment to disturb them! But without taking any notice Beatrice poured the spiced wine into the goblets with her slow gestures and offered one to Philippe of Poitiers. Mahaut, automatically, as she always did when there was any food or drink within reach of her hand, all but took the other goblet. Beatrice gave her a look and stopped her.

'No, I'm too ill, everything makes me feel sick,' she said.

Poitiers was reflecting. His mother-in-law's preoccupations were far from catching him off balance; these last weeks he had thought much about the succession. The long and short of it was that Mahaut was proposing to support him in the case of Louis's death. But what price was she demanding for her help?

'Oh, Philippe, save my daughter Jeanne from dying, I implore you,' cried Mahaut pathetically. 'She has not deserved such a fate.'

'But who's threatening her?' Poitiers asked.

'Robert, as always,' she replied. 'I have discovered that he was in league with the Queen of England, when she came to Pontoise to denounce her sisters-in-law. Which certainly brought Isabella no good luck, for her effeminate husband's army was defeated at Bannockburn immediately afterwards, and Isabella and Edward, as if it were the chastisement of God, have lost Scotland once again.'

She hesitated for a moment, because Poitiers had taken the goblet and raised it to his lips, but quickly went on, 'That devil Robert has improved on that since. Do you know that the day Marguerite was found dead in her prison, Robert, whom we believed to be in his house at Conches, had in fact been to Château-Gaillard that morning?'

'Is that true?' said Poitiers, arresting the goblet halfway to his lips.

'Blanche, who was confined on the storey immediately above, heard everything. The poor child, who has almost lost her senses since then, sent me a message the other day. Listen to me, Philippe, he'll kill both of them one after the other. His game is quite obvious. He wants my county. To diminish my power and disgrace me, he begins by having my daughters imprisoned. To make himself all-powerful with the King, his cousin, he rids him of the wife who prevented his marrying again by strangling her. Now, he'll attack my posterity, I am alone, widowed, with a son too young for me to lean upon,[14] and for whose life I fear as much as for the lives of my daughters. Could not so many fears and sorrows cause a woman to die before her time? God is my witness that I do not wish to die and leave my children at the mercy of that jackal. For Christ's sake take back your wife and protect her, and at the same time make it clear that I am not without an ally. For, if it so happened that I lost Jeanne (she touched her relic once again) and that Artois were taken from me as they are so determinedly trying to do, I should then be obliged to ask for the return, on behalf of my son, of the Palatinate of Burgundy, which was handed to you as a marriage portion in exchange for Artois.'

Poitiers could not but admire the dexterity with which his mother-in-law had aimed her last blow. The deal was clearly stated: 'Either you take Jeanne back, and I will help you to the throne should it become vacant, so that my daughter may be Queen of France; or you refuse to be reconciled to her, and I shall pursue the opposite policy of negotiating the return of your County of Burgundy against the loss of Artois.'

He gazed at her for a moment in silence, as she sat there, monumental beneath the great brocade curtains draped about the bed.

'She's as cunning as a fox and as obstinate as a boar; no doubt she has blood upon her hands, but I must admit I have always had a certain feeling of friendliness towards her. Behind her ruthlessness and deceit lies a certain quality of ingenuousness.'

To hide the smile which rose to his lips, he took a drink from the gilt goblet.

He promised nothing, concluded nothing, for he was reflective by nature and saw no reason to make an immediate decision. But at the very least he already saw a means of counteracting in the Council of Peers the Valois influence which he thought disastrous.

On his departure he said merely, 'We'll talk of all this again at the coronation, where we shall soon be meeting, Mother.'

And by his use of the word 'mother', which he now employed for the first time in fifteen months, Mahaut realized that she had won.

As soon as Poitiers had left, Beatrice came in and inspected the goblet.

'He drank it to the dregs,' she said with satisfaction. 'You will see, Madam, that Monseigneur of Poitiers will go straight off to Dourdan.'

'What I do see,' Mahaut replied, 'is that he would make us an excellent King, should we lose our present one.'

For anyone who knew the Countess Mahaut, to hear her utter such words meant that Louis X was as good as dead.

8

A Country Wedding

ON TUESDAY, AUGUST 13TH, 1315,[15] at first light, the inhabitants of the little town of Saint-Lye in Champagne were awakened by cavalcades coming from Sézanne in the north and Troyes in the south.

First to arrive were the masters of the King's Household who came at a gallop and disappeared into the castle with a large following of equerries, cellarmen, and valets. They were followed by a great convoy of furniture and plate under the command of the majordomos, the pantrymen, and the upholsterers; and finally came all the clergy from Troyes, riding mules and singing psalms, closely followed by the Italian merchants who, by reason of the famous fairs of Champagne, had one of their principal business centres in Troyes. The church-bell began to ring riotously; the King was shortly to be married at Saint-Lye.

Soon the peasants began shouting 'Hurrah!' and the women went of their own accord into the fields to gather flowers to strew upon the road, as if the Holy Sacrament were passing, while the commissariat officers spread over the countryside, acquiring all the eggs, meat, poultry, and fish from the fish-ponds they could find.

Luckily it had ceased raining; but the day was grey and overcast; the heat of the sun nevertheless came through the clouds. The King's people wiped their foreheads and the villagers, looking at the sky, prophesied that the storm would break before vespers. From the castle came the sound of carpenters hammering; the kitchen chimneys belched smoke, and high wagons of straw were being unloaded that it might be spread in the rooms as bedding for servants and even a gentleman or two.

Saint-Lye had not known such a bustle since the day that Philip Augustus, at the beginning of the previous century, had come to hand over the royal castle with due solemnity to the Bishops of Troyes. With only one great event every hundred years, memory had time to dim.

Towards ten o'clock the King, surrounded by his brothers-in-law, his two uncles, his cousins Philippe of Valois and Robert of Artois, galloped through the village without acknowledging the acclamations as they scattered the carpet of flowers which had to be replaced when he had gone by. He was hurrying on ahead of his new wife.

About two miles away, led by the Bishop of Troyes, appeared the cavalcade of the Princess Clémence of Hungary. The latter, leaning from her litter, asked the Comte de Bouville which of the horsemen coming to meet her was her future husband. Fat Bouville, somewhat fatigued by the journey and moved by the prospect of finding himself face to face once more with his King, explained badly, and Clémence at first took the Count of Poitiers for her fiancé, because he was the tallest of the three princes who were coming to meet them, and because he sat his horse with a natural majesty. But it was the least good-looking of the horsemen who first dismounted and came towards the litter. Bouville, leaping from his horse, rushed up to him, seized his hand in order to kiss it and, bending his knee, said, 'Sire, here is Madam of Hungary.'

Then beautiful Clémence looked at the young man with the stooping shoulders, the big pale eyes, and yellow complexion, with whom fate and court intrigue had sent her to share destiny, power, and bed.

Louis X gazed at her in silence with an expression of stupefaction which at first gave Clémence the impression that she was not pleasing to him.

It was she who decided to break the silence.

'Sire Louis,' she said, 'I am your servant for ever.'

Her words seemed to loosen The Hutin's tongue.

'I feared, Cousin, that the painted portrait of you they sent me was flattering and deceptive,' he said, 'but I now see that your grace and beauty surpass the reproduction.'

And he turned towards his following as if to make them acknowledge his good fortune.

Then the members of the family were presented.

A splendid corpulent lord, dressed in gold as if he were going to a tournament and who seemed somewhat short of breath, embraced Clémence, calling her 'niece' and told her that he had seen her as a child in Naples; Clémence realized that he was Charles of Valois, the principal artisan of her marriage. Philippe of Poitiers called her 'sister', as if he already considered her as united to his brother, and the ceremony no more than a formality. Then the horses of the litter shied. A colossal human frame, whose head Clémence could not see, masked the light for a moment, and the Princess heard a voice saying, 'Your cousin, Count Robert of Artois.'

They quickly set off again, and the King ordered the Bishop of Troyes, Monseigneur Jean d'Auxois, to go on ahead so that all might be ready at the church.

Clémence had expected the meeting to take place in quite a different way. She had imagined that tents would have been pitched in some previously selected spot, that heralds of arms would sound trumpets from both sides, and that she herself would alight from her litter to partake of a light meal, while gradually getting to know her fiancé. She had also thought that the wedding would be celebrated only after a few days and would be the prelude to two or three weeks of festivity, with jousting, jugglers, and minstrels, as was the custom at princely weddings.

The abrupt reception upon a country road in a forest, and the absence of all parade, surprised her a little. It was as if they had chanced to meet at a hunting party. She was still more disconcerted when she learnt that she was to be married within the hour in a neighbouring castle, where they would spend the night before leaving for Rheims on the morrow.

'My dear Sire,' she asked the King, who was now riding beside her, 'are you returning to the war?'

'Of course, Madam, I am returning – next year. If I pursued the Flemings no farther this year, and have left them to their terror, it was so that I could hasten to meet you and conclude our espousals.'

This compliment seemed to Clémence so exaggerated that she did not know what to think of it. She was meeting with one surprise after another. This King, who was so impatient to meet her that he demobilized a whole army, was offering her a village wedding.

In spite of the strewn flowers and the enthusiasm of the peasants, the castle of Saint-Lye, a small fortress with thick walls fouled by three centuries of damp, seemed sinister to the Neapolitan princess. She had barely an hour to change her clothes and rest before the ceremony, if one can call rest a sojourn in a room in which the upholsterers had not yet finished putting up the hangings embroidered with parrots, and in which Monseigneur of Valois buzzed about like a huge golden drone on the pretext of instructing his niece in a few minutes in all she must know about the Court of France and in the essential place that he, Charles of Valois, occupied at it.

Thus Clémence was to know that Louis X, if he had every quality that went to make a perfect husband, was no less the possessor of every virtue, particularly in political matters. He was easily influenced and needed to be encouraged in his good ideas while being defended from bad counsellors. In this Flanders affair, for instance, Valois considered that Louis had not sufficiently listened to him, while he had given too much credence to the counsels of the Constable, the Count of Poitiers, and even to Robert of Artois. As to the election of a Pope, Clémence had presumably passed through Avignon? Whom had she seen? Cardinal Duèze? Of course, it was

Duèze whom they must elect. Clémence must understand why Valois had been so determined, and indeed managed things so cleverly, that she had been chosen as Queen of France; he had counted upon her beauty, charm, and wisdom to help him lead the King in the way he should go. Clémence should discuss everything confidentially with himself. Was he not her nearest relation at the Court, since he had married, as his first wife, an aunt of Clémence, and was he not in the position of a father to the young King? Clémence and Valois should be close allies from now on.

But in truth Clémence was beginning to be dizzy from the flood of words, the names flowing out pell-mell, and from the restless activity of this gold-embroidered personage who so buzzed about her. She wondered whether the Constable was Robert of Artois, and which of the King's two brothers she had seen was called the Count of Poitiers. Her head was in turmoil from too many new impressions, too many glimpsed faces. And, what was more, she was going to be married in a few minutes. She was convinced of everyone's goodwill, and was touched that the Count of Valois should show her so much solicitude. But she would have liked to prepare her mind in prayer. Was this a Queen's marriage?

She had the courage to ask why the ceremony was to take place so hastily.

'Because you must be in Rheims on Sunday, where Louis will be crowned, and he wishes your marriage to take place first, so that you may be at his side,' Valois replied.

What he did not say was that the expenses of the wedding were paid by the Crown, while the expenses of the coronation were paid by the aldermen of Rheims. And the royal

Treasury, after the Muddy Army's setback, was more depleted than ever. This was the reason for the scamped marriage and the lack of pageantry; the rejoicings would be held with the citizens of Rheims as hosts.

Clémence of Hungary only managed to get a little peace by asking for her confessor. She had already confessed that morning, but she wished to be assured of going to the altar without sin. Had she not perhaps committed some venial fault during these last hours, failed in humility by being surprised at the lack of pomp with which she had been received, lacked in charity towards her neighbour in wishing to see Monseigneur of Valois at the devil rather than buzzing about her?

Louis X, the evening before, had had more serious things to confess to the Dominican father who had charge of his soul.

While the last preparations were being made, Hugues de Bouville was accosted in the courtyard of the castle by Messire Spinello Tolomei, the Captain-General of the Lombards in Paris. Still perfectly alert in spite of his sixty years and his enormous paunch, he also was going to Rheims, where he had heavily underwritten supplies for the coronation. He was going to see how his agents had carried out their business. He asked Bouville for news of his nephew Guccio.

'What the devil did he want to go and throw himself into the sea for? Oh, I miss him these days! It's he who ought to be dashing about the country,' Tolomei groaned.

'And don't you think I've missed him all the way from Marseilles?' Bouville replied. 'The escort spent twice as much as it would have done if he had been in charge of the cash.'

Tolomei was anxious. With his left eye shut, his thick lip thrust forward a little, he was complaining of events. In spite of what Monseigneur of Valois had promised, a new tithe had been exacted from the Lombard bankers; upon every sale, contract, exchange of gold or silver, both buyer and seller had now to pay twopence in the pound; and king's agents were to be set up everywhere to control the markets and receive the taxes. All this bore a considerable resemblance to the Orders in Council of King Philip.

'Why did they tell us that everything would be changed?'

Bouville left Tolomei to join the wedding procession.

It was a triumphant Monseigneur of Valois who led the bride to the altar. As for Louis X, he had to walk alone. There was no female member of the family present to give him her arm. His aunt, Agnes of France, daughter of Saint Louis, had refused to be present, and it was well enough known why: she was the mother of Marguerite of Burgundy. The Countess Mahaut had excused herself at the last moment owing to the difficulties created by the insurrection in Artois. She would come straight to Rheims for the coronation. As for the Countess of Valois, though imperiously directed to be present by her husband, she had either taken the wrong road, with the swarm of girls who attended her, or had broken the axle of her coach; the Chamberlain, ordered to accompany her, would hear more of it.

Monseigneur Jean d'Auxois, his mitre upon his head, officiated. During the whole service Clémence reproached herself with her lack of religious preparation. With an effort she raised her thoughts to heaven, asking God to vouchsafe her, throughout her whole life, the virtues of a spouse, the qualities of a sovereign, and the blessings of motherhood; but, in spite of herself, her eyes turned to the man who stood breathing heavily beside her, whose face she barely knew, and whose bed she would have to share that very night.

Every time he knelt he gave a short cough as if it were a tic; the deep furrow across his retreating chin was surprising in so young a man. His thin mouth was turned down at the corners; his long, straight hair was mouse-coloured. And when this man, to whom she was in process of being united, looked at her with his huge pale eyes, she felt embarrassed by the concentrated gaze he turned upon her hands, her throat, and her mouth. She wondered why she could not recover that state of supreme, unmitigated happiness which had been hers upon leaving Naples.

'Oh Lord, let me not be ungrateful for all the mercies Thou hast accorded me.'

But one cannot always control one's thoughts, and Clémence surprised herself by thinking in the middle of her marriage service that, if she had been allowed to choose among the three princes of France, she would undoubtedly have preferred the Count of Poitiers. She was seized with terror and nearly cried aloud, 'No, I do not, I am not worthy!' At that moment, she heard herself make the response 'I do', in a voice that seemed not to be her own, to the Bishop who was asking her whether she was prepared to take Louis, King of France and Navarre, as her lawful wedded husband.

The first crash of thunder sounded as the too-large ring was being placed upon her finger; those present looked at each other, and many crossed themselves.

When the procession emerged, the peasants were waiting,

gathered before the church, wearing coarse smocks, their legs bound in rags. Clémence was hardly conscious of saying, 'Should we not distribute alms?'

She was thinking aloud and it was remarked that her first words as Queen were words of kindliness.

To please her, Louis X ordered his Chamberlain, Mathieu de Trye, to throw them some handfuls of money. The peasants immediately scrambled for them upon the ground, and the first sight presented to the newly married Queen was one of savage fighting. There was a sound of ripping clothes, swine-like grunts, and the sharp impact of skulls meeting. The barons were much amused by the spectacle of the scuffle. One of the villeins, stronger and heavier than the rest, crushed a hand with a coin in it under his foot till it was compelled to open.

'There's a fellow who knows what he's about,' said Robert of Artois, laughing. 'Who does he belong to? I'd willingly buy him.'

And Clémence was displeased to see that Louis was laughing too.

'This is not the way to give alms,' she thought. 'I shall have to teach him.'

Rain started falling and the scramble ended in the mud.

Tables had been laid in the largest hall in the castle. The wedding breakfast lasted five hours. 'Here am I, Queen of France,' Clémence said to herself from time to time. She could not get used to the idea. She found it difficult to get used to her surroundings at all. She was amazed at the gluttony of the French lords. As the wine circulated, voices grew louder. The only woman at this banquet of warriors,

Clémence was conscious of being the cynosure of every eye, and realized that at the far end of the hall the conversation was taking a grosser turn.

From time to time one of the feasters would leave the room. Mathieu de Trye, the first Chamberlain, cried, 'The King our Lord desires that no one should piss upon the stairs by which he must pass.'

When they had reached the fourth service of six dishes each, of which a whole pig served on the spit and a peacock with all its tail feathers formed part, two equerries came in bearing a huge pie which they set before the royal couple. The crust was broken open and a live fox jumped out to the excited cries of all present. For lack of time to prepare set pieces and elaborate sweets, which would have taken many days to make, the cooks had hoped to create an effect in this way.

The frightened fox dashed round the hall, its tufted red brush sweeping the stone floor, its fine brilliant eyes pale with panic.

'Gone away! Gone away!' shouted the lords bounding from their seats.

They at once organized a hunt. It was Robert of Artois who caught the fox. He threw himself full length between the table and got up, holding the animal at arms' length. It snarled and revealed sharp teeth between black lips. Then Robert slowly closed his fingers; the vertebrae were heard to crack; the fox's eyes turned glassy, and Robert laid the dead animal upon the table in homage before the Queen.

Clémence, who was holding the too-large ring on her finger with her thumb, asked if it was the French custom that the women of the family should not attend weddings. It was explained to her what had happened and that those who had been coming had been unable to arrive in time.

'But in any case, my dear sister, you would not have had the opportunity of seeing my wife,' said the Count of Poitiers.

'And why not, brother?' Clémence asked, at once interested in all he said and finding some difficulty in conversing with him.

'Because she is still confined to the Castle of Dourdan,' replied Philippe of Poitiers.

Then turning to the King he said, 'Sire, my brother, upon this auspicious day I pray you to raise the ban imposed upon my wife Jeanne and to permit me to take her back. You know that she never forfeited her honour and that it would be an injustice to leave her any longer to pay for faults that were not hers.'

The Hutin frowned. He clearly knew neither what to answer, nor what to decide. In order to please Clémence, should he show mercy or firmness, both royal qualities? He sought his Uncle of Valois with his eyes to ask his counsel, but the latter had just gone out for a breath of fresh air. Robert of Artois was at the other end of the hall, explaining to Philippe of Valois, Charles's son, how to catch hold of a fox without getting bitten. Moreover, The Hutin did not much wish to bring Robert into a matter in which he was already too involved.

'Sire, my husband,' said Clémence, 'for my sake grant your brother the boon he asks. Today is a day of rejoicing, and I would wish every woman in your realms to have her share in it.'

She clearly had taken the matter to heart, and with

surprising warmth, as if she felt relieved that Philippe of Poitiers had a wife and wished to take her back.

She gazed at Louis. She was beautiful. Her blue eyes, huge between their fair eyelashes, rested upon him in a way that surpassed all other pleas.

Moreover, he had dined well and emptied his cup rather more often than he had intended. The moment was approaching when he would be able to sample the delights of this beautiful body of which he was now master. He had not the wit to weigh the political consequences of what was being asked of him.

'Beloved, there's nothing I won't do to please you,' he replied. 'Brother, you may take back Madame Jeanne and bring her among us as soon as you please.'

His younger brother, the young Count de la Marche, the best looking of the three, who had been following the conversation with attention, then said, 'What about me, brother; will you authorize the same thing on behalf of Blanche?'

'For Blanche, never!' the King said decisively.

'Merely permission to go and see her at Château-Gaillard and place her in a convent where she will be less hardly treated . . .'

'Never,' repeated The Hutin in a tone which forbade argument.

The fear that Blanche, once out of her fortress, would speak of the circumstances of Marguerite's death had caused him for once to take a decision that was both immediate and without appeal.

And Clémence, feeling that it was wiser to rest upon her first victory, did not dare to intervene further.

'Am I never to have the right to have a wife again?' Charles went on.

'Let fate take its course, brother,' replied Louis.

'Fate seems to be favouring Philippe more than me.'

And from that moment Charles de la Marche conceived a resentment, not so much against the King as against the Count of Poitiers, to whom he was in any case alien in temperament, and whom he was angry to see better treated than himself.

At the end of this exhausting day the young Queen was so tired that the events of the night seemed to take place in another life. She felt no fear, nor any particular suffering, nor any significant happiness. She merely submitted, feeling that things must take their course. Before relapsing into sleep, she heard mumbled words which allowed her to hope that her husband appreciated her. Had she not been so inexperienced, she would have understood that, for a time at least, she held complete sway over Louis X.

And indeed, the King was astonished to find a submissiveness in this daughter of kings which until then he had found only among servants. The appalling agonies of impotence which he had suffered in Marguerite of Burgundy's bed now disappeared. Perhaps after all he did not like brunettes. Four times he was triumphantly successful with this beautiful body which was so submissive to his desires and glowed faintly, as if made of mother-of-pearl, beneath the little oil-lamp hanging under the canopy of the bed. Never before had he accomplished such an exploit.

When he left the room, late in the morning, his head felt dizzy though he held it high. His glance was assured, and one might have thought that his marriage night had obliterated the memory of his military mortifications. What had been lost in war might be regained in love.

For the first time The Hutin felt capable of receiving without embarrassment the dubious jokes of his cousin of Artois, who was considered to be the most potent womanizer at Court.

Then, towards midday, they set out towards the north. Clémence turned a last time to look at the castle in which she had stayed but twenty-four hours and whose exact shape she would never be able to remember clearly.

Two days later they arrived at Rheims. The inhabitants, who had not seen a coronation for thirty years – that is to say that for at least half the population the spectacle was an entirely new one – had gathered at the gates and along the streets. The town was full of people from the surrounding country, who had come on foot or on horseback, of every kind of merchant, showmen with performing animals, jugglers, sergeants-at-arms, and officers of the Crown who were as pre-occupied as if they carried the whole weight of the Kingdom upon their shoulders.

The citizens of Rheims would not have believed that they were to have the opportunity of seeing a similar procession and what's more, paying its cost, three times over in less than fourteen years.

But never again would the threshold of the Cathedral of Rheims be crossed by a King of France together with the three successors history had designed for him. Behind Louis X, indeed, were the Count of Poitiers, the Count de la Marche, and Count Philippe of Valois, that is to say the future Philippe

V, the future Charles IV, and the future Philippe VI. The two Philippes, Poitiers and Valois, were twenty-two years old; Charles de la Marche, twenty-one. Before the latter reached the age of thirty-seven, the crown would have been placed on all their three heads in turn.

PART TWO

AFTER FLANDERS, ARTOIS

I

The Insurgents

Of all human functions that which consists in governing men, though the most envied, is the most disappointing, for it has no end and permits the mind no rest. The baker who has done his baking, the woodman before the oak he has felled, the judge who has delivered his judgement, the architect who has seen the last pinnacle in place, the painter once he has finished his picture, may all, for a night at least, know the relative relaxation which follows the satisfactory conclusion of a job. He who governs can never know it. Hardly has one political hurdle been surmounted than another, which was in course of formation while the first was being dealt with, demands immediate attention. The victorious general enjoys the honours of his victory for a long while; but a prime minister has to face the new situation born of that very victory itself. No problem can remain unresolved for long, for that which appears relatively unimportant today assumes tragic proportions tomorrow.

The exercise of power is comparable only to the profession of medicine, which is also subject to this unremitting cycle, this priority of urgencies, this constant watching of minor ills because they may be symptomatic of more serious affections; indeed, the perpetual taking of responsibility in fields where a solution must depend upon future circumstances. The organization of society, like the health of individuals, can never be taken as definitive or considered as a task finally accomplished.

The statesman's only moments of rest are in defeat, with all its bitterness and the anxious recapitulation of accomplished fact, often of a threatening future. There is no rest for those in power but in defeat.

What is true of today, when the task of directing a nation requires almost superhuman strength and talent, was doubtless true through the ages; and the profession of king, when kings themselves governed, consisted in equally ceaseless labour.

Hardly had Louis X, after his melancholy military adventure, allowed the affairs of Flanders to lapse, resigning himself to letting them go from bad to worse since he was unable to resolve them, hardly had he acquired the mystic prestige which the coronation conferred upon the sovereign, however deplorable a monarch he might be, than fresh troubles burst upon him in the north of France.

The Barons of Artois, in accordance with their promise to Robert, had not disarmed upon returning home from the army. They went up and down the country with their 'banners', trying to win over the population to their cause. The whole nobility was on their side and, through it, the countryside. The middle classes in the towns were divided in their allegiance. Arras, Boulogne, Thérouanne made common cause with the insurgents. Calais, Avesnes, Bapaume, Aire, Lens, and Saint-Omer remained faithful to the Countess Mahaut. The province was in a state of upheaval approaching insurrection.

The leaders were Jean de Fiennes, the lords of Caumont and Souastre, and Gérard Kierez, the cleverest of them all, who knew how to draw up petitions and understood how to manage the proceedings before the King's Councils.

Maintained, directed, and furnished with subsidies by Robert of Artois, they had, thanks to the latter, the support of the Count of Valois and of the whole reactionary faction surrounding Louis X.

Their demands were of two kinds. On the one hand they demanded a return to the customs of Saint Louis, desiring to go back to the times when they were answerable only to local courts, could declare war when they pleased and scarcely paid any taxes. On the other they demanded a change in local administration and particularly the resignation of Mahaut's Chancellor, Thierry d'Hirson, who was anathema to them.

Had their demands been met, it would have meant that the Countess Mahaut would have been deprived of all authority in her appanage, which was exactly what her nephew Robert wanted.

But Mahaut was not the woman to allow herself to be despoiled. By cunning, continual argument, unfulfilled promises, pretending to yield today what she would throw back into the melting-pot tomorrow, she sought to gain time by every means at her disposal. Customs? Of course she would grant them. But in order to do so there must, naturally, be a commission to determine what precisely these customs were in every lordship of the province. Her administrators? If they had transgressed or abused their powers, she would punish them without mercy. But for this, too, a commission was clearly necessary. And then the argument would be taken to the King, who understood nothing about it and thought of his other anxieties, while the judicial arguments flowed on. Countess Mahaut accepted the grievances of Master Gérard Kierez; she gave evidence of her goodwill. She wished to find out what it was all about, and they would have an interview in the near future at Bapaume. Why Bapaume? Because Bapaume was on her side and she had a garrison there. She insisted upon Bapaume. And then, on the appointed day, she failed to arrive at Bapaume, because she had had to go to Rheims for the coronation. And after the coronation she forgot all about the promised interview. But, nevertheless, she would go to Artois as soon as possible; let everyone be patient. The Commissions of Inquiry were pursuing their natural course, that is to say, the agents in her pay were compelling people, with threats of flogging, prison, or the gibbet, to sign themselves as witnesses in favour of the administration of the Canon-Chancellor, Thierry d'Hirson.

The barons lost their temper; they rebelled openly and forbade Thierry, who was in Paris with the Countess, to show his head in Artois on pain of death. Then they commanded the other Hirson, Denis, the Treasurer, to appear before them and he had the foolhardiness to comply; putting a sword to his throat, they obliged him to deny his brother upon oath.

The political conflict became a question of settling old

scores. Matters began to look so dangerous that Louis X went to Arras himself. He wished to arbitrate. But he could do very little, since he had no army, and the only 'banner' which remained mobilized was precisely that which was in revolt.

On September 19th Mahaut's people determined to surprise and arrest the lords of Souastre and Caumont, two gallants who were a perfect complement to each other, one being a brilliant speaker and the other strong of arm; they appeared to have become the leaders of the insurrection. Souastre and Caumont were thrown into prison. Robert of Artois immediately pleaded their cause before the King.

'Sire, my Cousin,' he said, 'you know that I have nothing whatever to do with these matters since I was so disgracefully deprived of my inheritance, which is now governed by my aunt Mahaut, and, it must be admitted, ill enough. But if Souastre and Caumont are kept in gaol, I tell you there will be war in Artois. I am only giving you my opinion because of the goodwill I bear you.'

The Count of Poitiers argued in the opposite sense.

'It may have been a mistake to have arrested these two lords, but it would be still more foolish to release them at this moment. It would encourage insurrection throughout the Kingdom; it is your authority, Brother, which is in question.'

Charles of Valois lost his temper.

'It is enough for you, Nephew,' he cried, addressing Philippe of Poitiers, 'that your wife, who has recently been released from Dourdan, should have been returned to you. Don't plead her mother's cause. You can't ask the King to open prison doors for those whom you like, and to close them upon those whom you do not.'

'I don't see the relevance, Uncle,' Philippe replied.

'I see it all right, and indeed one might think that Countess Mahaut is at the back of your demands.'

In the end The Hutin ordered Mahaut to free the two imprisoned lords. In the Countess's circle a bad pun was going the rounds: 'At the moment our lord King Louis is devoted to Clemency.'

Souastre and Caumont came out of their week's imprisonment with martyrs' haloes. On September 26th they ordered all their partisans, who now called themselves 'the allies', to meet at Saint-Pol. Souastre spoke at great length, and the scurrility of his speech and the violence of his language carried his audience away. They were to refuse to pay the taxes and were to hang the provosts, tax-collectors, and all the agents, sergeants-at-arms, or other representatives of the Countess, beginning of course with the Hirson family.

The King had sent two councillors, Guillaume Flotte and Guillaume Paumier, to counsel appeasement and negotiate a new conference at Compiègne. The allies accepted the conference in principle, but hardly had the two Guillaumes left the meeting than an emissary from Robert of Artois arrived, breathless and sweating from his long gallop. He brought the barons news: Countess Mahaut, surrounding her journey with great secrecy, was coming to Artois herself; and would be at the Manor of Vitz, staying with Denis d'Hirson, on the following day.

When Jean de Fiennes had made this news public, Souastre cried, 'We know now, my lords, what we have to do.'

That night the roads of Artois rang with the sound of horses' hooves and the clank of arms.

2

The Countess of Poitiers

THE GREAT TRAVELLING COACH, carved, painted, and gilded, trundled beneath the trees. It was so long that it sometimes had to manoeuvre to turn the corners, and the men of the escort had often to dismount to push it up the hills.

Though the huge oaken box was springless, the jolting of the road was not too uncomfortable because of the heaped rugs and cushions. There were six women inside it, almost as if in a room, gossiping, playing at knuckle-bones, or riddles. The low branches could be heard scraping along the leathern hood.

Jeanne of Poitiers drew aside the curtain, which was embroidered with fleurs-de-lys and the three golden castles which were the arms of the Artois family.

'Where are we?' she asked.

'We are skirting Authie, Madam,' replied Beatrice d'Hirson. 'We have just passed through Auxi-le-Château. Within the hour we shall be at Vitz, at my Uncle Denis's, who is expecting us and will be delighted to see you again. And perhaps Madame Mahaut will already be there with your husband.'

Jeanne of Poitiers gazed out at the countryside, the still green trees, the fields in which the peasants were making a thin gleaning under a brilliant sun, for, as often happens after wet summers, the weather had turned fine towards the end of September.

'Madame Jeanne, I implore you, don't look out of the coach all the time,' Beatrice went on. 'Madame Mahaut has strongly advised you not to show yourself while we are in Artois.'

But Jeanne could not help it. To gaze about her was all she had done during the eight days since she had come out of prison. As starving men stuff themselves with food, thinking that they can never have enough, she was once more taking possession of the universe through her eyes. The leaves on the trees, the fleecy clouds, a church steeple rising in the distance, the flight of a bird, the grass on a bank, all appeared to her in a guise of surpassing splendour because she was free.

When the doors of the Castle of Dourdan had opened in front of her, and the captain of the garrison, bowing low, had wished her a good journey and said how honoured he felt to have had her for guest, Jeanne had been seized with a sort of vertigo.

'Shall I ever get used to being free again?' she wondered.

In Paris she met with a disappointment. Her mother had had to leave hastily for Artois. But she had left her the travelling coach, several ladies-in-waiting and numerous servants.

While tailors, dressmakers, and embroiderers rapidly reconstructed her wardrobe, Jeanne had taken advantage of the several days' delay to enjoy the capital in Beatrice's company. She felt like a stranger who had arrived from the other end of the world, and was astonished by all she saw. The streets! She never tired of the spectacle of the streets. The booths in the Mercers' Gallery, the shops on the Goldsmiths' quay! She longed to touch everything, to buy everything. While still maintaining the somewhat distant, controlled manner which had always been hers, her eyes shone, and her body reacted with sensual pleasure to the touch of brocades, pearls, and gold knick-knacks. And yet she could not forget that she had wandered among these same booths with Marguerite of Burgundy, Blanche, and the brothers Aunay.

'In prison I often swore that if ever I were free I would not waste my time upon frivolous things,' she said to herself. 'Besides, in the old days I did not really care for them so much! What has caused in me this sudden, uncontrollable urge?'

She gazed long at the women's dresses, taking note of the new details of fashion, the shape head-dresses, gowns, and surcoats had assumed that year. She sought to read in men's eyes whether she was still capable of pleasing them. The unspoken compliments she received, the way young men turned their heads to gaze after her, were utterly reassuring. She found a hypocritical excuse for her coquetry. 'I need to know,' she thought, 'whether I still possess the power of charming my husband.'

And indeed she had come from her sixteen months of imprisonment physically unimpaired. The regimen at Dourdan was in no way comparable to that of Château-Gaillard. Jeanne was a little paler than she used to be, but this was in a sense an improvement, since her freckles had disappeared. Under the false tresses coiled about her ears – 'Women with poor hair always wear them,' Beatrice d'Hirson had told her reassuringly – her neck, the most beautiful neck in the Kingdom, still supported with all its old grace the little head with the high cheekbones and the blue eyes slightly tilted towards the temples. Her walk had all the supple grace of the pale grey-hounds of Barbary. Jeanne did not much resemble her mother, except in her robust health, and in appearance took after the family of the late Count Palatine, who had been a most elegant lord.

Now that she was almost arrived at the end of her journey, Jeanne found her impatience increasing; these last hours seemed to her longer than all the past months. Were not the horses going more slowly? Could not the postillions be urged on?

'Oh, Madam, I long to get to the journey's end too, but not for the same reason as yours,' said one of the ladies-in-waiting, sitting at the other end of the coach.

The lady, who was called Madame de Beaumont, was six months gone. The journey was becoming painful to her; from time to time she lowered her eyes to her stomach while uttering so heavy a sigh that the other ladies could not help laughing.

Jeanne of Poitiers asked Beatrice in a low voice, 'Are you sure that my husband has formed no other attachment during all this time? You haven't lied to me?'

'No, Madam, I assure you. And moreover, had Monseigneur of Poitiers turned his attention towards other women he could no longer think of them now, having drunk the philtre that will make him entirely yours. You know it was he who asked the King for your freedom.'

'Even if he has a mistress, I shan't care. I'll get accustomed to it. A man, even if one has to share him, is better than prison,' Jeanne said to herself. Once again she drew back the curtains as if this might of itself quicken the pace.

'I beseech you, Madam,' said Beatrice a second time, 'don't show yourself so much. We aren't much liked in this neighbourhood at the moment.'

'And yet the people seem friendly enough. These peasants saluting us look charming,' replied Jeanne.

She let the curtain fall back into place. She did not see that, as soon as the coach had passed, three of the peasants who had bowed so low ran into the undergrowth to get their horses and gallop away.

A moment later the coach entered the courtyard of the Manor of Vitz; the Countess of Poitiers's patience was put to a new test. Expecting to fall into her mother's arms, and above all prepared to greet her husband, Jeanne was met by Denis d'Hirson with the news that neither the Countess of Artois nor the Count of Poitiers had arrived but were waiting for her at the Castle of Hesdin, fifteen miles to the north. Jeanne turned pale.

'What does this mean?' she said to Beatrice apart. 'One might suspect a feint so as not to see me?'

Suddenly she was assailed by acute anxiety. This journey, the pint of blood that had been taken from her arm, the philtre, the respect paid her by the Chief Gaoler at Dourdan, were they not all part of an act in which Beatrice was the chief villain? After all, Jeanne had no proof that her husband had sent for her. Were they perhaps not in process of simply moving her from one prison to another, while surrounding this transference, for reasons peculiar to themselves, with all the appearance of freedom? Provided they had not – and Jeanne trembled at the thought – decided to assassinate her, having taken the precaution to show her free and pardoned both in Paris and in Artois. Beatrice had told her the circumstances in which Marguerite of Burgundy had died. Jeanne wondered whether they were not going to make away with her too, merely surrounding her death with different circumstances.

This was so much on her mind that she could not do justice to the meal that Denis d'Hirson set before her. The happiness of the last eight days had been suddenly replaced by appalling anxiety, and she tried to read her fate on the faces of those present. The beautiful Beatrice and the Treasurer, her uncle, seemed to have a perfect understanding between them; their embraces at meeting had endured longer than was normal even between relations. And there were two lords there, the squires of Liques and Nédonchel, who had been presented to Jeanne as her escort as far as Hesdin. They appeared somewhat embarrassed. Were they perhaps not also charged with some frightful deed to be carried out on the road?

No one spoke to Jeanne of her imprisonment; indeed, everyone affected to ignore the fact that she had ever been in prison, and this in itself she found scarcely reassuring. The conversation, of which she understood but little, was entirely concerned with the situation in Artois, with the ancient customs which were at stake, with the conference at Compiègne which the King's envoys had proposed, and with the insurrection fomented by Souastre, Caumont, and Jean de Fiennes.

'Madam, did you notice any excitement on the road or any assembly of armed men?' Denis d'Hirson asked Jeanne.

'I noticed nothing of the kind, Messire Denis,' she replied, 'and the countryside looked perfectly peaceful.'

'Nevertheless, I have information of activity yesterday and throughout the night; two of our provosts were attacked this morning.'

Jeanne was more and more inclined to believe that these were only words uttered to dispel her fears. She felt as though an invisible net were being drawn tightly round her. She wondered how she might escape. But where should she go? Who could help her? She was alone, appallingly alone, and she gazed round upon the assembled company without seeing anyone who might be a possible ally.

The pregnant lady-in-waiting was eating with extraordinary greed and still continued to sigh heavily as she contemplated her swollen stomach.

'I assure you, Messire Denis, that the Countess Mahaut will be forced to yield,' said the Lord of Nédonchel, who had long teeth, a yellow face, and stooping shoulders. 'Use your influence on her. She'll have to compromise. Difficult though it is to say it to you, she will have to part with your brother or at least pretend to, for the allies will never treat with her so long as he remains Chancellor. And, I assure you, we're risking everything in being faithful to the Countess while pretending to act with the other barons. The longer she delays, the more her nephew Robert will gain ascendancy over people's minds.'

At this moment a sergeant-at-arms, breathless and bare-headed, came running into the dining hall.

'What's the matter, Cornillot?' asked Denis d'Hirson.

Sergeant Cornillot whispered a few abrupt words in Denis d'Hirson's ear. The latter immediately turned pale, dashed away the cloth which covered his knees, and leapt from his bench, saying, 'One moment, Messeigneurs, I'm called away.'

He dashed through one of the little doors in the hall, with Cornillot hot on his heels. He was heard shouting, 'My sword, bring me my sword!'

Then he was heard running down the stairs.

A moment later, while the diners were still lost in surprise, a great clamour rose in the courtyard. It was as if a whole army had galloped into it. A dog, whom someone had doubtless kicked, was howling lugubriously. Liques and Nédonchel rushed to the windows, while the Countess of Poitiers's ladies-in-waiting took refuge in a corner like so many guinea-hens. Only Beatrice d'Hirson and the pregnant lady, who had turned ghastly pale, remained near Jeanne.

'It's a surprise attack,' Jeanne of Poitiers said to herself. Seeing how Beatrice had drawn close to her and how her hands trembled, Jeanne realized that she was certainly not in league with the attackers. This, however, did not materially improve the situation, and in any case there was but little time for thought.

The door flew open and twenty barons, with Souastre and Caumont at their head, entered with drawn swords, shouting, 'Where's the traitor? Where's the traitor? Where's he hiding?'

They stopped, somewhat disconcerted by what they saw.

There were several reasons for their surprise. In the first place Denis d'Hirson, whom they had been certain of finding, was absent. He seemed to have disappeared as if behind a magician's veil. Then the crowd of screaming, swooning women, all herded together and certain of being raped. And above all, the presence of Liques and Nédonchel, whom they believed to be on their side; at Saint-Pol the day before, these two lords had been among those summoned, and now they found them here, seated at dinner in a house belonging to the opposite camp.

The turncoats were grossly insulted; they were asked what they had made out of their perjury, whether they had sold themselves to Hirson for thirty pieces of silver; and Souastre hit Nédonchel's long yellow face with his iron gauntlet so that he bled from the mouth.

Liques made an attempt to explain matters and to justify himself.

'We came here to plead your cause; we wished to avert useless death and destruction. We could have achieved more by the spoken word than you can achieve with your swords.'

They swore at him and forced him to be silent. From the courtyard came the clamour of the other 'allies' who were waiting there. They amounted to at least a hundred.

'Don't mention my name,' Beatrice whispered to the Countess of Poitiers, 'because it's my uncle they're in search of.'

The pregnant lady had a fit of hysterics and fell back upon her bench.

'Where is the Countess Mahaut? She must listen to us! We know she's here, we followed her coach,' cried the barons.

Jeanne of Poitiers began to realize that these insurgents were not looking specially for her, and that it was not her life they sought. Her first feeling of terror passed, anger took its place; in spite of the sixteen months she had spent in prison, the Artois blood boiled once more in her veins with all its inherited violence.

'I am the Countess of Poitiers and it is I who have been travelling in my mother's coach,' she cried. 'And I take exception to your entering so noisily the house in which I happen to be staying.'

As the insurgents did not know that she had come out of prison, this unexpected announcement temporarily silenced them. They were meeting with surprise upon surprise. Those who had had the opportunity of seeing Jeanne in the past now recognized her.

'Would you please tell me your names,' Jeanne went on, 'for I am not accustomed to speaking with people whose names I do not know, and I find it difficult to recognize you beneath your harness of war.'

'I am the Lord of Souastre,' replied the leader with the thick red eyebrows, 'and this is my comrade Caumont; and here are Saint-Venant and Jean de Fiennes, and Messire de Longvillers; and we are looking for the Countess Mahaut.'

'What!' interrupted Jeanne. 'Do I hear the names of gentlemen! I would not have expected it from your manner towards ladies, whom it would behove you better to protect rather than attack! Look at Madame de Beaumont, who is in the last stages of pregnancy, and whom you have sent into a swoon. Aren't you ashamed of yourselves?'

A certain indecision became apparent among the barons.

Jeanne was a beautiful woman, and they were abashed by the way she confronted them. Besides, she was the King's sister-in-law and seemed to have regained his favour. Arnaud de Longvillers assured her that they wished her no harm, that they had a grudge against Denis d'Hirson alone, because he had sworn that he would deny his brother and had not kept his oath.

In fact, they had hoped to catch Mahaut in the trap and coerce her by force; and now they felt somewhat sheepish that their plan had misfired. Some of them, remounting their horses, went off to search the countryside for the Treasurer, while others, to avenge their discomfiture, sacked the house.

For an hour and more the Manor of Vitz resounded to the noise of banging doors, splintering furniture and breaking china. The tapestries and hangings were pulled from the walls; they looted the silver from the tables.

Then, somewhat calmer though still threatening, the insurgents made Jeanne and her ladies get into the great golden coach; Souastre and Caumont took command of the escort, and the coach started down the road to Hesdin surrounded by the clanking steel of the warriors' coats of mail.

Thus the allies were certain of reaching the Countess of Artois.

As they left the town of Ivergny, which was about two and a half miles on their road, there was a halt. They had caught Denis d'Hirson as he was attempting to cross the Authie among the marshes. He was covered with mud, wounded, bleeding, and laden with chains on hands and feet. He was stumbling along between two barons on horseback.

'What are they going to do to him? What are they going to

do to him?' Beatrice murmured. 'How they've ill-used him!'

And in a low voice she began to repeat curious prayers which made no sense either in Latin or in French.

After a good deal of argument, the barons agreed to keep him as a hostage, and shut him up in a neighbouring castle. But their murderous fury had need of a victim. They had no difficulty in finding one.

Sergeant Cornillot had been taken at the same time as Denis. It was his misfortune that, ten days earlier, he had himself arrested Souastre and Caumont. As his life was worth nothing in ransom, it was decided to put him to death on the spot. But it was necessary that his execution should serve as an example and give all Mahaut's agents pause for thought. Some wanted to hang him, others to break him on the wheel, others again to bury him alive. Rivalling each other in cruelty, they discussed the manner of his death in his presence, while Cornillot, upon his knees, his face pouring with sweat, screamed that he was innocent and besought them to spare him. Souastre found a compromise to which everyone, except the condemned man, could agree.

They went in search of a ladder. Cornillot was hoisted into a tree and tied there by the armpits; when he had been kicking for a bit, while the barons laughed, they cut the rope and let him fall to the ground. The unhappy man, his legs broken, screamed continuously while they dug his grave. He was buried upright, to the neck.

The Countess of Poitiers's coach was still waiting to continue the journey, while the ladies-in-waiting stopped their ears in order not to hear the victim's cries. The Countess of Poitiers, strong as she was, felt herself grow faint; and she did not dare to intervene for fear that the barons' anger should turn upon herself. Beatrice d'Hirson, in spite of the dangers of her position, followed the ceremony with singular attention.

At last Souastre handed his great sword to one of the men-at-arms. The blade flashed across the ground and Sergeant Cornillot's head rolled upon the grass, while a fountain of blood poured from the severed arteries.

As soon as the coach had set out once more, the pregnant lady was taken with pains; she began screaming, hurling herself upon her back, and raising her skirts. It was soon obvious that she would not reach the natural term of her pregnancy.

3

The Second Couple in the Kingdom

Hesdin was a considerable fortress surrounded by three lines of fortifications separated by fosses, bristling with flanking towers, enclosing a large number of outbuildings, stables, barns, and storehouses, and was connected by a number of underground passages with the surrounding countryside. A garrison of eight hundred archers could live there comfortably with all their supporting services and the necessary supplies for a siege of several months. Within the third court was the principal residence of the Counts of Artois, made up of several groups of lodgings, containing rare furniture, tapestries, works of art, and gold plate, accumulated during the course of three generations, an incalculable fortune.

'As long as I hold this place,' Mahaut was accustomed to say, 'my wicked barons will not get the better of me. They'll exhaust themselves before my walls are breached, and my nephew Robert is deluding himself if he thinks I'll ever let him get his clutches on Hesdin.'

'Hesdin belongs to me by right of inheritance,' Robert of Artois said on his side; 'my aunt Mahaut has stolen it from me, as she has all the rest of my county. But I'll fight on till I take it, and her wicked life into the bargain.'

When the allies, still escorting Jeanne's coach, came at dusk to the first fortifications, their number had already considerably decreased. The Lord of Journy had left the escort, on the excuse that he had to go home to see to the getting in of his harvest, and the Lord of Givenchy had done the same, not wishing to leave his wife alone for too long. Others, whose manors were within an arrow's flight of the road, went home to supper, taking their friends with them and swearing that they would rejoin the cavalcade later on. This had gone on to such an extent that the keenest among them were now no more than thirty in number; they had ridden for three days without quitting the company. Their armour began to weigh heavily upon their shoulders, and they felt in considerable need of a bath.

They had somewhat slaked their anger on Sergeant Cornillot, whose head was being carried on the point of a lance as a trophy.

They had to argue for some time with the outer guard before they were allowed to enter. Then they had to wait once more, with Jeanne of Poitiers in their midst, between the first and second lines of fortifications. The new moon had risen in the not yet dark sky. But shadows were gathering in the courtyards of Hesdin. All seemed quiet, even too quiet in the barons' eyes. They were surprised to see so small a number of armed men. A horse, smelling the presence of other horses, neighed from the far end of a stable.

The freshness of the evening fell upon them, and Jeanne recognized the scents of her childhood. Madame de Beaumont was still groaning that she was dying. The barons were arguing among themselves. Some were saying that they had done enough for the moment, that the whole business looked like a trap, and that they would do better to come back in greater strength another day. Jeanne saw the moment coming when she too would be taken away as a hostage, or would be involved in a night battle.

At last the second drawbridge was lowered, then the third. The barons hesitated.

'Is it really certain that my mother is here?' Jeanne whispered to Beatrice d'Hirson.

'I swear it to you, Madam, and indeed I am as anxious to find myself in her company as you can be.'

Jeanne then leant out of the coach.

'Well, Messeigneurs,' she said, 'do you still desire so much to speak to your suzerain, or does your courage fail at the moment of approaching her?'

These words urged the barons on and, so as not to lose face with a woman, they entered the third court, where they dismounted.

It does not matter how prepared for an event one is, it always takes place otherwise than one had imagined.

Jeanne of Poitiers had thought twenty times of the moment when she would be with her family again. She had been prepared for anything, from the cold reception usually accorded the freed gaolbird, to a great official scene of reconciliation and a new, intimate meeting amid joy and happy embraces. She had considered her attitude and her words for every eventuality. But she had never imagined that she would enter her family castle escorted by the riff-raff of a civil war and with, in the back of her coach, a lady-in-waiting in process of having a miscarriage.

When Jeanne entered the Great Hall, lit by candles, where the Countess Mahaut, arms crossed and tight of lip, watched the barons filing in, her first words were, 'Mother, Madame de Beaumont, who is in process of losing her child, must be given help. Your vassals have frightened her overmuch.'

The Countess Mahaut at once gave instructions to her god-child, Mahaut d'Hirson, a sister of Beatrice's who was with her (for the whole family of Hirson formed part of her court: Pierre was bailey of Arras, Guillaume was pantler, three other nephews and nieces held sinecures), to go and find Master Hermant and Master de Pavilly, her private physicians, that they might attend to the patient.

Then, pulling up her sleeves she addressed herself to the barons: 'Wicked lords, do you call this chivalry, attacking my noble daughter and the ladies of her household, and do you think that you can make me relent thereby? Would you like your own wives and daughters to be treated thus when they travel the roads? Answer me, explain your crimes, for which I shall ask the King to punish you!'

The barons nudged Souastre and whispered, 'Go on, tell her.'

Souastre coughed to clear his throat and rubbed his three days' growth of beard. He had talked so much, so vituperatively, held so many meetings to win over others, that now, on the most important occasion of all, he no longer knew what to say.

'As to that, Madam,' he began, 'we want to know if you are prepared to disavow your wicked chancellor who strangles our requests, and whether you will consent to recognize our customs as they were at the time of Monsieur Saint Louis . . .'

He broke off because a new personage had entered the room, and this was no less than the Count of Poitiers. His head a little to one side, he came forward with long steady strides. The barons, who were but small territorial lords and far from expecting the sudden appearance of the King's brother, nervously closed their ranks.

'Messeigneurs . . .' said the Count of Poitiers.

He stopped, having caught sight of Jeanne.

He went up to her and kissed her on the mouth in the most natural manner in the world, before all those present, in order to prove once and for all that his wife was wholly taken back into favour and that at the same time, as far as he was concerned, Mahaut's interests were a family matter.

'Well, Messeigneurs,' he went on, 'you appear discontented. Well, so are we! And therefore if we are both stubborn, and if we use violence, we shall never arrive at a happy issue. Ah, I know you, Messire de Balliencourt; I saw you with the army. I hope you're in good health? Violence is the resource of people who are unable to reflect. How do you do, Messire de Caumont?'

As he spoke, he was moving among them, looking them straight in the eyes, addressing by name those whom he recognized, and extending his hand to them that they might kiss it in sign of homage.

'It would be easy for the Countess of Artois to punish you for your ill-behaviour towards her should she so wish. Just have a look out of that window, Messire de Souastre, and tell me what chances of escape you have.'

Some of the barons went to the window and saw that the walls had suddenly become lined with men whose helmets made a frieze across the evening sky. A company of archers was drawn up in the courtyard, and sergeants-at-arms were ready, upon a signal, to raise the bridges and lower the portcullises.

'Let us fly, if there is still time,' some of the barons murmured.

'No, Messeigneurs, don't try to escape,' said the Count of Poitiers; 'your flight would take you no farther than the second wall. Once more I tell you that we do not want to use violence, and I am asking your suzerain not to use arms against you. Is not that so, Mother?'

The Countess Mahaut nodded approval.

'Let us endeavour to resolve our differences in another way,' the Count of Poitiers continued, sitting down.

He prayed the barons to do likewise, and ordered refreshments to be brought them.

As there were not enough seats for all, some sat on the floor. The alternation of threats and politeness bewildered them.

Philippe of Poitiers talked to them at length. He showed them that civil war could bring nothing but disaster, that they were the King's subjects before they were the subjects of Countess Mahaut, and that they must submit to the Sovereign's arbitration. The latter had sent two emissaries, Messire Flotte and Messire Paumier, to conclude a truce. Why had they refused it?

'We no longer had confidence in the Countess Mahaut,' replied Jean de Fiennes.

'The truce was demanded of you in the King's name; it is therefore the King you are affronting by doubting his word.'

'But Monseigneur Robert of Artois had assured us . . .'

'Ah, I was waiting for that! Take care, my good lords, not to listen too much to the advice of Monseigneur Robert, who is inclined to talk rather too easily in the King's name, and is using you for his own ends, paying, perhaps, with his own money, but very little with his own person. Our cousin of Artois lost his case against Madame Mahaut six years ago, and the King my father, God rest his soul, judged the case himself. Whatever happens in this county is between yourselves, the Countess, and the King only.'

Jeanne de Poitiers was watching her husband. She listened with joy to the level cadences of his voice; she noted once more his manner of suddenly raising his eyelids to mark a phrase, and his nonchalance of attitude which, and she now realized it for the first time, was merely a cloak to hide his strength. He seemed to her strangely matured. His features had set; his long thin nose was sharper than ever; his face was beginning to acquire its definitive shape. At the same time Philippe seemed to have achieved an extraordinary authority as if, since his father's death, some part of the dead king's natural authority had been passed on to him.

At the end of a full hour's discussion the Count of Poitiers had obtained what he wanted, or at least the most that could be obtained. Denis d'Hirson would be set at liberty; Thierry, provisionally, would not reappear in Artois, but the Countess's administration would continue to function till the

Commissions had made their report. Sergeant Cornillot's head would be immediately returned to his family to receive Christian burial. 'For,' said the Count of Poitiers, 'to behave as you have is to act as infidels rather than as defenders of the true faith. Such deeds open the way to acts of vengeance of which you yourselves will shortly be the victims.'

The lords of Liques and Nédonchel were to be left in peace, for they had only desired the good of all and the avoidance of useless bloodshed. The ladies of both sides would be respected as they should be in a chivalrous country. And then everyone was to meet at Arras, in a fortnight's time, that was to say on October 7th, to conclude a truce which would be maintained until the celebrated conference of Compiègne, so often rejected, could be held, and this was now fixed for November 15th. If the two Guillaumes, Flotte and Paumier, had not succeeded in rallying the barons to the King's wishes, other negotiators would be sent.

'There's no need to sign anything today; I trust your word, Messeigneurs,' said the Count of Poitiers, who knew that the best way of gaining the confidence of opponents is to pretend to accord them your own. 'You are reasonable and honourable men; I know very well that you, Balliencourt, and you, Souastre, and you, Loos, and all the rest of you will be determined not to disappoint me or allow me to approach the King in vain. And I count upon you to make your friends see sense and show respect for our agreement.'

He managed them so well that they thanked him as they left, almost as if they had found in him a defender. They mounted their horses, crossed the three drawbridges, and disappeared into the night.

'My dear son,' said Mahaut. 'You have saved me. I could not have been so patient with them.'

'I've gained you a fortnight,' said Philippe, shrugging his shoulders. 'The customs of Saint Louis! Really, I'm beginning to get tired of the whole lot of them with their customs of Saint Louis! You might think my father had never existed. When a great King has brought progress to the land, must there always be idiots who are determined to be reactionary. And my brother encourages them!'

'What a pity that you're not King, Philippe!' said Mahaut.

Philippe did not reply; he gazed at his wife. She, now that her fears had been dissipated and so many months of hope at last realized, suddenly felt overcome with weakness and was fighting against the tears which mounted to her eyes.

To hide her distress she walked about the room, gazing once more upon the scene of her childhood. But her emotion was only exacerbated by every object she recognized. She saw once again the chessboard of jasper and chalcedony on which she had learned to play.

'Nothing is changed, you see,' Mahaut said.

'No, nothing has changed,' Jeanne repeated, her throat constricted, turning towards the bookcase.

It contained a dozen volumes and thereby formed one of the most important private libraries in France. Jeanne stroked the bindings with her fingers: *Les Enfances d'Ogier*, *Le Roman de la Violette*, the Bible in French, *The Life of the Saints*, *Le Roman de Renart*, *Le Roman de Tristan*.[16] She had so often, with her sister Blanche, looked at the beautiful illuminations painted on the sheets of parchment! While one of Mahaut's ladies had read to them.

'You know this one. Yes, I had already bought it. It cost me three hundred pounds,' said Mahaut, showing her *Le Voyage au Pays du Grand Khan* by Messire Marco Polo.

She was trying to dissipate the embarrassment that had come upon the three of them.

At that moment Mahaut's dwarf, who was called Jeannot le Follet, came in, carrying the wooden hobbyhorse on which he was supposed to caracole about the house. He was over forty years of age with a large head, big spaniel eyes, and a little flat nose; he was just about the height of a table, and he wore a robe embroidered with 'bestelettes' and a round cap.

When he saw Jeanne he was overcome with amazement; his mouth opened, but no sound came, and instead of advancing into the room making the capers which were his duty, he rushed towards her and threw himself on the ground to kiss her feet.

Jeanne's fortitude and self-control yielded on the spot. She suddenly began sobbing and, turning to the Count of Poitiers, and seeing that he was smiling at her, threw herself into his arms stammering, 'Philippe! Philippe! At last, at last, I am with you again.'

The tough old Countess Mahaut felt a little pang at the heart that her daughter should have rushed towards her husband, rather than towards herself, to weep with joy.

'But what else did I hope for?' thought Mahaut. 'After all, that's the most important thing. I've succeeded.'

'Philippe, your wife is tired,' she said. 'Take her to your apartments. Supper will be brought up to you.'

And as they passed her, she added in a low voice, 'I told you she loved you, didn't I?'

She gazed after them as they passed through the door, leaning against each other. Then she signed to Beatrice d'Hirson to follow them discreetly.

Later, during the night, when the Countess Mahaut, to compensate herself for her exhausting day, was in process of eating her sixth and last meal of the day, Beatrice came in, a half-smile on her lips.

'Well?' said Mahaut.

'Well, Madam, the philtre has had the effect we expected. They are now asleep.'

Mahaut leant back among her pillows.

'God be praised,' she said. 'We have brought the second couple in the Kingdom together again.'

4

A Servant's Friendship

THERE FOLLOWED SEVERAL weeks of comparative peace in the Kingdom. The opposing parties met at Arras, then at Compiègne, and the King promised to announce his arbitration over Artois before Christmas. The barons of the north, temporarily satisfied, returned to their manors.

The fields were black and deserted; the flocks were gathered in the folds. The land of France slept in the silence of winter. These were the shortest days of the year; the misty December dawns were like smoke from greenwood fires; night fell early upon the royal residence of Vincennes as it lay surrounded by its forest.

Queen Clémence spent the hours of the afternoon at her embroidery. She had started upon a great altar-cloth which was to depict Paradise. The elect strolled about beneath a pure blue sky among orange and lemon trees; Paradise bore a peculiar resemblance to the gardens of Naples.

'One does not become a queen to find happiness,' Queen

Clémence often thought, repeating the words of her grandmother, Marie of Hungary. She was not really unhappy in the proper sense of the term; she had no reason to be so. 'These are wicked thoughts,' she said to herself, 'and it is wrong of me not to thank God for all He has given me.' She could not understand the reason for the lassitude, the melancholy, and the boredom which oppressed her day after day.

Was she not surrounded by every possible care? She had always about her at least three ladies-in-waiting, chosen from among the most noble ladies of the Kingdom, to carry out her smallest desires, foresee her least wishes, carry her missal, thread her needle, hold her mirror, do her hair, and place a cloak about her whenever the temperature dropped.

The best minstrels succeeded each other in telling her of the adventures of King Arthur, Sir Lancelot, and the Golden Legend of the saints.

There were ten couriers with but one duty: to carry her correspondence with her grandmother, her uncle, King Robert, and her other relatives between Naples and Vincennes.

She had for her own use four white horses, harnessed with silver bits and silken reins woven with gold thread; and, that she might accompany the King to the meeting at Compiègne, so exquisitely luxurious a travelling coach had been built for her that, with its wheels shaped like flaming suns, Countess Mahaut's seemed no more than a haywain beside it.

And was not Louis really the best husband upon earth? Once she had said, upon visiting Vincennes, that the castle delighted her and that it was there she would like to live, Louis had decided at once to abandon Paris and make it his permanent residence. All the great lords had immediately set about buying land round Vincennes and building themselves houses. It was even said that Messire Tolomei had considerably assisted them in their purchase of land and that, thanks to him, the neighbourhood had gained enormously in prosperity. And Clémence, who had not realized what a winter at Vincennes could be like, now no longer dared admit that she would have preferred to return to Paris, fearing to disappoint all the people who had been put to considerable expense so as to live in her vicinity.

The King was overwhelmingly kind. Not a day passed but he bought her some new present; she was almost embarrassed by it.

'Dearest,' he had said, 'I want you to be the best endowed woman in the world.'

But did she really need three golden crowns, one encrusted with ten huge balas rubies, the second with four great emeralds, sixteen small ones, and twenty-four pearls, and the third with pearls again, and emeralds and rubies?[17]

For her table Louis had bought her twelve silver-gilt goblets enamelled with the arms of France and Hungary. And because she was devout and he so much admired her piety, he had given her a great reliquary, for which he had paid eight hundred pounds, containing a fragment of the True Cross. It would have discouraged his good intentions to tell him one could pray equally well in the middle of a garden, and that the most beautiful monstrance in the world, in spite of all the arts of goldsmiths and all the fortunes of kings, still remained the sun shining brilliantly down upon the Mediterranean.

A month ago Louis had made her a present of lands which she had not yet had time to visit: the houses and manors of Maneville, Hébicourt, Saint-Denis de Fermans, Wardes, and Dampierre, the forests of Lyons and of Bray.

'Why, my dear lord,' she had asked him, 'do you dispossess yourself of so much property in my favour, since I am but your servant, and can only profit by them through you?'

'I am not dispossessing myself of anything,' Louis had replied. 'All these lordships belonged to Marigny, from whom I took them back by a judgement of the court, and I can dispose of them as I wish. In case something happened to me, I want to leave you the richest woman in the Kingdom.'

In spite of the repugnance she felt at inheriting the possessions of a man who had been hanged, could she refuse them when they were given her as gauges of love? And the King insisted upon proclaiming his love even in the deed of gift itself: 'We, Louis, by the Grace of God, King of France and Navarre, make known to all by these presents that we, in consideration of the happy and agreeable companionship that Clémence humbly and amiably brings us, by which she merits well that we should courteously make deed of gift . . .'

Could a state paper be more charmingly composed? And he had also made over to her the houses at Corbeil and Fontainebleau. Every night he spent with her seemed to be worth a castle. Yes, indeed, Messire Louis loved her well. Never had he shown himself to be The Hutin in her presence, and she could not understand how he had earned that nickname. There was never quarrel nor anger between them. God had given her a good husband indeed.

And yet, in spite of it all, Clémence was bored. She did not hear the minstrels' voices and sighed as she drew golden threads to embroider her lemons.

She had tried in vain to interest herself in the affairs of Artois concerning which Louis, night after night, discoursed alone in her presence as he strode up and down the room.

She was terrified by the great bawling speeches of Count Robert which he uttered in a voice loud enough to blow the roofs off Vincennes, calling her 'Cousin!' the while, as if he were cheering on his pack of hounds, crying that Madame Mahaut and Madame of Poitiers were no more than a couple of harlots, which Clémence indeed refused to believe.

She was irritated by Monseigneur of Valois, who buzzed round her saying, 'Well, Niece, when are you going to give us an heir to the throne?'

'When God wills, Uncle,' she replied gently.

The fact was, she had no friends. She realized, because she was intelligent and without vanity, that every mark of affection shown her was interested. She learnt that kings are never loved for themselves, and that those who kneel before them have but one thought: that of picking up the crumbs of power that fall from the august lips.

'One does not become a queen to find happiness; it may even be that being a queen prevents one from finding it,' Clémence was saying to herself again one afternoon, when Monseigneur of Valois, who always seemed to be in a hurry, as if he were about to repulse some enemy from the frontiers, came in to see her and said, 'Niece, I am bringing you news which will upset the Court: your sister-in-law, Madame of Poitiers, is pregnant. The matrons have certified it this morning. Your neighbour, the Countess Mahaut, is already bedecking her castle of Conflans with flags as if the feast of Corpus Christi was to take place there.'

'I'm delighted for Madame of Poitiers's sake,' said Clémence.

'And I hope she's grateful to you,' went on Charles of Valois, 'because it's to you she owes her present condition. If you had not asked for her pardon on your wedding day, I very much doubt whether Louis would have granted it.'

'God proves that I did well since he has blessed their union.'

Valois, who was warming himself at the fireplace, turned round suddenly, making his cloak fly about him as if he were unfurling a standard.

'It seems that God is less eager to bless yours,' he replied. 'When are you going to make up your mind, Niece, to follow your sister-in-law's example? It's a great pity that she's got there first. Clémence, you must allow me to talk to you as a father. You know I don't like beating about the bush. Between ourselves, does Louis fulfil his duties as a husband?'

'Louis is as attentive as a husband could be.'

'Listen, Niece, understand me well; I'm talking of a husband's Christian duties, physical duties if you prefer it.'

Clémence blushed. She stammered, 'I don't understand your meaning, Uncle. I have but little experience, but I cannot see that Louis is in any way at fault in the matter. I have barely been married five months and I hardly think there is yet reason for your alarm.'

'Yes, but does he regularly honour your bed?'

'Nearly every night, Uncle, if that is what you want to know, and I cannot do more than be at his service when he desires it.'

'Well, we must hope! We must hope!' said Charles of Valois. 'But you must realize, Niece, that it is I who arranged your marriage. And I would not like to be blamed for having made a bad choice.'

Then, for the first time, Clémence showed some signs of anger. She pushed her embroidery to one side, stood up straight in front of her chair and, in a voice in which could be detected the tones of old Queen Marie, replied, 'You seem to forget, Messire of Valois, that my grandmother of Hungary had thirteen children, that my mother Clémence of Hapsburg had already had three when she died at about my age. The women of our family are fruitful, Uncle, and if there is any impediment to what you so much desire, it cannot come from my heredity. And what's more, Messire, we have spoken enough upon this subject for today, and for ever.'

And she went and shut herself up in her room.

It was there that Eudeline, the linen-maid, coming to prepare the bed, found her two hours later, sitting before a window beyond which night had now fallen.

'What, Madam,' she cried, 'haven't they brought you a light? I'll call them!'

'No, no, I don't want anyone,' said Clémence wearily.

The linen-maid revived the fire which was dying on the hearth, plunged a resinous branch into the faggots and used it to light a candle standing in an iron candlestick.

'Oh, Madam, you're weeping!' she said. 'Has someone wounded you?'

The Queen dried her eyes; she seemed absent, her thoughts far away.

'Eudeline, Eudeline,' she cried, 'my mind is troubled with wicked thoughts; I am jealous.'

Eudeline looked at her in surprise.

'You, Madam, jealous? What possible reason can you have to be jealous? I am sure that our Lord Louis is not deceiving you. The idea hasn't even entered his head.'

'I am jealous of Madame of Poitiers,' Clémence replied. 'I am envious of her because she's going to have a child, while I still am not expecting one. Oh, I am happy for her. Oh, yes, I'm delighted. But I didn't know that someone else's happiness could hurt one so much.'

'Oh, indeed, Madam, other people's happiness can cause one much sorrow!'

Eudeline said this with a curious inflexion, not like a servant who approves the words of her mistress, but like a woman who has suffered the same hurt and understands it. Her tone of voice did not escape Clémence.

'Have you too no child?' she asked.

'Yes, indeed, Madam, indeed, I have a daughter who bears my name and who is eleven years old.'

She turned away and busied herself with the bed, smoothing down the coverings of brocade and miniver.

'Have you been linen-maid to the castle long?' Clémence went on.

'Since the spring, immediately before your arrival. Until then I was in the Palace of the Cité, where I looked after the linen of our Lord Louis, after having looked after his father, King Philip's, for six years.'

They fell silent and there was no sound but the linen-maid beating up the pillows.

'She must know all the secrets of the house and of the alcove,' the Queen said to herself. 'But no, I will not ask her, I will not question her. It's never right to make servants talk. It would be unworthy of me.'

But who indeed was there who could tell her the truth, if it were not a servant, one of those beings who share a king's intimacy without sharing his power? She would never have had the audacity to question the princes of the family about the particular matter which weighed upon her mind since her conversation with Charles of Valois; moreover, she was quite sure she would not get an honest answer. Of the great ladies of the court none really had her confidence, because none of them had really shown herself to be her friend. She felt herself a stranger, oppressed with vain flattery, but watched, observed, her slightest fault or weakness never to be forgiven. Moreover, she felt she could not let herself go except with her servants. Eudeline, in particular, seemed to deserve her friendship; her gaze was frank, her manner simple, her movements calm and sure; the first linen-maid had shown herself daily more attentive, and there was no ostentation about the services she rendered.

Clémence suddenly made up her mind.

'Is it true,' she asked, 'that little Madame of Navarre, who is kept away from the Court and has only been shown me once, is not my husband's daughter?'

And at the same time, she was thinking, 'Should I not have been warned earlier of these secrets of the Crown? My grandmother should have sought more information; indeed, I was allowed to embark upon this marriage ignorant of many things.'

'Indeed, Madam,' replied Eudeline, still shaking up the pillows and as if the question in no way surprised her, 'I don't believe anybody knows, not even our Lord Louis. Everyone hold the point of view that happens to suit him best; those who assert that Madame of Navarre is the King's daughter have an interest in doing so, and so have those who hold that she is a bastard. There are even some, like Monseigneur of Valois, who change their opinion once a month, concerning a matter which can have but one truth. The only person who could have told for certain was Madame of Burgundy and she is now laid deep in the ground.'

Eudeline stopped and glanced at the Queen.

'Madam, you are anxious to know if our Lord the King . . .'

She hesitated, but Clémence encouraged her with her eyes.

'Be reassured, Madam,' said Eudeline, 'Monseigneur Louis is not incapable of having an heir, as wicked tongues in the Kingdom and even in the Court affirm.'

'Is it known . . . ?' Clémence murmured.

'I know it,' Eudeline replied slowly, 'and care has been taken to see that I am alone in knowing it.'

'What do you mean?'

'I want to speak the truth, Madam, because I too carry a heavy secret. Doubtless, I should still keep silence. But it is no offence to a lady such as yourself, of such high birth and such great charity, to admit to you that I had a child by Monseigneur Louis, in his youth, eleven years ago now.'

The Queen looked at Eudeline in immeasurable astonishment. That Louis should have had a first wife had not created any problem, except possibly a dynastic one, for Clémence. That union was on the plane of established things. Louis had

had a wife who had behaved badly; first prison, and then death, had separated them. But during the whole of the five months since she had married the King of France, Clémence had never once asked herself what Louis and Marguerite of Burgundy's intimate life had been like. She had never pictured to herself the fact of their physical relations nor had she felt any curiosity about them; she had never connected the fact of their marriage with love. And now love and, what was more, love outside marriage, was standing before her in the person of this beautiful fair woman with her rosy skin, and her luxuriant thirty years; and now Clémence began to think.

Eudeline took the Queen's silence for disapproval.

'It was not I who wanted it, Madam, I assure you; it was he who compelled me to it. Besides, he was so young, he had no discernment, and a great lady would doubtless have frightened him.'

With a gesture of her hand Clémence signified that she desired no further explanations.

'And the child,' she asked, 'that's the one you were telling me about a moment ago?'

'Yes, Madam, it's Eudeline.'

'I want to see her.'

An expression of fear appeared upon the linen-maid's face.

'You can, Madam, you can of course, since you are Queen. But I do ask you not to insist, because it will become known that I have talked to you. She is so like her father that Monseigneur Louis, for fear of upsetting you, had her shut up in a convent just before you arrived. I see her only once a month and, as soon as she is of age, she will take the veil.'

Clémence's first reactions were always generous. For the moment she forgot her own troubles.

'But why,' she asked in a low voice, 'why did he do that? How could anybody think that such a thing would please me, to what kind of women are the Princes of France accustomed? So it's on my account, my poor Eudeline, that your daughter has been torn from you! I sincerely ask your forgiveness.'

'Oh, Madam,' Eudeline replied, 'I know very well that you had nothing to do with it.'

'I had nothing to do with it, but it was done because of me,' said Clémence thoughtfully. 'We are each responsible not only for our own bad actions, but also for the harm of which we are the cause, even unknowingly.'

'And as for myself, Madam,' Eudeline went on, 'I was first linen-maid at the Palace of the Cité, and Monseigneur Louis sent me here to this lesser post than the one I held in Paris. No one has the right to question the King's wishes, but it is small thanks for my having kept silence. Doubtless Monseigneur Louis wishes to conceal me too; it did not occur to him that you would prefer living here among the woods to the great Palace of the Cité.'

Now that she had begun her confidences, she could no longer stop.

'I don't mind admitting,' she went on, 'that when you arrived, I was prepared to serve you out of duty but certainly not with pleasure. You must be a very noble lady, and as kind-hearted as you are beautiful, for me to feel affection for you growing upon me. You have no idea how much you are loved by the lower orders; you ought to hear them talking of the Queen in the kitchens, the stables, and the laundries! It's there, Madam, that you have devoted friends, much more so than among the great barons. You have conquered all our hearts, even mine that was most closed against you, and you have now no more devoted servant than I am,' said Eudeline, going down on her knees and kissing the Queen's hand.

'I'll get your daughter back,' said Clémence, 'and I'll protect her. I shall speak to the King.'

'Please do nothing, Madam, I beseech you,' cried Eudeline.

'The King loads me with so many presents I don't want! He can very well give me one I do!'

'No, no, I beseech you, do nothing,' repeated Eudeline. 'I would rather see my daughter behind the veil than beneath the earth.'

Clémence, for the first time since the beginning of their conversation, smiled, indeed she almost laughed.

'Are people of your condition so frightened of the King in France? Or is it the memory of King Philip, who was said to be without mercy, which still weighs upon you?'

If Eudeline had real affection for the Queen, she had a no less real grievance against The Hutin, and here was the opportunity to satisfy both these feelings at the same time.

'You don't yet know Monseigneur Louis as everyone here knows him; he hasn't yet shown you the reverse of his character. No one has forgotten,' she said, lowering her voice, 'that our Lord Louis tortured his household servants after the case against Madame Marguerite, and that eight corpses, all broken and mutilated, were fished out of the river at the foot of the Tower of Nesle. Do you think they were thrown into it by chance? I shouldn't like chance to push my daughter and me in the same direction.'

'That is merely gossip invented by the King's enemies . . .'

But as she uttered the words, Clémence remembered the allusions made by Cardinal Duèze, and the way in which Bouville, on the Lyons road, had replied to her question concerning Marguerite's death. Clémence recollected what her brother-in-law, Philippe of Poitiers, had let fall about the merciless tortures and unjust sentences suffered by Philip the Fair's ex-ministers.

'Have I married a cruel man?' she wondered.

'I'm sorry if I've said too much,' Eudeline went on. 'May God spare you hearing anything worse, and may your great goodness leave you in ignorance.'

'What worse could I hear? . . . Madame Marguerite . . . is that true?'

Eudeline sadly shrugged her shoulders.

'You are the only person at Court, Madam, who has any doubt of it; if you haven't yet been told of it, it is because some people are waiting till the moment's ripe, perhaps, to injure you the more. He had her strangled, it's well known.'

'My God, my God, can it possibly be true? Can he possibly have committed murder in order to marry me?' groaned Clémence, hiding her face in her hands.

'Oh, don't start weeping again, Madam,' said Eudeline. 'It will soon be supper-time, and you cannot appear thus. You must wash your face.'

She went and fetched a basin of cold water and a looking-glass, dabbed wet towels on the Queen's cheeks, and rearranged a blonde tress which had come loose. Her gestures had a curious gentleness, a sort of protective tenderness.

For a moment the faces of the two women appeared

side by side in the looking-glass, two faces of the same blonde complexion and golden hair, each with the same large blue eyes.

'You know, we're very much alike,' said the Queen.

'That is the finest compliment that has ever been paid me, and I only wish it were true,' Eudeline replied.

As they were both much moved, and were equally in need of friendship, the wife of King Louis X and his first mistress stood for a moment clasped in each other's arms.

5

The Fork and the Prie-dieu

His head held high, a smile on his lips, his feet in slippers, and wearing a fur-lined dressing-gown over his nightshirt, Louis X entered Clémence's room.

He had thought the Queen strangely silent during supper. She had been distant, absent almost, barely following the conversation and scarcely replying when spoken to. He had not, however, been unduly perturbed: 'Women are moody creatures,' he said to himself, 'and the present I bought her this morning will restore her good humour.' For The Hutin was one of those husbands who are so lacking in imagination and have so small an opinion of women, that they believe a present will solve anything. He therefore arrived, in as gracious a mood as he was able to assume, carrying a little oval jewel-case decorated with the Queen's arms.

He was somewhat surprised to find Clémence kneeling on her prie-dieu. She had generally said her evening prayers before he arrived. He signed to her with his hand, intending to indicate: 'Don't put yourself out for me, finish at your leisure.' And he remained at the other end of the room, somewhat embarrassed, turning the jewel-case over in his hands.

The minutes went by; he went and took a sweet from a jar by the bedside, and ate it. Clémence was still on her knees and Louis began to get bored with waiting. He went over to her, and saw that she was not in fact praying. She was looking at him.

'Look, dearest,' he said, 'look at the surprise I've brought you. Oh, it's not a jewel, but a curiosity, a rare piece of goldsmith's work. Look!'

He opened the case and took from it a long shining object with two points. Clémence, upon her prie-dieu, started back in fear.

'Dearest!' cried Louis, laughing, 'don't be frightened, this is no weapon for wounding; it's a little fork to eat pears with. Look at the workmanship,' he added, placing on the wooden back of the prie-dieu a fork with two sharp steel prongs set in a handle of ivory and chased gold.

Louis was disappointed; the Queen seemed to show very little interest in his present, nor did she seem to appreciate its novelty.

'I had it made specially,' he went on, 'through the good offices of Messire Tolomei, who ordered it directly from a Florentine goldsmith. There are apparently only five of these forks in the world, and I wanted you to have one so that you should not stain your pretty hands when you eat fruit. It's particularly suitable for a lady; a man would never dare, nor indeed know how, to use so precious a tool, except my effeminate brother-in-law Edward of England who, I am told, possesses one and does not fear the mockery his using it at table arouses.'

He had hoped to amuse her by telling her this anecdote, but the joke fell flat. Clémence neither moved from her prie-dieu nor took her eyes off him; never had she looked more beautiful, her long golden hair falling to her waist. Louis began to find himself at his wits' end.

'By the way,' he went on, 'Messire Tolomei has just told me that his young nephew, whom I sent with Bouville to fetch you from Naples, is now recovered. He will shortly be on his way to Paris and in every letter to his uncle speaks of your kindness to him.'

'What can be the matter with her?' he wondered. 'She might at least have said thank you.' With anyone else but Clémence he would have already lost his temper, but he could not as yet resign himself to having the first quarrel of their married life. He took it upon himself to make another effort.

'I really believe that this time the affairs of Artois will be settled,' he said. 'I feel reasonably confident and things seem to be going well. The conference at Compiègne, to which you were kind enough to accompany me, has had the effect I expected and I shall soon summon my Grand Council in order to make my arbitration and seal the agreement between Mahaut and her barons.'

'Louis,' Clémence said suddenly, 'how did your first wife die?'

Louis leant forward, as if someone had hit him in the stomach, and gazed at her in momentary stupefaction.

'She died,' he said, 'she died' – and he waved his hands about – 'she died of a pleurisy which choked her, or so I'm told.'

'Louis, can you swear it before God?'

'What do you want me to swear?' said The Hutin, raising his voice. 'There is no reason why I should swear anything. What are you getting at? What do you want to know? I have said what I have said, and I hope you will be content with that; there is nothing more you need know.'

He was pacing up and down the room. At the opening of his nightshirt, the base of his neck had turned red; his huge pale eyes had suddenly become disquietingly bright.

'I do not wish,' he cried, 'I do not wish her spoken of! Ever! And by you in particular. I forbid you, Clémence, ever to mention Marguerite's name in my presence.'

He was interrupted by a fit of coughing.

'Can you swear to me before God,' Clémence repeated in a voice that she had to make carry to the end of the room, 'can you swear that you had no hand in her death?'

With Louis anger soon clouded judgement. Instead of simply making a denial and pretending to laugh it off, he replied violently, 'And what if it were true? You're the last person to have any right to blame me. It was not my fault, it was the fault of Madame of Hungary!'

'My grandmother?' murmured Clémence. 'What has my grandmother to do with it?'

The Hutin realized at once that he had made a mistake, which served merely to increase his fury. But it was too late to turn back. He felt himself cornered.

'Of course it was Madame of Hungary's fault!' he repeated.

'She insisted that your marriage should take place before the summer. Therefore, I hoped – make no mistake about it, I only hoped – that Marguerite would die before then. I hoped it aloud, and I was heard, that's all! If I had not expressed that hope, you would not today be Queen of France. So don't pretend to be so innocent, and don't throw the blame in my face for something that has turned out very well for you; it has raised you to a higher place than you could ever have hoped for.'

'I would never have accepted it,' cried Clémence, 'if I had known that it was at such a cost. It is because of that crime, Louis, that God has not given us a child!'

Louis turned about and stood rigid in astonishment.

'Because of that crime, and of all the others you have committed,' continued the Queen, rising from her prie-dieu. 'You have had your wife murdered! On false evidence you have had Messire de Marigny hanged, and have thrown into prison your father's ministers who, I am assured, were good servants. You have tortured those who displeased you. You have attacked the lives and liberties of God's creatures. And that is why God is now punishing you by preventing you from fathering others.'

Louis, horrified, watched her come towards him. There was thus a third person on the earth who was not terrified of his rages, who could stand four-square to his anger and take the upper hand. His father, Philip the Fair, had dominated him by his authority; his brother, the Count of Poitiers, dominated him through his intelligence; and here was his second wife dominating him through her faith.

Never could he have believed that his judge would appear

in the marriage chamber in the form of so beautiful a woman, her hair trailing behind her like a comet.

Louis's face crumpled; he looked like a child about to cry.

'And what do you want me to do now?' he asked in a shrill voice. 'I can't bring the dead back to life. You don't know what it is to be a King! Nothing that has happened has been done altogether by my will and yet you blame me for everything. What do you expect to get by it? What's the use of blaming me for things that cannot be undone? Leave me, go back to Naples, if you can't stand the sight of me any longer. And wait till there's a Pope, so that you can ask him to untie the knot that binds us! Oh, the Pope! The Pope they've never succeeded in making,' he added, clenching his fists. 'You don't know how hard I tried! None of this would have happened if there had been a Pope.'

Clémence placed her hands on his shoulders. She was a little taller than he was.

'I would never think of leaving you,' she said. 'I am your wife to share your lot, your sorrows as well as your joys. What I desire is to save your soul, to inspire you with repentance, without which there is no forgiveness.'

He gazed into her eyes, and saw there nothing but goodness of heart and a great strength of compassion. He felt relieved; he had been so frightened of losing her! And he drew her to him.

'Dearest, dearest,' he murmured, 'you are better than I, oh how much better, and I don't know how I should live without you. I promise to mend my ways and to repent of the harm of which I have been the cause.'

As he spoke, he hid his head in the hollow of her shoulder and touched her neck lightly with his lips.

'Oh, dearest,' he went on, 'how good you are! How wonderful you are to love! I promise I will be such as you would wish. Of course I have fits of remorse, and sometimes they terrify me! I can forget only when I am in your arms. Come, dearest, let's make love.'

He tried to lead her to the bed, but she stood still and he felt her grow rigid in refusal.

'No, Louis, no,' she said very softly. 'We must do penance.'

'But we *will* do penance, dearest; we'll fast three times a week if you like. Come, I want you so badly!'

She tore herself from his grasp and, as he tried to hold her by force, a seam of her nightdress gave way. The noise of its rending frightened Clémence who, covering her naked shoulder with her hand, ran to take refuge, to barricade herself behind the prie-dieu.

Her gesture of timidity released The Hutin's anger once more.

'Really, what's the matter with you?' he cried. 'And what must I do to please you?'

'I don't want to sleep with you again till we have been upon a pilgrimage to Monsieur Saint-Jean who has already saved me from the sea. And you will come with me, and we shall go on foot; then we shall know if God forgives us by giving us a child.'

'The best pilgrimage we can make for the purpose of having a child is here!' said Louis, indicating the bed.

'Oh, don't make a mock of religion,' Clémence replied, 'you won't persuade me that way.'

'Your religion is a very strange one if it commands you to refuse yourself to your husband. Have you never been told that there are certain duties from which you must not swerve?'

'Louis, you don't understand me!'

'Yes, I do!' he shouted. 'I understand that you are refusing yourself to me. I understand that I no longer please you, that you are behaving towards me as did Marguerite . . .'

She saw his eyes fixed on the fork with its two long sharp points as it still lay upon the prie-dieu. And at that moment she really felt afraid. She slowly put out her hand to take it before he did so himself. But, luckily, he did not notice her gesture. He was only thinking of the overwhelming panic, the appalling despair in which he was submerged.

Louis was never certain of his potency except in contact with a docile body. Not to be wanted, not to be suffered, destroyed his powers; the tragedy of his first marriage had no other origin but this. Supposing this infirmity attacked him again? There is no greater anguish than being unable to possess the person one most desires. How could he explain to Clémence that, for him, the punishment had preceded the crime? He was terrified at the idea that the appalling cycle of refusal, impotence, and hatred was about to begin all over again. He muttered, as if to himself, 'Am I damned and accursed not to be able to be loved by those I love?'

Then, yielding to pity as much as to fear, Clémence left the protection of the prie-dieu, and said, 'Very well, I do as you wish.' She went to snuff the candle.

'Let them burn,' said The Hutin.

'Really, Louis, do you wish . . .'

'Take all your clothes off.'

Decided now to submit to everything, she took her clothes off with the feeling that she was giving herself to the devil. Louis led her towards the bed; her body was beautiful with sculptured shadows, and it was once more in his power. In order to thank Clémence, he murmured, 'I promise you, dearest, I promise you to free Raoul de Presles, and all my father's ministers. Basically you always want the same things as my brother Philippe does!'

Clémence thought that her surrender would at least be compensated for by some good and that, in default of penance, innocent people would be set free.

A great cry arose that night from the royal bedchamber. Having been married five months, Queen Clémence discovered only now that one was not Queen only to be unhappy, and that the portals of marriage might open upon unknown joys.

For long minutes she rested exhausted, breathless, amazed, almost beside herself, as if the sea of her native shores had washed her up on some golden strand. It was she who sought the King's shoulder in order to rest her head upon it in sleep, while Louis, overwhelmed with gratitude for the pleasure he had given her, and feeling more like a king even than on the day of his coronation, knew his first wakeful night free of the fear of death.

But this night of felicity was, alas, but a solitary one. From the following day, and without having recourse to a confessor, Clémence came to the conclusion that her pleasure partook of sin. She was doubtless more neurotic by nature than she appeared for, from that time, her husband's approach caused her intolerable suffering, which made her incapable of accepting the royal homage, not through any lack of willingness, but from physical intolerance. It sincerely saddened her. She apologized, made every effort, but in vain, to gratify Louis's insistent ardours.

'I assure you, my dear Lord, I assure you,' she said to him, 'that we must go on a pilgrimage; till then I cannot.'

'Very well, dearest, we shall go, and soon, and as far as you please, with ropes round our necks if you like; but let me first settle the affairs of Artois.'

6

Arbitration

TWO DAYS BEFORE CHRISTMAS, in the largest room in the Manor of Vincennes, transformed for the occasion into a hall of justice, the principal lords of the Kingdom and a great number of lawyers were awaiting the King.

A delegation of barons from Artois, at their head Gérard Kierez and Jean de Fiennes, as well as the inseparable Souastre and Caumont, had arrived that morning. It seemed as if a solution had been found. The King's emissaries had worked well, finding points of agreement between the two sides; the Count of Poitiers had inspired much wise compromise and had counselled his mother-in-law to yield on a number of points in order to restore peace in her territories and, when all was said and done, to remain mistress of them.

Obeying the King's instructions which, though somewhat vague in form, were clear in intention: 'I want no more blood spilt; I no longer want people to be held in prison unjustly; I want everyone to have his rights, and that peace and friendship should reign everywhere,' the Chancellor, Etienne de Mornay, had drawn up a long document of which The Hutin, when it was shown to him, had felt extremely proud, as if he had dictated all its articles himself.

At the same time Louis X had freed Raoul de Presles and the six other ministers of his father who had been languishing in prison since April. As he now seemed unable to desist from his new policy of mercy, he had even, in spite of Charles of Valois's opposition, freed the wife and son of Enguerrand de Marigny, who had also been held in gaol.

Such a change of attitude surprised the Court and no one could discover a reason for it. The King had even gone so far as to receive Louis de Marigny in audience, embracing him in the presence of the Queen and several dignitaries and saying, 'Godson, the past is forgiven.'

The Hutin now used this particular formula on every possible occasion, as if he wished to persuade himself and others that a new phase of his reign had begun.

His conscience felt particularly good that morning, while they put on his crown and draped about his shoulders the great robe decorated with lilies.

'My sceptre! My sceptre!' he said. 'Have they unpacked my sceptre?'

'It's the Hand of Justice you need today, Sire,' replied Mathieu de Trye, his first Chamberlain, handing him the great golden hand with the two raised fingers.

'How heavy it is,' said Louis. 'It seemed lighter on the day of my coronation.'

'Your barons are ready, Sire,' went on the Chamberlain. 'Will you first give audience to Master Martin, who has just arrived from Paris, or will you see him after the Council?'

'Is Master Martin here?' cried Louis. 'I'll see him at once. And leave me alone with him.'

The personage who then appeared was a man of some fifty years, rather corpulent, dark of complexion, and with dreamy eyes. Though he was extremely simply dressed, almost as a monk might have been, he had, in his manners and gestures, which were at once humble and assured, in the way in which he held his cloak in the crook of his arm and bowed in salutation, something of the oriental. Master Martin had travelled widely in his youth, had reached Cyprus, Constantinople, and Alexandria. There was some doubt about the name of Martin by which he was known; had he always borne it?

'Have you studied the question I placed before you?' the King asked him as he looked at his reflection in a hand-mirror.

'I have, Sire, I have; with a great sense of the honour it is to have been consulted by yourself.'

'Well, then? Tell me the truth, I have no fear even if it should be disagreeable.'

An astrologer such as Master Martin knew very well what to think of such an opening, particularly when uttered by the King.

'Sire,' he replied, 'our science is not an absolute one. And, even if the stars never lie, our human understanding may fall into error as we observe them. Nevertheless, I can see no sound reason for your anxiety, there seems to be nothing to prevent your having an heir. The conjunction of the planets at your birth is wholly favourable to such an issue, and the stars appear admirably disposed upon the question of your fertility. Indeed, Jupiter is at the apex of Cancer, which is significant of fecundity, and Jupiter, which was ascendant at your birth, is in amical triangulation with the moon and the planet Mercury. You must therefore not despair of producing a child, far from it, indeed. Nevertheless, the opposition of the moon and Mars does not mean to say that your son will have a life free from difficulties, and it will be necessary to surround him, from his earliest youth, with extreme vigilance and faithful servants.'

Master Martin had acquired a considerable reputation by having announced long beforehand, though in extremely ambiguous words, the death of Philip the Fair, as coinciding with an eclipse of the sun which was to take place in November 1314. He had written: 'A powerful monarch of the West', taking great care to be no more precise. Louis X, who looked upon the death of his father as a happy occurrence in his life, had ever since held Master Martin in great favour. But, if he had been more perspicacious, he would have realized, from the astrologer's prudent reserve, that the latter, in his study of the heavens, had doubtless seen more than he was prepared to say.

'Your advice is precious to me, Master Martin, and your counsel gives me great comfort,' said The Hutin. 'Have you been able to discern the most auspicious moment for the conception of the heirs I desire?'

Master Martin hesitated for a moment.

'Let us talk only of the first, Sire, I cannot speak with sufficient assurance of the others. I lack the hour of the Queen's birth which you tell me she does not know, and which no one else can give me; but I do not think I am gravely in error if I tell you that, before the sun's entry into the sign of

Sagittarius, you will have a child, which would place the time of conception at about mid-February.'

'Before then we shall go on a pilgrimage to Saint-Jean of Amiens as the Queen wishes. And when do you think, Master Martin, that I should begin my war against the Flemings again?'

'I think that in that, Sire, you must follow the dictates of your own wisdom. Have you chosen a date?'

'I don't think that I can mobilize the army again before next August.'

Master Martin's absent look concentrated itself for a moment on the King's face, his crown, and the hand of justice which seemed to embarrass him since he held it over his shoulder as a gardener holds his spade.

'Before the month of August, we have June to get through . . .' the astrologer said to himself.

'It may well be, Sire,' he replied, 'that before next August the Flemings will no longer be bothering you.'

'I would willingly believe that!' cried The Hutin, taking the reply in a favourable sense. 'Because of the fear with which I inspired them last summer, they will undoubtedly come to terms without battle before the season for renewing operations.'

There is no more curious sensation than to be face to face with a man who will almost certainly be dead within six months, hearing him make useless plans for a future he will in all probability never see. 'As long as he does not die before November . . .' said Martin to himself. For, besides the terrifying conjunction in June, the astrologer could not ignore another disastrous portent, the unhappy position of Saturn at twenty-seven years and forty-four days from the King's birth. 'The misfortune may be for him, his wife, or the child he may have between now and then. In any case, these are not things that should be said.'

Nevertheless, before leaving, while his fingers played with the weight of the purse the King had given him, Master Martin hesitated once more, almost from remorse, and felt it incumbent upon him to add, 'Sire, one more word in connection with your health. Beware of poison, particularly towards the end of spring.'

'I should therefore avoid mushrooms and edible fungi of all varieties, though I am very fond of them but which, now I come to think of it, have given me stomach-aches to which I am much subject.'

Then, suddenly anxious: 'Poison! You don't mean a viper's bite?'

'No, Sire. I'm talking of the food that may pass your lips.'

'Thank you, Master Martin, I shall take care.'

And as he went to the Council, Louis ordered his Chamberlain to redouble his watchfulness upon the kitchen, to take care not to use supplies which were not perfectly fresh and came from known sources, and to see that all foods were tasted twice instead of once before they were served to him.

As he went into the Great Hall, everyone rose to their feet and remained standing till he had taken his place upon the dais.

Once installed upon his throne, the skirts of his robes across his knees, the Hand of Justice somewhat askew in the crook of his arm, Louis felt himself at that moment equal in majesty to the representations of Christ which glow in cathedral glass. Seeing to right and left of him his barons, so exquisitely dressed though so humble in demeanour, and feeling that they were subject to his power, Louis discovered that in spite of everything there were certain days upon which it was a pleasure to be a king.

'Now,' he thought, 'I shall deliver my judgement, everyone will conform to it, and I shall restore peace and harmony among my subjects.'

Before him were gathered the two parties between whom he was to arbitrate. On one side, the Countess Mahaut, also wearing a crown, and standing head and shoulders above the Councillors grouped about her. On the other, the delegation of the 'allies' of Artois. Among them there was a certain lack of conformity in dress, for they had all put on their best suits for the occasion, but they were not all of the latest fashion. The lesser lords smacked of provincialism; Souastre and Caumont had dolled themselves up as if they were about to appear in a tournament, huge helms surmounted in one instance by an eagle with spread wings and in the other by a female bust; they looked about them from beneath their raised visors, somewhat embarrassed by the solecism.

The great barons, who had been selected to attend the Council, had been carefully chosen in equal numbers from the two sides. Charles of Valois and his son Philippe, Charles de la Marche, Louis de Clermont, the Lord of Mercœur, the Count of Savoy and, above all, Robert of Artois, Count of Beaumont-le-Roger, were the supporters of the 'allies'. It was known that on the other side Philippe of Poitiers, Louis of Evreux, Henri de Sulli, the Count of Boulogne, the Count of Forez, and Messire Miles des Noyers were supporting Mahaut.

The Chancellor Etienne de Mornay was sitting a little in front of the King with his parchments before him upon a table.

'In nomine patris et filii . . .'

Those present looked at each other in surprise. It was the first time that the King had opened a Council with a prayer and asked for divine approval of his decisions.

'He's changed,' whispered Robert of Artois to his cousin Philippe of Valois. 'He's now become a priest in a pulpit.'

'My very dear Brothers and Uncles, my good lords and beloved subjects,' began Louis X, 'we are most desirous, and indeed it is our duty, by divine right, to maintain peace within our Kingdom and to condemn division among our subjects . . .'

Instead of stuttering in public as he normally did, he was today expressing himself in slow but clear terms; indeed he felt inspired, and those present wondered as they listened to him whether his true destiny would not have been to make an excellent country priest.

He first turned to the Countess Mahaut and prayed her to follow his counsel. Mahaut rising, replied, 'Sire, I have always done so and shall always continue to do so.'

Then the King turned towards the 'allies' and made a similar recommendation.

'As true and faithful subjects, Sire,' replied Gérard Kierez, 'we humbly pray you to act and command in accordance with your will.'

Louis looked about him at his uncles, brothers, and cousins, with an expression that seemed to say, 'See how well I have arranged matters.'

He then invited the Chancellor de Mornay to read the document of arbitration.

The Chancellor Etienne de Mornay, though still young, was shortsighted. He raised the great roll of parchment to his eyes and began, 'The past is forgotten. Hatreds, offences, and rancours are forgiven by both sides. The Countess Mahaut recognizes her obligations towards her subjects; she must maintain peace in the province of Artois, must do no harm to or take any act of revenge upon the "allies", nor must she seek any occasion to do so. She will guarantee, as the King has done, the customs which were in use in Artois at the time of Monsieur Saint Louis and which will be proved before her by witnesses of good faith, knights, clerics, townspeople, lawyers . . .'

Louis X was no longer listening. Having dictated the first phrase, he was under the impression that he had drawn up the whole. They were now coming to legal considerations of which he understood nothing. He was engaged in thinking, as he counted upon his fingers, 'February, March, April, May – it looks as if an heir will be born to me about November.'

'As for guarantees,' went on Etienne de Mornay, 'if complaint is laid against the Countess, the King will have the complaint examined by commissioners and, if it is well founded, and she refuses to give justice, the King will compel her to do so by force. On the other hand, the Countess shall declare the amount of each subvention for the taxes she imposes. The Countess shall return to the lords the lands she has sequestrated without legal proceedings . . .'

The Countess was beginning to become excited, but the

brothers Hirson, who were sitting beside her, calmed her down.

'There was never any question of these things at the conference at Compiègne!' said Mahaut.

'It's better to lose a little than to lose all,' Denis whispered.

The memory of the journey he had made in chains, on the day of Sergeant Cornillot's death, inclined him towards compromise.

Mahaut turned back her sleeves and went on listening, restraining the anger which was mounting within her.

The reading had been going on for a quarter of an hour. Kierez from time to time turned to look at the 'allies' and reassure them with a nod of the head that all was going well.

A shiver of interest passed through the hall when the question of Thierry d'Hirson was reached in the judgement. All eyes were turned upon Mahaut's Chancellor and his brothers.

'As regards Master Thierry d'Hirson, whom the allies have demanded should be placed upon trial, the King has decided that the accusations must be brought before the Bishop of Thérouanne, under whose jurisdiction Thierry, as Provost of Ayré, is; but he cannot go to Artois to present his defence, because the said Master Thierry is much hated in that county. His brothers, sisters, and nieces also may not go there so long as the judgement has not been delivered by the Bishop of Thérouanne and ratified by the King . . .'

From that moment the Hirsons abandoned the conciliatory attitude they had so far observed.

'Look at your nephew; see how triumphant he is!'

And indeed Robert of Artois was exchanging smiles with Charles and Philippe of Valois.

Such calm and impudent complacency succeeded in making Mahaut lose her temper. Silencing the Hirsons with a gesture of both her hands, she replied in a low voice, 'All has not yet been said, my friend! Have I abandoned you, Thierry? Be patient.'

The Chancellor's monotonous voice ceased; the reading of the judgement of arbitration was over. The Bishop of Soissons, who had taken part in the negotiations, came forward, carrying a Bible, and went over to present it to the barons; the latter rose in a concerted movement and raised their right hands, while Gérard Kierez, in their name, swore upon the Book that they would scrupulously respect the King's judgement. Then the Bishop went over to Mahaut.

At that moment the King's thoughts were upon the roads. 'As to this pilgrimage to Amiens, we shall make it on foot, of course, during the last couple of miles or so. As for the rest of the journey we shall travel in a coach, with plenty of warm rugs. We shall also need furred boots. And I'll have made for Clémence a cloak of ermine which she can put over her coat to protect herself from taking cold ... We must hope that she will be freed of the pains which prevent her making love.' He was dreaming as he gazed upon the golden fingers of the Hand of Justice when, suddenly, he heard a loud voice saying, 'I refuse to swear; I shall not ratify this wicked sentence!'

A heavy silence fell upon the assembly and every eye was fixed upon The Hutin. The audacity of this refusal, thrown in the sovereign's teeth, terrified even the most courageous with its enormity. Everyone wondered what terrible sanction would fall from the royal lips.

'What's going on?' asked Louis, leaning towards the Chancellor. 'Who is refusing? The arbitration seemed to me to be wholly fair.'

He gazed round at those present with his large pale eyes and they, seeing him so absent, so lacking in all reaction, thought, 'Really, what a poor creature the King is.'

Then Robert of Artois rose to his feet, pushing his chair aside with a wide gesture of his arm; he went to take up his position immediately before the King, and the flagstones shook beneath his red boots. He took a deep breath as if he were imbibing all the air in the room at a single gulp, and declaimed in his warrior voice, 'Sire, my Cousin, how much longer are you going to allow people to cross you and laugh in your face? We, your relations and counsellors, will not tolerate it. You see the thanks you get for your forbearance! You know that for my part I was opposed to any diplomatic agreement with Madame Mahaut, of whom I am ashamed as being of my blood; for she takes every mark of goodwill shown her as a sign of weakness and is merely encouraged to greater villainy. Will I be believed, Messeigneurs,' he went on, taking the whole assembly to witness, and striking his breast till it resounded beneath his scarlet coat, 'Will I be believed when I say, when I assert, as I have done for so many years, that I have been defrauded, betrayed, and despoiled by that monster in female form who has respect neither for the King's authority nor for the power of God! But one need not be surprised at such behaviour from a woman who has failed to obey the wishes of her dying father, has appropriated an inheritance which was not hers, and profited from the fact that I was a child to rob me, an orphan!'

Mahaut, on her feet, her arms akimbo, gazed at her nephew in scorn while two paces away the Bishop of Soissons, his heavy Bible under his arm, did not know which way to look.

'Do you know, Sire,' went on Robert, 'why Madame Mahaut refuses to accept today the judgement to which she yesterday agreed? It is because you have added to it sentence upon Master Thierry d'Hirson, upon that damned and bartered soul, upon that master knave whom I should like to see unshod that we may determine whether he has a cloven hoof or not! It is he who, upon the order of Madame Mahaut, secretly helped her conceal the will of my grandfather, Count Robert II, by which he left me his County, his powers of justice, and his goods. The secret of this theft is the link between them, and that is why the Countess Mahaut has laden all the brothers and relations of Thierry with benefices so that they may shamefully fleece this unhappy people, once so prosperous, and now so wretched that they have no resource but in rebellion.'

The barons of Artois had risen to their feet with delighted expressions; and one felt that they were upon the point of acclaiming Robert as if he had been a great minstrel who had just recited an heroic passage.

'If you have the impudence, Sire,' Artois went on, passing from rage to irony, 'if you have the audacity to injure Master Thierry, to deprive him of the least part of the fruits of his larcenies, to threaten even the smallest nail on the smallest finger of the smallest of his nephews, then, Sire, you are committing an imprudence! Here is Madame Mahaut showing all her claws and ready to spit in the face of God. For the vows she made at your baptism and the homage she paid you upon her knees count for nothing beside her allegiance to Master Thierry, who is her true suzerain!'

He had finished his peroration. Mahaut had not moved. The eyes of aunt and nephew met in a long moment of defiance.

'Lies and calumnies, Robert, drool like saliva from your mouth,' said the Countess calmly. 'Take care never to bite your tongue, you might die of it.'

'Be quiet, Madam!' cried The Hutin suddenly, not wishing to be surpassed in violence by his cousin. 'Be quiet! You have deceived me! I forbid you to return to Artois before you have subscribed to the judgement I have made and which, so I am told on all sides, is a sound one. And you will reside until that time either at Paris or at Conflans, but nowhere else. This is enough for today, the Council is adjourned.'

He was seized with a violent fit of coughing which bent him double on his throne.

'I hope to God he dies of it!' said Mahaut between her teeth.

The Count of Poitiers had not uttered a word. He was swinging one of his legs and thoughtfully stroking his chin.

PART THREE

THE TIME OF THE COMET

I

The New Master of Neauphle

ON THE SECOND THURSDAY after Epiphany, which was market-day, there was a considerable commotion in the Lombard bank at Neauphle-Château. The office was being cleaned from top to bottom as if for the visit of a prince; the village painter was giving a new coat to the heavy front door; the strong-boxes were being polished till their iron bands shone brighter than silver; the cobwebs were being swept away from the door-frames; the walls were being whitewashed and the counters polished; and the clerks, whose account-books, balances, and abaci had been pushed aside, found it difficult to attend to clients with normal serenity.

A young girl of about seventeen, tall, handsome, her cheeks coloured by the frost, crossed the threshold and halted in amazement at the sight of all the activity. From the brown camlet cloak in which she was muffled and the silver clasp at her neck, indeed from all her bearing, one could tell at a glance that she was a daughter of the nobility. Seeing her the villagers removed their hats.

'Oh, Demoiselle Marie!' cried Ricard, the head clerk. 'Welcome! Come in and warm yourself. Your basket is ready, as it is every week, but, with all this going on, I have had it put on one side for safe-keeping.'

Then, turning to a fat peasant who was asking for some silver pieces in exchange for a *Louis d'or*, 'Yes, you'll be attended to, Master Guillemard,' and turning towards the second clerk he cried, 'Piton! Attend to Master Guillemard.'

He led the girl into a neighbouring room, which served as a common-room for the bank's employees and in which a big fire was burning. From a cupboard he took a basket of osiers, covered with a cloth.

'Nuts, oil, fresh bacon, spices, wheat-flour, dried peas, and three large sausages,' he said to Marie. 'As long as we have enough to eat, you shall have it too. Those are the orders of Messire Guccio. And I am putting it all down to his account as usual. The winter is dragging on and I shall be much surprised if it doesn't end in famine as it did last year. But this year we shall have made better provision.'

Marie took the basket. 'Is there no letter?' she asked.

The first clerk – he was by birth half-Italian and half-French, and his real name was Ricardo – shook his head in assumed sorrow.

'No, my fair Demoiselle, no letter this time!'

He smiled at her disappointed expression, and added, 'No, no letter, but good news!'

'Is he recovered?' the girl cried.

'And for whom do you think we are making all these

preparations in the very middle of January, when we never normally do any painting till April?'

'Ricard, is it really true? Your master's coming?'

'*Santo dio*, yes, he's coming! He's already in Paris and has sent us word that he is arriving tomorrow. It would seem that he is most eager to get here, since it appears that he has hardly halted on the journey.'

'Oh, how happy I am! How happy I shall be to see him again!'

Then, controlling herself, as if to give way to her joy were to be lacking in modesty, Marie added, 'All my family will be delighted to see him.'

'Yes, but I've got earache today,' replied Ricard, 'and it's market-day too. I could have done without all this extra trouble. Look, Demoiselle Marie, I would like your opinion upon the decorations of the room we have prepared for him, whether it's to your taste or not.'

He led her upstairs and opened the door of a well-proportioned room, though it was somewhat low of ceiling, in which the beams had just been waxed. The room was furnished with a few rather coarse oak pieces, with a narrow bed, whose coverlet was nevertheless a fine piece of Italian brocade, and with a few pewter ornaments and a candlestick. Marie looked round the room.

'This all looks very nice,' she said. 'But I think, indeed I hope, that your master will soon be lodged at the manor.'

Ricard once more gave a slight smile.

'I expect so too,' he replied. 'I promise you that everyone here is very intrigued by Messire Guccio's arrival and by the news that he is going to settle here. Since yesterday there has been a ceaseless flow of people coming here on every kind of pretext, taking up our time for nothing at all, to such an extent that you might think there was no one else in the town who could count out a dozen pennies for a shilling. All this merely to gaze in astonishment at the decorating we are doing and to be told the reason for it all over again. I must say that Messire Guccio is much beloved in the neighbourhood since he had Provost Portefruit dismissed: everyone complained of him. He will be warmly welcomed and I can see him becoming the real master of Neauphle, after your brothers of course,' he added as he saw the girl out by the garden door.

Never had the road between the town of Neauphle and the Manor of Cressay seemed so short.

'He's coming, he's coming . . .' she repeated to herself like a song, jumping from one rut to another. 'He's coming, he loves me, and we shall soon be married. He will be the true master of Neauphle.' The basket of food felt light upon her arm.

As she went into the courtyard of Cressay, she met her brother Pierre.

'He's coming!' she cried, putting her arms round his neck.

'Who's coming?' asked the great lout in amazement.

It was the first time in months that he had seen his sister show any real sign of happiness.

'Guccio's coming!'

'Oh, that's good news,' cried Pierre de Cressay. 'He was a good friend and I shall be delighted to see him again.'

'He's coming to live in Neauphle, where his uncle has given him charge of the branch. And above all . . .'

She stopped, but, incapable of keeping her secret any longer, she pulled her brother's ill-shaven face down towards her and whispered in his ear, 'He's going to ask for my hand.'

'What nonsense!' said Pierre. 'Where did you get that idea from?'

'It is not an idea, I know it . . . I know it . . . I know it . . .'

Attracted by the noise, Jean de Cressay, the eldest of them, came out of the stables, where he was in process of grooming his horse. He had a wisp of straw in his hand.

'Jean, it seems that a brother-in-law is arriving from Paris,' said the younger brother.

'A brother-in-law? Whose brother-in-law?'

'That's just it! Our sister has found herself a husband!'

'Well, that would be no bad thing!' Jean replied.

He entered good-humouredly into the game and believed that it was merely a piece of girlish nonsense.

'And who is this powerful baron,' he went on, 'who covets the honour of uniting himself to our ruined towers and our fine heritage of debt? I only hope, sister, that he's rich, because we need it.'

'Oh, yes, he is,' replied Marie. 'It's Guccio Baglioni.'

From her elder brother's expression she knew at once that she was in for a scene. She suddenly felt cold and her ears began humming.

For a few more seconds Jean de Cressay pretended to treat the whole matter as a joke, but the tone of his voice had changed. He wanted to know why his sister had spoken thus. Was she particularly attracted to Guccio? Had she had any conversation with him which went beyond the limits of propriety? Had he written to her without the family's knowledge?

To every question, Marie replied 'No,' but her anxiety was increasing. Even Pierre felt a certain uneasiness.

'I've been stupid again,' he said to himself. 'I'd have done better to keep my mouth shut.'

All three of them went into the Great Hall of the Manor where their mother, Dame Eliabel, was spinning wool by the fireplace. The lady of the manor had during these last months recovered her natural stoutness as a result of the food which Guccio had sent Marie every week since the famine of the preceding winter.

'Go up to your room,' said Jean de Cressay to his sister.

As the eldest, he had the authority of a head of the family, and Marie obeyed without discussion.

When they heard the door shut on the first floor, Jean told his mother what he had just learned.

'Are you quite sure, my son? Can it be true?' she cried. 'Who could possibly imagine that a girl of our rank, whose ancestors have formed part of chivalry for three centuries, could marry a Lombard? I am sure that young Guccio, who indeed is an extremely nice boy, and keeps his station, has never even thought of it.'

'I don't know whether he has thought of it or not,' replied Jean, 'but I know that Marie is thinking of it.'

Dame Eliabel's fat cheeks grew red.

'The child's imagining things!' she said. 'My sons, if that young man has come here to visit us several times and shown us so much friendliness, it is because, I am sure, he is more interested in your mother than in your sister. Oh, without any impropriety of course,' she hastened to add, 'and not a single word that could offend me has passed his lips. Nevertheless, these are things one knows when one is a woman and I have been well aware that he admires me.'

So saying, she sat straight and bridling upon her stool.

'Without wishing to doubt your judgement, Mother,' replied Jean de Cressay, 'I am not so sure. Do you remember that the last time Guccio came here, we left him alone several times with our sister, when she seemed to be so ill; and it was after that time that she recovered her health.'

'It's perhaps because from that moment she began to have enough to eat again, and we too,' Pierre remarked.

'Yes, but I realize also that since then it has always been through Marie that we have heard news of Guccio. His Italian journey, the accident to his leg . . . It is always Marie whom Ricard informs and never one of us. And the way she always insists on going to get the food from the bank herself! I tell you there's something behind all this to which our eyes have been closed.'

Dame Eliabel left her distaff, shook the bits of wool from her skirt, and, rising, declared in an outraged voice, 'Indeed, it would be extremely dishonest of this young man to have made use of his ill-gotten fortune to suborn my daughter, and try to buy our alliance by a few gifts of food and clothing, when the honour of being our friend should suffice to repay him.'

Pierre de Cressay was the only member of the family who had a sense of the realities of the situation. He was simple, loyal, and without prejudices. So much bad faith, in conjunction with such vain pretensions, began to make him impatient.

'They're each jealous of Marie in their own way,' he said to himself, looking at his mother and his brother who were engaged in mutually encouraging each other's indignation.

'You seem to forget, both of you,' he said, 'that Guccio's uncle is still our creditor to the extent of three hundred pounds which he has been kind enough not to demand, nor has he asked for the interest which is increasing all the time. And if we were not distrained upon by Provost Portefruit and turned out of our house, it's to Guccio that we owe it. And remember that he has saved us from dying of hunger with food for which we have never paid. Before sending him about his business, just think whether you can discharge your debts. Guccio is rich and will become more so as time goes on. He is under high protection, and if the King of France thought he cut a sufficiently good figure to send him with an embassy to Naples to fetch the new Queen, I don't see why we should be so difficult about it.'

Jean shrugged his shoulders.

'It was Marie who told us that too,' he said. 'He must have gone there as a merchant on business.'

'And even if the King did send him to Naples, that doesn't mean that he would give him his daughter's hand!' cried Dame Eliabel.

'My dear mother,' replied Pierre, 'as far as I know Marie is not the daughter of the King of France! She is very good-looking, of course . . .'

'I refuse to sell my sister for money,' cried Jean de Cressay.

He had one eyebrow higher than the other and when he was angry the asymmetry became very apparent.

'Naturally you won't sell her,' replied Pierre, 'but you'll

select some old dotard for her, and fail to be offended by the fact that he is rich, provided he can wear spurs on his gouty heels. If she loves Guccio, you won't be selling her! Nobility? Great God, surely we two boys can uphold it. I don't mind telling you that, as far as I'm concerned, I would not be altogether averse from their marriage.'

'And you wouldn't be averse from seeing your sister installed at Neauphle, in our very own fief, behind the counter of a bank, weighing coins, and trafficking in spices? You're out of your mind, Pierre, and I don't know where you can have acquired your lack of respect for what we are,' said Dame Eliabel. 'In any case, as long as I'm alive, I shall never consent to such a misalliance! Nor will your brother, will you, Jean?'

'Even to discuss the matter is going too far, and I ask you, Pierre, never to speak of it again.'

'All right, all right, you're the eldest, do as you think best,' said Pierre.

'A Lombard! A Lombard!' went on Dame Eliabel. 'Young Guccio's coming, you say? Leave it to me, sons. The debt we owe him and the obligations we are under prevent our closing our doors to him. Very well, we'll receive him well; indeed we'll receive him too well; but if he is deceitful, I shall be so too. And I guarantee I'll prevent his ever desiring to come here again, if it is for the motive we fear!'

2

Dame Eliabel's Reception

FROM DAWN THE FOLLOWING day one might have thought that the feverish activity which had taken charge of the bank at Neauphle had been caught by the Manor of Cressay. Dame Eliabel harried her maid, and six peasants from the neighbourhood had been summoned to forced labour for the day. The flagstones were being thoroughly scrubbed, the tables were being set as if for a wedding, tree trunks were being stacked each side of the chimney-piece; fresh straw had been laid in the stables, the courtyard brushed with birch-brooms, and, in the kitchen, a young wild boar and a whole sheep were already turning on the spit; pies were cooking in the oven; and in the village the rumour was abroad that the Cressays were expecting an envoy from the King.

The day was cold and bracing, with a pale January sun which nevertheless lit up the leafless branches and illuminated points of light in the puddles on the roads.

Guccio arrived towards the end of the morning, wearing a

coat lined with expensive fur, and a lavish bonnet of green cloth whose peak fell upon one shoulder. He was riding a fine bay horse which seemed to be in beautiful condition and was richly harnessed. He was followed by a servant, also on horseback, and you could see from a mile off that he was a rich man.

He found Dame Eliabel and her two sons in their best clothes and was delighted with his welcome. From the ampleness of the fare provided, from the attentiveness of the servant, the embraces of Dame Eliabel, and the evident pleasure at his presence, he drew happy auguries.

Marie must have informed them of his intent and it had been received with enthusiasm. It was known why he was come, and he was already being treated as her fiancé. Only Pierre de Cressay seemed somewhat embarrassed.

'My dear friends,' cried Guccio, 'how delighted I am to see you again! But you should not have put yourselves to all this expense. Treat me exactly as if I were a member of the family.'

This speech displeased Jean, who secretly exchanged a glance with his mother.

Guccio had somewhat changed in appearance. His accident had given him a slight stiffness of the right leg which nevertheless gave a certain haughty elegance to his walk. Also, in hospital he had grown to his full height; he was now an inch taller, his features were set, and his face had acquired that more serious and mature expression which is the result of a long ordeal of physical suffering. He had outgrown his adolescence and had now taken on the appearance of a man.

Without having lost any of his previous assurance, rather the contrary, he now took less pains to impose himself on others. His French had grown more correct; he spoke with less accent and somewhat more slowly, though he still gesticulated as much as before.

Guccio looked at the walls about him as if he were already their master. He inquired about Pierre's and Jean's plans. Had they no plans for the reconditioning of the Manor? Alterations which would make it conform to the taste of the day?

'In Italy,' he said, 'I saw some painted ceilings which would be most effective here. And don't you think you ought to rebuild your bathroom? They build little ones today which are extremely convenient and, in my opinion, a bathroom is indispensable to people of quality.'

It was to be understood that he was implying, 'I am prepared to pay for all this, for this is how I like living.'

He also had ideas about the furniture, and tapestries with which to decorate the walls. He was beginning seriously to annoy Jean de Cressay, and even the huge Pierre himself thought that it was going a bit too far to begin speaking immediately about reconditioning the whole house.

Guccio had been there half an hour, and Marie had not yet appeared. 'Perhaps,' he thought, 'I should declare myself at once . . .'

'Am I to have the pleasure of seeing Demoiselle Marie; will she be of our company at dinner?'

'Of course, of course; she is dressing, she'll be down soon,' replied Dame Eliabel. 'You will find her much altered; she is completely obsessed by her new-found happiness.'

Guccio rose to his feet, his heart beating, his complexion

turning dark. Where others turned red, he became olive-coloured.

'Really?' he cried. 'Oh, Dame Eliabel, what happiness you give me!'

'Yes, and we too are delighted to be able to share the good news with a friend such as yourself. Our dear Marie is affianced . . .'

She paused in order to savour the pleasure of seeing Guccio change countenance.

'She is affianced to a relation of ours, the Lord of Saint-Venant, a gentleman of Artois of the most ancient nobility who has fallen in love with her, as she has with him.'

Aware that they were all looking at him, Guccio made an effort to ask, 'And when is the wedding to be?'

'In the first days of summer,' replied Dame Eliabel.

'But to all intents and purposes it's an accomplished fact,' said Jean de Cressay, 'because promises have been exchanged.'

For a moment Guccio felt bewildered, incapable of speech, fiddling automatically with the golden reliquary given him by Queen Clémence, which now shone brightly upon his parti-coloured jerkin of the latest Italian fashion. He heard Jean de Cressay open a door and call his sister. Then he recognized the sound of Marie's footsteps; pride coming to his aid, he compelled himself to put a good face on it.

Marie came in, her manner stiff and distant, but her eyes red. She greeted Guccio composedly. He congratulated her as naturally as he could, while she received his compliments with as much dignity as she could muster. She was not far from bursting into tears, but was alone in knowing it, and she succeeded so well in controlling herself that Guccio took for real coldness what in reality was Marie's fear of betraying herself and of suffering the punishments she had been threatened with.

The too copious meal was a long agony. Dame Eliabel, delighting in her own duplicity, pretended to a false gaiety, obliging her guest to take second helpings of every dish, constantly ordering the servant to bring another slice of mutton or boar for his hunk of bread.

'Have you lost your appetite on your long journeys?' she cried. 'Come now, Messire Guccio, at your age you must eat well. Isn't it to your liking? Take a larger helping of that pie!'

Guccio wanted to throw his bowl in her face.

He was not once able to meet Marie's eyes.

'She's apparently not too proud to have gone back on her word to me,' thought Guccio. 'Have I escaped death only to receive an affront such as this! Oh, I had good reason for my fears when I despaired in the Hôtel-Dieu. And the letters I sent her! But why did she reply through Ricard that she was still the same and longed to see me, while in fact she was getting engaged elsewhere? This is a betrayal that I shall never be able to forgive! Oh, what a filthy dinner this is! I can never remember a worse!'

The search for vengeance is frequently a by-product of sorrow. Guccio wondered how he could respond to the humiliation inflicted upon him. 'I could, of course, demand the immediate payment of the debt, and this perhaps might place them in such difficulties that they would have to give up the wedding.' But the plan seemed to him inadmissibly vulgar. Had he been dealing with a middle-class family, he might perhaps have used them thus; but with gentlemen, who wished to inflict their nobility upon him, he wanted to find a gentlemanly answer. He wanted to prove to them that he was a greater gentleman than all the Cressays and Saint-Venants on earth.

His anxiety continued throughout the pudding and the cheese. When they came to the end of the meal, he suddenly took off his reliquary and gave it to the girl, saying, 'Here, my fair Marie, is my wedding present to you. It was Queen Clémence' – and Guccio made the name ring out – 'it was the Queen of France who placed it round my neck with her own hands because of the services I rendered her and because of the friendship with which she honours me. Within it is a relic of Saint John the Baptist. I never thought that I should come to part with it; but it seems that one can gladly part with all one holds most dear; and I shall be happy to think that you are wearing it from now on. May it protect you, and the children I hope you will have with your gentleman from Artois.'

This was the only way he could find of showing his contempt. It was paying a high price merely for the opportunity of turning a phrase. And indeed, as far as the Cressays, who hadn't a sixpence between them, were concerned, Guccio's emotional disturbances were always apt to end in costly gestures. Having come to take, he invariably left having given.

If Marie did not at that moment burst into tears, it was because the fear of her mother and brother weighed more heavily upon her than did her sorrow; but her hand trembled as she took the reliquary from Guccio's fingers. She carried it to her lips; this she could do because it contained a relic. But

Guccio did not see her gesture; he had already turned away.

On the pretext of his recent wound, the fatigue of his journey, and the necessity of returning to Paris on the following day, he immediately took leave of them, called his servant, put on his fur coat, leapt on his horse, and left the courtyard of Cressay with the certainty that he would never set foot in it again.

'And now we shall have to write to our cousin Saint-Venant,' said Dame Eliabel to her son Jean when Guccio had passed the gate.

Having reached the bank at Neauphle, Guccio said not a word all evening. He had the books brought him and pretended to be absorbed in examining the accounts. Ricard, the clerk, who had seen him leave so joyfully in the morning, realized that things had gone badly. Guccio told him that he would set off again the following morning; he did not seem to wish to make confidences and Ricard judged it wiser not to question him.

Guccio spent a sleepless night in the room that had been prepared so carefully for a long stay. He now regretted his reliquary and thought that his expensive gesture had merely been absurd. 'She didn't deserve so much; I've been a fool. And what will Uncle Spinello think of the situation?' he wondered as he tossed about among the crumpled sheets. 'He'll say that having besought him to give me this branch I don't now know what I want. I shall certainly never ask him for another. I might have returned in the Queen's escort and made myself a place in her household; I missed the quay by trying to jump too quickly, and then spent six months in hospital. Instead of returning to Paris and looking after my affairs, I rush headlong to this little town in order to marry a country girl about whom I've been crazy for nearly two years, as if there were no other woman in the world! And all this merely to find that she prefers some nitwit of her own sort. *Bel lavoro! Bel lavoro!* This'll be a lesson to me; it's time I grew up.' By dawn he had almost persuaded himself that fate had done him a great service. He called his servant, had his luggage strapped up, and his horse saddled.

While he was drinking a bowl of soup before leaving, a servant he had seen at Cressay the day before entered the bank and asked to speak to him alone. She came with a message: Marie, who had succeeded in escaping for an hour, was awaiting Guccio halfway between Neauphle and Cressay by the bank of the Mauldre at 'the place you know well', she added.

As Guccio had seen Marie but once outside the Manor, he realized that she meant the orchard by the river where they had kissed for the first time. But he replied that there must be some mistake, that as far as he was concerned he had nothing to say to Madame Marie, and that she should not have put herself to the trouble of coming out to meet him.

'Madame Marie is in a sad state,' said the servant. 'I swear to you, Messire, that you should go and meet her; if you have been offended, it has nothing to do with her.'

Without deigning to reply, he leapt on to his horse and started off down the road.

'The quay at Marseilles! The quay at Marseilles!' he kept repeating to himself. 'Enough of this foolishness; who knows what I shall be in for if I see her again. Let her consume her own tears if she wants to weep!'

Thinking thus, he galloped a few hundred yards towards Paris; then, suddenly, to his valet's amazement, he turned his horse and set out at a gallop across country.

In a few minutes he came to the bank of the Mauldre; he saw the orchard and Marie waiting for him beneath the apple trees.

3

The Midnight Marriage

When, a little after vespers, Guccio dismounted in the Rue des Lombards before the Tolomei bank, his horse was foaming.

Guccio threw the reins to his servant, crossed the great gallery where the counters were, and climbed, as quickly as his stiff leg would let him, the stairs leading to his uncle's study.

He opened the door; the light was masked by Robert of Artois's back. The latter turned about.

'Ah, Providence has sent you, friend Guccio,' he cried, extending his arms. 'I was just asking your uncle for a sure and diligent messenger to go at once to Arras to Jean de Fiennes. But you'll have to be prudent, young man,' he added, as if Guccio's consent were not in question; 'for my dear friends, the Hirsons, are far from taking things easily. They let loose their hounds on anyone who comes from me.'

'Monseigneur,' Guccio replied, still breathless from his

ride, 'Monseigneur, only a year ago I nearly brought up my soul at sea while going to England on your service; I have just spent six months in bed as a result of going to Naples on the service of the King, and neither of these journeys has resulted in any good fortune to myself. For this once you will allow me not to obey you, for I must attend to my own affairs which will not permit of delay.'

'I'll pay you so well that you won't regret it,' said Robert.

'Doubtless with the money that I shall have to lend you, Monseigneur,' softly interposed uncle Tolomei, who was standing in the shadow, his hands crossed over his stomach.

'I wouldn't go for a thousand pounds, Monseigneur!' cried Guccio. 'And particularly not into Artois.'

Robert turned to Tolomei.

'Tell me, friend banker, have you ever heard such a thing in your life? A Lombard to refuse a thousand pounds, which I haven't even offered him! Clearly he must have sound reasons. I suppose your nephew isn't in the pay of Master Thierry, may God strangle him, and with his own guts if possible!'

Tolomei burst out laughing.

'You needn't fear, Monseigneur; I suspect my nephew of being in love and even of having won the heart of a high-born lady.'

'Oh, if it's a matter of a woman, there's nothing I can do about it, and I shall have to forgive him his refusal. All the same, I need someone to go on the business I told you of.'

'Don't worry, I have someone who will do; an excellent messenger, who will serve you all the more discreetly for the fact of knowing you. Besides, a monk's robe is not much noticed upon the roads.'

'A monk?' said Robert, looking doubtful.

'An Italian.'

'Ah, that's better. You see, Tolomei, I'm playing for high stakes. Since the King has forbidden my aunt Mahaut to leave Paris, I'm going to take the opportunity of having her château of Hesdin, or rather *my* château of Hesdin, taken by the "allies"! I've bought – yes, and with your gold, you'll say! – I've bought the consciences of two of the dear Countess's sergeants-at-arms, two rascals, as are all the others she employs, who'll sell themselves to the highest bidder. They'll let my friends into the place. And if I can't enjoy what belongs to me, at least I can promise you a splendid sack and I'll give you the job of selling the loot.'

'Oh, Monseigneur, you're mixing me up in a very pretty business!'

'Nonsense! You might as well be hung for a sheep as a lamb. Since you're a banker you're a thief, and you're not the man to be afraid of receiving stolen goods; I never divert people from their natural bent.'

Since the arbitration he had been in the greatest good humour.

'Goodbye, my friend, I'm very fond of you,' he went on. 'Oh, I was forgetting: the names of the two sergeants-at-arms. Give me a sheet of paper.' And as he wrote out his message, he added, 'To the lord of Fiennes, you understand, and to no one else. Souastre and Caumont are watched too closely.'

He got to his feet, closed the gold clasp of his coat, and

then, placing his hands on Guccio's shoulders, which made Guccio feel as if he were sinking halfway into the floor, he said, 'You're quite right, my boy, amuse yourself with the lady of high degree, it's proper to your age. When you're a few years older, you'll know that they're only harlots like the rest, and that the pleasures they sell can be bought for tenpence in a brothel.'

He went out, and for several seconds afterwards his great laugh could be heard shaking the staircase.

'Well, nephew, when's the wedding to be?' asked Messire Tolomei. 'I didn't expect you back so soon.'

'Uncle, you must help me!' cried Guccio. 'Those people are absolute monsters, they've forbidden Marie to see me again, their cousin in the north is hideously deformed and she'll certainly die!'

'What people? What cousin?' asked Tolomei. 'It seems to me, my boy, that your affairs have not gone as well as you expected. Tell me what's happened and try to be a little clearer.'

So Guccio told his uncle the story of his visit to Neauphle. With his Latin sense of tragedy he made everything seem even blacker than it was. The girl was shut up; she had risked death to cross the fields to meet him and had begged him to save her. The Cressay family, having discovered Marie's intentions, wished to marry her by force to a distant relation, a man of appalling morality and hideous physical appearance.

'An old man of forty-five!' cried Guccio.

'Thank you,' said Tolomei.

'But Marie loves no one but me, she's told me so, she's said it often. She doesn't want anyone else for husband, and

I know that she'll die if she's forced to marry someone else. Uncle, you must help me.'

'But how can I help you, my boy?'

'You must help me to abduct Marie. I'll take her to Italy and live there.'

Spinello Tolomei, one eye almost shut, the other wide open, looked at his nephew with a half-anxious, half-amused expression.

'I told you, my boy, that it wouldn't be as easy as you thought, and that you were making a mistake by going and becoming infatuated with a daughter of the nobility. Those people haven't got a shirt of their own to their backs; they can only eat thanks to us. Oh yes, I know all about it. They owe us everything down to their beds, but they spit on our faces if one of our boys wants to sleep in it. Believe me, forget the whole thing. When we're insulted, it's generally because we've stuck our necks out. Choose a beautiful girl from one of our families, well provided with gold from our bank, who will give you equally beautiful children, and whose coach will splash the feet of your country lass with mud.'

Guccio had a sudden idea.

'Saint-Venant, isn't he one of the "allies" of Artois?' he cried. 'Supposing I took Monseigneur Robert's message, and could find this Saint-Venant, challenge him, and kill him!'

He put his hand to his dagger.

'A fine thing,' said Tolomei, 'and it wouldn't make a noise, of course. And then the Cressays would choose another fiancé in Brittany or in Poitou, and you'd have to go and kill him too. You're taking on quite a job!'

'I'll marry Marie or not at all, Uncle, and I won't let anyone else marry her.'

Tolomei raised his hands above his head.

'So like the young! In fifteen years' time your wife will be ugly in any case, *figlio mio*; and you'll ask yourself, when you look at her, if that lined face, that fat stomach, and those hanging breasts were really worth all the trouble you took about her.'

'It's not true! It's not true! Besides, I'm not thinking of fifteen years hence, but of my life today, and I know that nothing in the world can take Marie's place. She loves me.'

'She loves you, does she? Well, my boy, if she loves you so much – and don't go repeating my words to our good friend the Archbishop of Sens – if she loves you so much, believe me, marriage is not an indispensable condition of happiness for two people. You should rejoice rather that they have chosen for her a husband who is imbecile, deformed, and losing his teeth, according to the portrait you have painted of him without ever having seen him. There could be no better solution to your problem.'

'*Schifoso! Queste sono parole schifose! Vengono da un uomo che non conosce Maria!** You don't know how pure she is, the strength of her religion. She can only be mine through marriage, and she will never belong but to him to whom she will be united before God. If that's how things are, I shall abduct her without your help, and we shall travel the roads

---

* Ignoble! How ignoble your words are! They could only be uttered by someone who does not know Marie!

like miserable tramps, and your nephew will end by dying of hunger and cold while crossing the mountains.'

He was now talking in a mixture of Italian and French and gesticulating even more with his hands than usual.

'Anyway,' he went on, 'I don't need your help, I shall go and see the Queen.'

Tolomei hit the table lightly with the palm of his hand.

'Now, you shut up,' he said, hardly raising his voice, but his eye which was normally shut had suddenly opened. 'You'll go and see no one, and certainly not the Queen, for our affairs have not been going all that well since her arrival that we can afford to attract attention to ourselves with a scandal. The Queen is kindness itself, she is charitable and religious, I know it well! She gives alms to everyone she meets, but in the meantime, since she has gained ascendancy over the King's mind, we, the poor Lombards, are fleeced to the bone. It's with our wealth that the Treasury gives alms! We are accused of being usurers, and every opportunity is taken of blaming the follies of others upon us. Monseigneur of Valois to begin with, who has much disappointed me. Queen Clémence will give you fair words and her blessing; but there are too many people about her who would be happy to have you arrested and subjected to the punishment reserved for those who seduce the daughters of nobles, even if it were only to do me an injury. Have you forgotten that I am Captain-General of the Lombards of Paris? The wind has changed while you have been away. Marigny's best friends, who don't exactly love me, have been freed and form a party about the Count of Poitiers . . .'

But Guccio wasn't listening; for the moment he was

reckless of taxes, Orders in Council, lawyers, and the fluctuations of power. He was determined to carry out his intention: he would abduct Marie without anyone's help.

'*Segnato da Dio!*' said Tolomei, touching his forehead as if he were dealing with a halfwit. 'But, my poor afflicted boy, you wouldn't get twenty miles without being arrested. Your girl would be taken from you and placed in a convent; as for you . . . You want to marry her? Very well! You shall marry her, since it seems to be the only way to cure you. I'll help you.'

And his left eye closed again.

'Folly for folly, since it is folly, it's likely to be less serious than if I leave you to act alone,' he added. 'But why should one have to be responsible for the follies committed by one's family?'

He rang a bell; a clerk came in.

'Go to the Monastery of the Augustin fathers,' Tolomei said to him, 'and find me Fra Vincento who arrived from Pérouse the other day.'

Two days later Guccio took the road again to Neauphle, in company with an Italian monk who was going to deliver Monseigneur Robert's message in Artois. His journey was well paid and Fra Vincento had not hesitated to make a detour to render Tolomei two services instead of one.

Moreover the banker had succeeded in putting the matter before him in a most acceptable light. Guccio, having seduced a young girl, had committed with her the sins of the flesh, and Tolomei did not wish these two young people to live any longer in a state of sin. But it was necessary to proceed with discretion in order not to awaken the suspicions of the family.

These admirable reasons being accompanied by a small purse of gold, Fra Vincento found them wholly convincing. Moreover, like all his compatriots, whether in holy orders or not, he was always ready to lend a hand to an amorous intrigue.

Guccio and his monk appeared at the Manor of Cressay at nightfall. Dame Eliabel and her children were about to go to bed. The young Lombard asked them for hospitality for the night, saying that he had not had time to warn Ricard, and that his house at Neauphle was not ready to entertain a priest in a sufficiently dignified fashion. As Guccio, in the past, had on several occasions slept at the Manor, and upon the invitation of the Cressays themselves, his action now was not particularly surprising; the family did their best to welcome the travellers.

'Fra Vincento and I don't in the least mind sleeping in the same room,' said Guccio.

Fra Vincento's round face inspired confidence as much as did his habit; moreover, he spoke only Italian, which enabled him to give no reply to indiscreet questions.

He said grace in an extremely pious manner before touching the food set before him.

Marie dared not look Guccio in the face; but the young man took advantage of a moment when she passed close by him to whisper to her, 'Don't go to sleep tonight.'

At the moment of going to bed, Fra Vincento said something to Guccio which was incomprehensible to the Cressays; the words *chiave* and *capella* were mentioned.

'Fra Vincento asks me,' Guccio translated for the benefit of

Dame Eliabel, 'if you would give him the key to the Chapel, because he must leave early and would like to say his Mass before going.'

'Of course,' replied the lady of the Manor, 'one of my sons will rise early in order to help him say his office.'

Guccio expostulated that no one must be put to any trouble. Fra Vincento would really be getting up so early, at the crack of dawn, and Guccio looked upon it as an honour to act as his acolyte himself. Pierre and Jean took care not to insist.

Dame Eliabel gave the monk a candle, the key of the Chapel, and that of the ciborium; then everyone parted.

'Really, I think that we have misjudged Guccio,' said Pierre to his mother as they parted for the night; 'he is extremely attentive to matters of religion.'

Towards midnight, when the whole Manor seemed plunged in sleep, Guccio and the monk crept from their rooms. The young man went to scratch gently upon Marie's door; the girl appeared at once. Without a word Guccio took her by the hand; they went down the spiral staircase and gained the open air by the kitchens.

'Look, Marie,' murmured Guccio, 'look at the stars. The Brother is going to marry us.'

She did not even appear surprised. He had promised to come back and he had come back; to marry her, and he was about to do so. The circumstances did not matter; she completely and utterly deferred to him. A dog began barking but, having recognized Marie, fell silent again.

The night was freezing but neither Guccio nor Marie felt the cold.

They entered the Chapel. Fra Vincento lit a candle from the tiny lamp which burnt above the altar. Though no one could hear them, they went on talking in low voices. Guccio translated for Marie the priest's question as to whether she had been to confession. She said that she had done so two days before, and Fra Vincento gave her absolution for the sins that she might have committed since, with all the more confidence for the fact that, had she avowed them, he would have been incapable of understanding her. As far as Guccio was concerned the formality had been complied with before they came downstairs.

A few minutes later, by exchanging the word 'yes' in low voices, the nephew of the Captain-General of the Lombards and beautiful Marie de Cressay were united before God, if not in the sight of men.

'I would have liked to give you a more sumptuous wedding,' Guccio murmured.

'As far as I am concerned, darling, there could be no finer wedding,' replied Marie, 'since it joins me to you.'

As they were leaving the Chapel, the monk gave signs of a lively disquiet.

'*Che cosa?*' Guccio whispered to him.

Fra Vincento pointed out that the door had been closed during the wedding.

'*E allora?*'

The monk explained to him that, for a marriage to be valid, the doors of the church must be left open, so that any stranger could theoretically be a witness to the fact that the vows had been properly given and without constraint. If this were not done, there was a case for annulment.

'What is he saying?' Marie asked.

'He's counselling us to go quietly back to the house,' said Guccio.

They entered the house again and went up the stairs. When they arrived before Marie's door, the monk, whose scruples seemed to have disappeared, took Guccio by the shoulders and pushed him gently into the room.

Marie had been in love with Guccio for two years. For two years she had thought of no one but him and lived only in the longing to be his. Now that her conscience was set at rest and the fear of damnation had been put aside, there was nothing to prevent her giving free rein to her passion.

Marie had been brought up in isolation in the country, and had been spared the gallant speeches which so often create a false bashfulness. She was in love with love without ever having known it; and she now abandoned herself to it frankly and with delight.

The pain suffered by girls at the moment of their true marriage is more often due to fear than nature. Marie did not know this fear. Guccio, though he was only nineteen, had already sufficient experience to avoid being clumsy, but not enough to have forgotten emotion. That night he made Marie a happy woman, and as, in matters of love, what one receives is always in proportion to what one gives, his own cup of happiness was overflowing.

Towards four o'clock in the morning the monk came and woke them up, and Guccio went back to his room on the other side of the house. Then Fra Vincento went downstairs making as much noise as possible, and going by the Chapel went and took his mule from the stable and rode off into the night.

At the first light of dawn Dame Eliabel, somewhat suspicious, opened the door of the travellers' bedroom and had a look. Guccio was breathing regularly in a deep sleep; his black hair curling upon the pillow; his face wearing an expression of childish peace.

'Oh, what a handsome fellow!' thought Dame Eliabel, sighing.

Guccio was so deeply asleep that she dared approach the bed on tiptoe and place a kiss upon the young man's hair which had for her all the seductiveness of sin.

4

The Comet

In the same last days of January in which Guccio had secretly married Marie de Cressay, the Queen, the King, and some of the Court had gone on a pilgrimage to Amiens.

Having walked through the mud, the procession had gone up the Cathedral nave on its knees; the pilgrims had meditated for a long time in an icy chapel before the relic of the Baptist which had been brought back from the Holy Land a century earlier by a certain Wallon de Sartou, who had been a Crusader in 1202, and had sought out pious remains in the Holy Land, bringing back in his baggage three pieces of inestimable value: the head of Saint Christopher, that of Saint George, and part of that of Saint John. The Amiens relic consisted only of the bones of the face; it was enshrined in a silver-gilt reliquary whose domed top was a substitute for the skull. This skeleton face, black beneath its crown of emeralds and sapphires, seemed to be laughing and was singularly terrifying. Above the left eye-socket there was a hole which, according to tradition, was the mark of a dagger-blow given it by Herodias when the head of the Baptist was presented to her. The whole reposed upon a golden charger. Clémence, lost in devotion, seemed to be unaware of the cold, and Louis X himself, a prey to religious fervour, succeeded in remaining still throughout the ceremony, his mind moving on a plane to which it was not normally accustomed. But fat Bouville acquired a cold in the chest which it took him nearly two months to get rid of.

Good results from this pilgrimage did not fail to become manifest. Towards the end of March the Queen showed symptoms which seemed to be a direct answer to prayer; she recognized in them the results of a beneficent intercession on the part of Saint John the Baptist.

None the less, the physicians and midwives who were keeping Clémence under observation could not as yet make any pronouncement, and declared that they needed a full month before they could be sure.

As the time of waiting went on, the Queen's mysticism seemed to affect her husband. To attract the divine blessing, The Hutin governed as if he had determined to be canonized.

It must be acknowledged that it is in general a bad thing to try to alter people's nature; it is better to leave the wicked to their wickedness than to transform them into sheep. Indeed, the King, thinking thereby to absolve himself of his sins, had undertaken to empty the prisons; as a result crime flourished in Paris, where one could no longer go out at night without running the risk of being robbed. There were more robberies, assaults, and murders than had been known for forty years, and the Watch had its work cut out. Since the prostitutes had been confined to the precise limits of the district which Saint Louis had assigned to them, clandestine prostitution had developed in the taverns, and particularly in the public baths, to the point at which an honest man could no longer go and take his warm bath without being exposed to overt temptations of the flesh.

Charles of Valois felt himself outmatched; but having been the champion of religion and of ancient customs for his own purposes, he found it difficult to oppose measures taken in the name of morality.

The Lombards, feeling that they were not in good odour, were more reluctant than ever to open their coffers for the need of the Court. In the meantime the old ministers of Philip the Fair, Raoul de Presles at their head, were forming an opposition party round the Count of Poitiers, and the Constable Gaucher de Châtillon had frankly declared himself to be on their side.

Clémence had even gone so far as to ask Louis to take back from her Marigny's lands, which he had given her, and restore them to the heirs of the late Rector of the Kingdom.

'That, my dear, I cannot do,' The Hutin had replied, 'and I cannot alter my judgement on that point; the King can do no wrong. But I promise you, as soon as the state of the Treasury permits it, to give my godchild Louis de Marigny a pension that will amply compensate him.'

In Artois the situation was growing no better. In spite of every agreement, all the proceedings and proposals, the Countess Mahaut remained undefeated. She complained that the barons had tried to take her castle by surprise.[18] The treachery of two sergeants-at-arms, who were to deliver the place to the 'allies', had been discovered in time; and now two skeletons were hanging from the battlements of Hesdin as an example. Nevertheless, the Countess, obliged to submit to the King's decision, had not returned to Artois since the arbitration at Vincennes, nor had any of the Hirsons. Moreover, there was great disorder in all the country about Arras, everyone joining whichever side he pleased; and fair words had no more effect on the barons than would milk flowing down their breastplates.

'No bloodshed, my dear lord, no bloodshed!' counselled Clémence. 'Bring your people to reason through prayer.'

This, however, did not prevent lawlessness upon the northern roads.

The Hutin's store of new-found patience was beginning to wear thin. He might perhaps have put more energy into solving the problem if, at the same time, round about Easter, his whole attention had not been absorbed by the situation in the capital.

The summer of 1315 had been as disastrous for the harvest as it was for the war, and if the King had lost his victories in the mud, the people had lost their bread there. Moreover, taught by the experience of the previous year, the country people, however poor they might be, had not given up the little wheat gathered once the harvest was over. Famine left the provinces and settled upon the capital. Never had wheat been so dear and never the population so thin.

'Oh God, oh God, let them be fed,' said Queen Clémence, when she saw the starving crowds that dragged themselves as far as Vincennes to beg a pittance.

So many came that soldiers had to be called out to forbid

access to the castle. Clémence advised that there should be great processions of clergy through the streets and imposed upon the whole court after Easter the same fast as during Lent. Monseigneur of Valois agreed to this happily enough, and had the news spread throughout the population so as to let them know that their sufferings were being shared. But he himself was negotiating satisfactory deals in bread from his own county.

Robert of Artois, when he had to go to Vincennes, first had a meal sufficient for four men served him by his faithful Lormet, and swallowed it down repeating one of his favourite maxims: 'Live well and we'll die fat.' After which he was able to appear to be doing penance at the Queen's table.

In the middle of this disastrous spring, a comet passed across the sky of Paris, remaining visible for three nights. The imagination stops at nothing in calamity. The population saw in it a sign of worse disasters, as if those it was undergoing were insufficient. The mob panicked and riots broke out in several places, though no one knew precisely against whom they were directed.

The Chancellor advised the King to return to his capital, even if it were only for a few days, so as to show himself to the people. Therefore, at the moment when the woods about Vincennes were beginning to turn green once more and Clémence was recapturing her first delight in the place, the whole Court moved to the great Palace of the Cité which seemed to the Queen so hostile and so cold. It was there that the consultation between the physicians and the midwives, who were to pronounce upon her pregnancy, took place.

The King was extremely anxious on the morning of the

consultation and, to mask his impatience, had organized a game of lawn tennis in the garden of the Palace. The ground he was playing on gave into the Island of Jews. But in two years memories become blurred; and Louis felt no uneasiness, now that he was assured of redemption by conversion, in running after a leather ball at the very place he and his father, twenty-five months earlier, had heard themselves cursed from amid the flames.

He was running with sweat and vaunting himself upon a point his gentlemen had permitted him to win, when Mathieu de Trye, his first Chamberlain, hurriedly approached. Louis interrupted the game and asked, 'Is the Queen pregnant?'

'It is not yet known, Sire, since the physicians have only just begun to consult on the matter. But Monseigneur of Poitiers wished you to join him urgently, if you please. He is closeted with your two brothers and Messire des Noyers.'

'I don't want to be bothered; I don't feel like attending to business at the moment.'

'The matter is grave, Sire, and Monseigneur of Poitiers has assured me that it concerns you closely. Things are to be discussed which you must hear with your own ears.'

Louis looked with regret at the leather ball, wiped his face, and put his robe on over his shirt, saying, 'Go on playing without me, Messeigneurs!'

Then he went into the Palace, saying to his Chamberlain, 'As soon as they know, Mathieu, come and tell me.'

5

The Cardinal's Spell

THE MAN STANDING AT the end of the room had a twitching face, dark narrow eyes close to his nose, and a shaved skull like a monk. He was tall, but was unable to stand at his full height owing to a shortening of his right leg.

Unlike an ordinary prisoner, who would have been guarded by two sergeants-at-arms, he was escorted by two esquires of the Count of Poitiers, Adam Heron and Pierre de Garancière.

Louis X barely acknowledged his presence. He nodded to his uncle of Valois, his brothers of Poitiers and la Marche, his cousin of Clermont, and Miles des Noyers, brother-in-law of the Constable and a Councillor of Parliament, who had risen at his entry.

'What is going forward?' he asked, taking his place among them and signing to them to be seated.

'A grave matter of sorcery, or so we are assured,' replied Charles of Valois in a somewhat ironic tone.

'Could not the Keeper of the Seals be instructed to examine the matter himself without bothering me today of all days?'

'That was just what I was telling your brother Philippe,' said Valois.

The Count of Poitiers calmly rested his chin on his joined hands.

'Brother,' he said, 'this is a serious matter, not only because of the sorcery, which is common enough, but because this particular manifestation of it is taking place within the Conclave itself, and thereby shows what the attitude of certain of the Cardinals is towards us.'

A year earlier, at the mere word 'Conclave', The Hutin would have been most concerned. But since Marguerite's death it had become a question in which he felt no interest at all.

'This man is called Everard,' went on the Count of Poitiers.

'Everard,' the King repeated automatically to show that he was listening.

'He is a clerk at Bar-sur-Aube; but he was once a member of the Order of the Templars, in which he held the rank of Knight.'

'A Templar, I see!' said the King.

'A fortnight ago he gave himself up to our people in Lyons, who have sent him to us.'

'Who sent him to *you*, Philippe,' corrected Charles of Valois.

The Count of Poitiers appeared to pay no attention to this remark. It was a question of a conflict of power, and Valois was annoyed that the matter had been dealt with over his head.

'Everard has said that he has revelations to make,' went on Philippe of Poitiers, 'and he was promised that he would come to no harm on condition that he told the truth, a promise which we will certify now. From his avowals . . .'

The King's eyes were fixed on the door, awaiting the appearance of his Chamberlain; the hope of becoming a father was, at the moment, his sole preoccupation. His great fault as a Sovereign lay perhaps in the fact that he always had his mind upon something other than the question under discussion. He was incapable of concentration, which is the gravest of all faults in the powerful.

He was surprised by the silence which had fallen upon them and ceased smiling.

'Well, Brother . . .' he said.

'Brother, I have no desire to interrupt your thoughts. I shall wait till you have terminated your reflections.'

The Hutin blushed a little.

'No, no, I'm listening, go on,' he said.

'According to the statements of this man,' Poitiers went on, 'Everard went to Valence to seek the protection of a Cardinal upon a matter in which he had had a difference with his Bishop . . . This needs going into further,' he added, addressing himself to Miles des Noyers, who was in charge of the interrogation.

Everard heard but gave no sign of grasping the implication.

Poitiers went on, 'It was only by chance, he says, that he made the acquaintance of Cardinal Francesco Caetani.'

'The nephew of Pope Boniface,' said Louis, to show that he was following.

'That is so. And he has become an intimate friend of the Cardinal, who is an alchemist of note, since he has in his house, so Everard tells us, a room full of cauldrons, retorts, and diverse chemicals.'

'All the Cardinals are more or less alchemists; it's their peculiar hobby,' said Charles of Valois, shrugging his shoulders. 'Monseigneur Duèze has himself, it appears, written treatises upon it.'

'He has, indeed, Uncle; I have read part of his *Authoritative Treatise upon the Art of Transmutation* without, I must admit, understanding much of it. But the present business goes much further than alchemy, which is an extremely useful and respectable science. Cardinal Caetani wanted to find someone who could evoke the devil in order to cast spells.'

Charles de la Marche, emulating the ironic attitude of his uncle Valois, said, 'There's a Cardinal who smacks of the bonfire.'

'All right, burn him,' said The Hutin indifferently, looking at the door again.

'Who do you want to burn, Brother? The Cardinal?'

'Oh, it's the Cardinal, is it? No, you can't do that.'

Philippe of Poitiers sighed in exasperation before going on, emphasizing his words.

'Everard told the Cardinal that he knew a man who made gold to the profit of the Count of Bar.'

Hearing that name, Valois rose to his feet in indignation and cried, 'Really, Nephew, we're wasting our time! I know the Count of Bar well enough to be quite sure that he would never indulge in that sort of foolishness! We are merely confronted with a false accusation of black magic, such as are made twenty times a day, and it is really not worth our while listening to it.'

Though trying to remain calm, Philippe finally lost patience.

'You listened to denunciations of sorcery all right when they were attributed to Marigny,' he replied dryly; 'you might at least listen to this one. In the first place, it is not a question of your friend the Count of Bar, as you will see. Everard did not go and find the man he had mentioned, but brought to the Cardinal's notice a certain Jéhan du Pré, another ex-Templar, who happened by chance to be at Valence. That's right, isn't it, Everard?'

Bowing his dark head, the witness silently agreed.

'Don't you agree, Uncle,' went on Poitiers, 'too great a concatenation of risks to be fortuitous, and too many Templars in the neighbourhood of the Conclave and in close proximity to Boniface's nephew?'

'Well, yes, I suppose so,' murmured Valois, somewhat subdued.

Turning to Everard, Poitiers suddenly asked him, 'Do you know Messire Jean de Longwy?'

Everard's face gave its customary twitch, and his spatulate fingers gripped the cord of his habit. Nevertheless, he replied without hesitation, 'No, Monseigneur, he's only a name to me. I know that he is a nephew of our late Grand Master.'

'Are you sure that you have never had any contact with him?' Poitiers insisted. 'Or received, through ex-members of your Order, any communications from him?'

'I have heard that Messire de Longwy has tried to keep contact with some of us; but nothing else.'

'And you have not learnt, through Jéhan du Pré for instance, the name of some ex-Templar who came to the army in Flanders to deliver messages to Longwy and take others from him?'

Both the Charleses, Valois and de la Marche, looked equally surprised. Without doubt, Philippe knew a great deal more than other people about a number of things; but why did he always keep his information to himself?

Everard had maintained a bold front to the Count of Poitiers's scrutiny. But the latter said to himself, 'I'm almost certain that it is he, the description I've been given fits him too nearly. And he's lame.'

'Were you ever tortured?' he asked.

'My leg, Monseigneur, bears witness for me!' cried Everard, beginning to tremble.

The Hutin was becoming anxious. 'The physicians are taking too long. Clémence is not pregnant and no one dares to come and tell me.' His attention was re-engaged by Everard, who had fallen to his knees before him and was screaming, 'Sire! Sire, have mercy, don't have me tortured again! I swear to God that what I am saying is the truth!'

'You mustn't swear, it's a sin,' said the King.

The two esquires forced Everard to his feet.

'Noyers, you must clear up that point about the army,' said Poitiers, addressing the Councillor of Parliament. 'Continue with the interrogation.'

Miles des Noyers, a man of some thirty years, with thick hair and two deep furrows across his forehead, said, 'Well, Everard, what did the Cardinal say to you?'

The ex-Templar, barely recovered from his panic, replied

in a rapid voice, and it was unlikely that he was lying, 'The Cardinal said to us, to Jehan du Pré and myself, that he wished to avenge the memory of his uncle, and become Pope; and that to do so he must destroy the enemies who stood in his way; and he promised us three hundred pounds if we would help him. And the two principal enemies whom he indicated were . . .'

Everard looked at the King in some hesitation.

'All right, go on,' said Miles des Noyers.

'He indicated the King of France and the Count of Poitiers, and said that he would be delighted to see them turning up their toes.'

The Hutin automatically looked at his shoes; then he started in his chair and cried, 'Turn up my toes? The wicked Cardinal wants my death!'

'Precisely so, Brother,' said Poitiers smiling; 'and mine too.'

'And you, cripple, don't you realize that for a crime such as that you would be burnt in this world and damned in the next?' The Hutin continued.

'Sire, Cardinal Caetani assured us that, when he became Pope, he would see that we had absolution.'

Leaning forward, his hands upon his knees, Louis looked at the ex-Templar in amazement.

'Do people dislike me so much that they want to kill me?' he said. 'And how did the Cardinal propose to do it?'

'He said that you were too well guarded, Sire, for either steel or poison to be effective, and that it must be brought about by casting a spell. To this end he had a pound of pure wax delivered to us, which we put to melt in a basin of hot water in the room where the cauldrons were. Then Jéhan du Pré moulded an admirable likeness with a crown on its head . . .'

Louis X quickly crossed himself.

'And then another smaller one, with a smaller crown. While we were working the Cardinal came to see us; he appeared to be in extremely good spirits, and he even began laughing when he saw the first image and he said to us, "He has an enormous privy member."'[19]

Charles of Valois could not retain a burst of laughter.

'All right, we'll leave that,' said The Hutin nervously. 'What did you do with the images?'

'We put papers inside them.'

'What papers?'

'The papers which have to be placed in the image with the name of the person it represents and the words of the spell. But I promise you, Sire,' cried Everard, 'that we wrote neither your name nor that of Messire of Poitiers! At the last moment we took fright, and we wrote the names of Giacomo and Pietro Colonna . . .'

'The two Colonna cardinals?' asked Poitiers.

'. . . because the Cardinal had also mentioned them as enemies of his. I swear, I swear it was so!'

Louis X was now listening to every word that was said and seemed to be looking for support from his younger brother.

'Do you believe, Philippe, that the man is telling the truth?'

'I don't know,' replied Philippe.

'He must be properly interrogated by the tormentors,' said Louis.

The word 'tormentors' seemed to have a fatal effect on

Everard, for he once more fell to his knees and dragged himself towards the King, his hands joined in supplication, repeating over and over again that he had been promised that he would not be tortured if he made a complete avowal! There was a little white froth at the corner of his lips, and fear had made him wild-eyed.

'Stop him! Don't let him touch me!' cried Louis X. 'The man's possessed.'

It would have been difficult to tell which of the two, the King or the caster of spells, was the more frightened.

'Torture serves no purpose,' cried Everard; 'it's because of torture that I denied God.'

Miles des Noyers made a note of this unsolicited admission.

'But now it's remorse that drives me,' continued Everard, still upon his knees. 'I'll tell you everything. We had no holy oil with which to baptize the images. We had the Cardinal, who was sitting in Consistory in the big church, secretly told this, and he replied that we should approach a certain priest in a certain church behind the slaughter-yard, pretending that the holy oil was required for a sick man.'

There was no need to ask Everard questions. Of his own accord he was giving them the names of the people in the Cardinal's service. He cited the chaplain-secretary Andrieu, Father Pierre, and Brother Bost.

'Then we took the two images and the two sacred candles, and a pot of holy water, hiding them under our habits, and we went to the Cardinal's goldsmith, a man named Boudon, who had an extremely beautiful young wife, and who was to act as godfather while his wife acted as godmother. We baptized the images in a barber's bowl. After which we took them back to the Cardinal, who was extremely grateful to us, and himself placed the pins in the heart and the vital parts.'

There was a moment's silence; the door half-opened and Mathieu de Trye's head appeared. But the King signed to him with his hand to retire.

'And what happened then?' asked Miles des Noyers.

'The Cardinal then asked us to proceed to further spells,' replied Everard. 'But I began to be anxious because too many people knew about it, and I left for Lyons, where I gave myself up to the King's people, who sent me here.'

'Did you get the three hundred pounds?'

'Yes, Messire.'

'Good God!' said Charles de la Marche. 'What on earth could a clerk want three hundred pounds for?'

Everard bowed his head.

'Women, Monseigneur,' he answered in a low voice.

'Or for the Temple perhaps . . .' the Count of Poitiers said as if to himself.

The King, overwhelmed by private anxieties, said nothing.

'To the Petit Châtelet!' said Poitiers to his two esquires, indicating Everard.

The latter allowed himself to be taken away without any resistance whatever. He seemed suddenly to have come to the end of his strength.

'These ex-Templars appear to be quite a gang of sorcerers,' Poitiers went on.

'We ought not to have burnt the Grand Master,' murmured Louis X.

'I said as much as the time,' cried Valois.

'Of course, Uncle, you did say so,' replied Poitiers. 'But

that is not the question now. It's perfectly clear that the refugees from the Temple have formed a secret society, and that they will go to all lengths to serve our enemies. Everard has not said half of what he knows. His story has been rehearsed beforehand, that's quite clear, and he only began to tell the whole truth towards the end. But it is also quite clear that this Conclave, which has been moving from town to town for almost exactly two years, is now bringing Christianity into contempt as much as it is beginning to injure the Kingdom; and that the Cardinals, in their eagerness to obtain the tiara, are behaving in a manner deserving of excommunication.'

'Is it not possible that Cardinal Duèze,' said Miles des Noyers, 'has sent us this man in order to damage Caetani?'

'Perfectly possible,' said Poitiers. 'Everard appears to be one of those demented people who will support any cause provided it is a rotten one.'

He was interrupted by Monseigneur of Valois, whose expression had suddenly become both reflective and extremely grave.

'Don't you think, Philippe,' he said, 'that you should go yourself to visit the locality of the Conclave, whose affairs you seem to know so well, introduce some sort of order into it, and give us a Pope? You seem to me perfectly cut out for the part.'

Philippe gave the ghost of a smile. 'Uncle Charles thinks he's being very clever!' he thought. 'He's at last found an opportunity of removing me from Paris, and sending me into a wasp's nest.'

'Oh, how wise your advice is, Uncle!' cried Louis X. 'Of

course, Philippe must do us this service, and he's the only man who can. Brother, I shall be very grateful to you if you will undertake this business. Make an inquiry on your own account into the matter of the papers which have been placed in the images, and find out whether these have really been baptized in our names. Yes, indeed, this must be done at once, and it's as much to your interest as mine. Do you know what religious procedure should be invoked to protect oneself against a spell? After all, God is stronger than the devil.'

He did not give the impression of being completely certain of it.

The Count of Poitiers considered the matter. At heart he was tempted by the proposal. To leave the Court for a few weeks, where he had no power to prevent the follies that were committed, and where he was in perpetual conflict with the faction in power, and go to fulfil what was clearly a useful mission, attracted him. He would take with him his faithful adherents, Gaucher de Châtillon, Miles des Noyers, Raoul de Presles, and who could tell what might not happen? He who has made a Pope is well placed to receive a crown. The throne of the German Empire, which his father had already considered for him, and for which he had, in his capacity of Count Palatine, the right to stand, might one day become vacant.

'Very well, Brother, I accept, in order to do you service,' he replied.

'What a good brother I have!' cried Louis X.

He rose to embrace Philippe, and stopped in the middle of the gesture with a loud cry.

'My leg! My leg! It's gone cold; it's trembling; I can no

longer feel the ground under my foot!' It was as if the devil had already caught him by the calf of the leg.

'What's the matter, Brother?' said Philippe. 'You've got pins and needles, that's all. Give your leg a good rub!'

'Oh, do you think that's all it is?' said The Hutin.

And he went out, limping like Everard.

On reaching his apartments, he learnt that the physicians had given an affirmative decision, and that he would become, God willing, a father in November. At the moment he showed less pleasure in the prospect than had been expected.

6

'I Assume Control of Artois'

THE FOLLOWING DAY Philippe of Poitiers visited his mother-in-law in order to wish her goodbye. The Countess Mahaut was at the moment living in her new castle of Conflans, so called because it was situated immediately at the confluence of the Seine and the Marne, at Charenton.

Beatrice d'Hirson was present at their interview. When the Count of Poitiers recounted the cross-examination of the spell-maker, she exchanged a rapid glance with Mahaut. Both women had the same thought. The creature of Cardinal Caetani seemed to bear a singular resemblance to the man they had used, two years earlier, to poison Guillaume de Nogaret.

'It would be most surprising if there were two ex-Templars of the same name, both versed in sorcery. The death of Nogaret must have made a good introduction to the nephew of Boniface. I expect he's done a bit of blackmailing in that direction! What an unfortunate business!' Mahaut said to herself.

'What did this Everard look like?' she asked.

'Thin, dark, with a mad look about him,' replied Poitiers; 'and he was lame.'

Mahaut was watching Beatrice. The latter nodded imperceptibly; it was clearly the same man. The Countess of Artois felt a sudden dismay; Everard was bound to be subjected to special tortures designed for vivifying the memory of such people. Even if they weren't in process of doing it already. And supposing he talked? Not that Nogaret was much regretted by Louis X and his counsellors. But they would be delighted to use the murder as an occasion for proceeding against her! What play her nephew Robert would make with it! Her imagination working with astonishing rapidity, she at once began making plans. 'To kill a prisoner immured in a royal prison is far from easy. And who, even if there is still time, will help me to do it? Philippe, there's no one but Philippe; I must admit the whole business to him. But how will he take it? If he refuses to support me, I am finished.'

Beatrice also felt her throat turn dry.

'Has he been tortured?' asked Mahaut.

'They haven't had time,' replied Poitiers, who was leaning down to rebuckle his shoe; 'but . . .'

'God be praised,' thought Mahaut, 'nothing is yet lost. I must take the plunge!'

'My son . . .' she said.

'. . . but it's most unfortunate,' continued Poitiers, still leaning down, 'for we shall now learn nothing more. Everard hanged himself last night in the prison of the Petit Châtelet. From fear doubtless of being put to the question again.'

He heard two deep sighs; he sat up straight, rather surprised that these two women should show so much compassion for the fate of an unknown and so low a creature into the bargain.

'You were about to say something, Mother, and I interrupted you.'

Mahaut instinctively touched the relic she wore upon her breast through her dress.

'I was about to say . . . what was I going to say?' replied Mahaut. 'Oh, yes. I wanted to talk to you of Jeanne. In the first place, are you taking her with you?'

She had gathered her wits, and spoke in a natural voice. But, good God, what an escape!

'No, her condition forbids it,' replied Philippe. 'As a matter of fact I wanted to talk to you about her. She's three months from her lying-in, and I don't want to take any risks on the bad roads. I shall be moving about a lot.'

In the meantime Beatrice d'Hirson was concerned with her memories. She saw once more the back room in the shop in the Rue des Bourdonnais; she could smell the odour of wax, tallow, and candles; she felt the hard contact of Everard's hands on her skin and the strange impression she had had of being united with the devil.

'Why are you smiling, Beatrice?' the Count of Poitiers asked suddenly.

'No particular reason, Monseigneur, except that it's always a pleasure to see you and listen to you talk.'

'In my absence, Mother,' went on Philippe, 'I should like

Jeanne to live here with you. You can give her the care she needs and you will be able to afford her the protection she requires. To tell you the truth, I am somewhat afraid of the plots of our cousin Robert who, when he can't get the better of men, attacks women.'

'Which means, my son,' replied Mahaut, 'that you place me among the men. If it's a compliment, it doesn't displease me at all.'

'Of course it's a compliment,' said Philippe.

'Anyway you'll be back for Jeanne's lying-in?' asked Mahaut.

'I hope so, and will do my best; but I can't guarantee it, since the Conclave has all the appearance of being such a tangled skein that it will take me more than a few days to unravel it.'

'I'm very disquieted at your being away for so long, Philippe, because my enemies will assuredly take advantage of it concerning Artois.'

'Yes, I have no doubt they will. Plead my absence as an excuse for yielding nothing,' said Philippe as he took his leave.

The Count of Poitiers left for the south two days later and Jeanne came to live at Conflans.

As Mahaut had foreseen, the situation in Artois immediately gave reason for alarm. With the return of good weather the barons felt a need to disport themselves. Guided by Robert from a distance, and knowing the Countess to be in exile, they had now decided to administer the province themselves and were doing it extremely ill. They were perfectly content with the anarchy that reigned, and it was to be feared that the example would spread to the neighbouring provinces.

Louis X, who had returned to reside at Vincennes, determined to put an end to it once and for all. He was much encouraged in this by his treasurer, because the Artois taxes were not being paid. Mahaut could plead that she had been placed in a situation where she could not collect the taxes; and the barons said the same thing. Indeed, it was the only point upon which the adversaries were in agreement.

'I want no more Grand Councils, no more discussions by Parliamentary delegates, at which everyone lies and nothing gets done,' Louis X had declared. 'This time I propose to negotiate directly, and I'm going to make the Countess Mahaut yield.'

The impression made upon the King's mind by the Caetani affair, though violent, had been but of short duration.

During the weeks that followed the avowals of the ex-Templar, Louis had been in better health than for a long time past. He had but few symptoms of the stomach trouble to which he was subject; the pious fasts which Clémence imposed upon him had certainly been salutary. He succeeded in persuading himself that a spell had not been cast upon him. Nevertheless, as a precaution, he took Communion several times a week.

He had surrounded the Queen not only with the most famous midwives in the Kingdom, but also with the most competent saints in heaven: Saint Leon, Saint Norbert, Saint Colette, Saint Julienne, Saint Marguerite, and Saint Felicity, the last because she had only had male children. New relics arrived every day; tibias and molars accumulated in the

Chapel Royal. The prospect of having an heir whom he was certain was his own had an admirable effect upon The Hutin; Clémence, by making him a father, had completed his transformation. She had not succeeded in making him intelligent; that would have been an impossible task. But she had made a normal man of him; surrounded with better ministers, he might have become, in the long run, a moderately good king.

His manner, on the day he sent for the Countess Mahaut, appeared calm, courteous, and relaxed. It was no great distance from Charenton to Vincennes. To give the interview an air of greater intimacy, he received Mahaut in the Queen's apartment. The latter was engaged on her embroidery. There was a family atmosphere about the occasion. Louis talked conciliatingly.

'For form's sake put your seal to the document of arbitration, Cousin,' he said, 'for it seems that we cannot have peace but at that price. And then we shall see! The customs of Saint Louis are, after all, not all that well defined and you will always find means of taking back with one hand what you have appeared to give with the other. That's what I did with the people of Champagne, when the Count of Champagne and the Lord of Saint-Phalle came to demand my assent to their charter. We merely added "*except in those cases which touch Our Royal Majesty*"; and now when any litigation arises, it always does touch Our Royal Majesty.'

At the same time, with a friendly gesture, he pushed towards her the bowl of sweets from which he was helping himself as he talked.

'Wasn't it your brother Philippe who thought out that ingenious formula?' asked Mahaut.

'Yes, yes, of course it was Philippe who put it into words; but I thought of it, and he did no more than meet my thoughts.'

'But you must realize, Sire my Cousin, the circumstances are not the same in my case,' said Mahaut calmly. 'I have not the majesty of royalty; I am suzerain, yes, but no queen.'

'Nevertheless, you can put the phrase "the royal majesty" since I exercise it above you! Should there be dissension, it will be brought before me and I shall resolve it.'

Mahaut took a handful of sweets from the bowl, since there was no other food within reach of her hand.

'They're excellent, quite excellent,' she said, her mouth full, trying to gain time. 'I'm not really fond of sweets, but I must admit that they're quite delicious.'

'My dearest Clémence knows that I like nibbling them all the time, and she always sees that they are provided in her room,' said Louis, turning towards the Queen with the expression of a husband who wishes to underline the fact that he is properly cherished.

Clémence raised her eyes from her embroidery and returned Louis's smile.

'Well, Cousin,' went on Louis, 'are you going to put your seal to the document?'

Mahaut finished chewing a sugared almond.

'Well, no, Sire my Cousin, I can't put my seal to it,' she said. 'Though today we have in you an admirable King, and though I have no doubt that you will act in accordance with the sentiments you have expressed and would exercise the royal majesty in my favour, you will not last for ever and I a lesser time still. And after you, who knows, though God willing not for many years . . .' she added, making the sign of the Cross, 'there may be kings whose judgements will be less equitable. I must think of my heirs and cannot submit them to the discretion of the royal power for more than we already owe to it.'

However diplomatic the form in which it was couched, the refusal was none the less categorical. Louis, who had told his entourage that he would gain the upper hand of the Countess by personal diplomacy more successfully than by great public hearings, was rapidly losing patience; his vanity was at stake. He began striding up and down the room, raised his voice, brought his fist down on a piece of furniture; but, meeting Clémence's eyes, he stopped, blushed, and compelled himself to reassume a royal demeanour.

In the interplay of argument Mahaut was stronger than he; he'd never get anywhere by that method.

'Put yourself in my place, Cousin,' she said. 'You're about to have an heir; would you tolerate transmitting him diminished powers?'

'That's exactly it, Madam! I will not leave him either diminished powers or the memory of having had a weak father. And when all's said and done, you're going too far! And since you are so obstinate in your effrontery, I assume control of Artois myself! I have spoken! And you can turn up the sleeves of your dress, but you won't frighten me. From now on, your county will be governed in my immediate name by one of my lords whom I shall appoint. As for you, you will no longer have the right to go more than five miles away from the residences I have assigned you. And don't come into my presence again, for I shall not be pleased to see you. You may now retire.'

The blow was annihilating and Mahaut was not expecting it. Clearly, The Hutin had changed considerably.

Misfortunes come in series. Mahaut had been so suddenly dismissed that, as she came out of the Queen's apartment, she still had a sweet in her hand. She automatically put it in her mouth and bit upon it so violently that she broke a tooth.

For a whole week Mahaut remained at Conflans like a panther in a cage. With huge mannish paces she went from the living rooms, which gave upon the Seine, to the principal courtyard, which was surrounded by galleries and from which she could see the weathercocks upon the royal castle above the treetops of the forest of Vincennes. Her rage knew no bounds when, on May 15th precisely, Louis X, putting his plans into execution, named the Marshal of Champagne, Hugues de Conflans, as Governor of Artois. Mahaut saw in the choice of this particular governor, whose name was the same as that of her castle, a deliberately derisive gesture, and a supreme outrage.

'Conflans! Conflans!' she kept on repeating. 'I am shut up in Conflans, and a Conflans is nominated to steal my property from me.'

In the meantime her broken tooth was giving her severe pain because an abscess had formed. She constantly probed it with her tongue and exacerbated the pain. She vented her fury upon her attendants; she smacked Master Renier, one of the choristers in her chapel, because she thought that he sang flat during a service; Jeannot le Follet, her dwarf, hid in corners whenever he saw her coming afar off; she raged at Thierry d'Hirson whom she accused, him and his innumerable family, of being the cause of her immediate troubles; she even reproached her daughter Jeanne for not having prevented her husband from going to the Conclave.

'What the hell do we want a Pope for,' she cried, 'when we're being robbed? No Pope will give us back Artois!'

Then she turned on Beatrice.

'And can't you do anything, eh? All you're good for is to take my money, rig yourself out in fine clothes, and waggle your bottom at the first whipper-snapper who comes along! Can't you be of any use?'

'What, Madam?' said Beatrice gently. 'Haven't the cloves I brought you helped to stop the pain?'

'If my tooth were all I had to worry about! I've got a bigger one than that to draw, and you know his name. Oh yes, when it's a question of making love-philtres, you get busy, you take trouble, you find me witches! But when I want something important done . . .'

'You're being unjust, Madam; you very quickly forget how I poisoned Messire de Nogaret, and the risks I have run for you.'

'I haven't forgotten; I haven't forgotten at all; but Nogaret seems small beer today . . .'

If Mahaut did not hesitate before the idea of crime, she nevertheless disliked being forced to speak of it. Beatrice, who knew her well, subtly led her on to do so.

'Really, Madam?' she said, looking from beneath her long

black lashes. 'Do you really wish for the death of someone so highly placed?'

'What on earth do you imagine I've been thinking about for the last week, you fool? What else can I do now, except pray to God from morning till night, and night till morning, that Louis will break his neck in a fall from his horse or choke himself to death with a dried nut?'

'There may be more rapid methods, Madam . . .'

'Go and find them, if you've got the stomach. Oh, in any case, the King's not fated to make old bones; one has only to listen to him cough to know that. But it's now that I want him to die. I shan't be at peace till I've seen him to Saint-Denis.'

'And in that case, Monseigneur of Poitiers would probably become Regent of the Kingdom.'

'Of course!'

'And he would give you back Artois.'

'Exactly! My dear Beatrice, you perfectly understand me; but you also see that it's not easy. Oh, I assure you I shall not be sparing in my reward to anyone who will find me the means of deliverance.'

'Dame Isabelle de Férienne knows many good recipes for inducing oblivion.'

'Bah! By magic, wax, and incantations! Louis has already had a spell cast upon him, or so it appears, and look at him! He's never been in better health than he is this spring. You might think he was in league with the devil.'

Beatrice seemed to be reflecting.

'If he's in league with the devil, it would perhaps be no great sin to send him to hell by means of some suitably prepared food.'

'And how do you propose to set about it? I suppose you'll go to him and say: "Here's a nice pie that your cousin Mahaut who loves you so much has sent you." And he'll eat it out of hand. You might as well know that since the winter, owing to some sudden fear, he has all the food set before him tasted three times, and that two armed equerries accompany each dish from the oven to his table. Oh, he's as much of a coward as he's wicked. You don't imagine I haven't taken steps to be informed!'

Beatrice looked upwards, stroking her throat with the ends of her fingers.

'He often goes to Communion, so I'm told, and the Host is generally swallowed with confidence.'

'Do you imagine I haven't thought of that? That's the kind of thing one thinks of at once,' said Mahaut. 'But the chaplain always carries the key to the ciborium in his purse. Do you propose to go and get it from there?'

'Well, one never knows,' said Beatrice. 'Purses are worn below the belt. All the same, it's a somewhat hazardous method.'

'If we strike, my child, it's got to be a sure blow, and one which no one will ever know was struck by our hands, or at least not until it's too late,' added Mahaut, waving her hand above her head.

For a moment they were both silent, each seeking a solution in her own way.

'You were complaining, the other day,' Beatrice suddenly said, 'that the deer were infesting your woods and eating your young trees. I can't see any harm in asking Isabelle de Férienne for some sound poison into which arrows may be dipped in order to kill the deer. The King is very fond of venison.'

'Yes, and the whole Court'll die of it! Oh, there won't be any danger as far as I'm concerned; I'm no longer invited. But, I repeat, every dish is tried by the servant and touched with the unicorn's horn.[20] It would soon be discovered from which forest the deer had come. To get the poison is one thing, to introduce it in the right place is another. Order it at once, and let it be rapid and leave no trace. By the way, Beatrice, you liked that cloak of watered silk I wore at the coronation, didn't you? Very well, it's yours!'

'Oh, Madam, Madam! How wonderfully kind you are!' cried Beatrice, putting her arms round Mahaut's neck.

'Mind my tooth!' cried the Countess, putting her hand to her cheek. 'And do you know how I broke it? On one of those beastly sweets Louis gave me.'

She stopped short and her grey eyes glowed beneath her eyebrows. 'The sweets!' she murmured. 'Yes, that's it, that's it; have the poison prepared and say that it's for my deer. Whatever happens, it'll come in useful.'

7

In the King's Absence

On a day towards the end of May, when the King was away hawking, Jeanne called upon her sister-in-law Queen Clémence. The interdict which applied to the Countess Mahaut did not extend to her daughter; the Queen and the Countess of Poitiers saw each other fairly frequently, and Jeanne never failed to show her royal sister-in-law her gratitude for having obtained her pardon. Clémence, from her side, felt herself linked to the Countess of Poitiers by that particular tenderness one feels towards people to whom one has done a good turn.

If the Queen had felt a moment's jealousy, or more exactly a feeling of the injustice of fate, when she heard that Jeanne was pregnant, the feeling had been quickly dissipated when she found herself in a similar condition. Indeed, their pregnancies seemed to have brought the sisters-in-law closer to each other. They talked together at length about their health, the regimen they followed, the precautions they took, and

Jeanne, who had already had two daughters before her condemnation, gave Clémence the benefit of her experience.

The distinction with which Madame of Poitiers carried her burden at seven months was much admired. She came in to the Queen her head held high, her step firm, her complexion fresh, her appearance as elegant as always; her dress seemed to flow about her.

The Queen rose to receive her, but the smile on her lips vanished when she saw that Jeanne of Poitiers was not alone; behind her followed the Countess of Artois.

'Madam my Sister,' said Jeanne, 'I wanted to ask you to show my mother the finely wrought tapestries with which you have hung and newly divided your room.'

'Indeed,' said Mahaut, 'my daughter has spoken so much of them that I wished to have the opportunity of admiring them myself. You know that I am something of an expert in these matters.'

Clémence was in some perplexity. She did not wish to infringe, even accidentally, her husband's decisions, and he had forbidden Mahaut to appear at Court; but on the other hand she thought it would be stupid to send her away now that she had got so far, sheltering as she was behind her daughter's pregnancy as behind a buckler. 'There must be some serious reason for her visit,' thought Clémence. 'Perhaps she wishes to make a settlement and is looking for some way of regaining favour without losing face. Her wish to see my tapestries can be no more than a pretext.'

She therefore pretended to believe in the pretext and led her two visitors to her room which had been newly decorated.

The tapestries were not only used to decorate the walls, but were hung from the ceiling in such a way as to make of the vast hall a number of cosy little rooms which were easier to heat, allowing the sovereigns a certain privacy from their attendants and deadening their voices to the ears of the indiscreet. The effect was rather as if nomad princes had established their tents within the building.

Clémence's set of tapestries showed hunting scenes in exotic countrysides where numerous little lions disported themselves beneath orange-trees and birds of strange plumage frolicked among the flowers. The hunters and their arms appeared only in the background of the tapestries, half-hidden by the foliage, as if the artist had been ashamed to depict men indulging in their lust for killing.

'Oh, how beautiful they are,' cried Mahaut, 'and how delightful it is to see high warped cloth so admirably worked.'

She went up to the tapestry, felt it, caressed it.

'Look, Jeanne,' she went on, 'how pliant and consistent it is; look at the charming contrast between the flowered background, those florets stitched in indigo, and the fine kermes red of the parrot's feathers. It is truly an artistic triumph in the use of wools!'

Clémence looked at her in some astonishment. The Countess Mahaut's grey eyes shone with pleasure, her hand seemed to touch tenderly; her head a little bent forward, she lingered in contemplation of the delicacy of the drawing and the contrast of the colours. This strange woman, tough as a warrior, clever as a monk, fierce in her appetites and hatreds, was now, suddenly disarmed, giving herself up to the enchantment of a tapestry. And she was, indeed, quite certainly the greatest expert in the matter to be found in all the Kingdom.

'They really are a most excellent selection, Cousin,' she said, 'and I congratulate you. These tapestries would give the most hideous walls a festal air. They are in the manner of Arras, and yet the wools seem to glow more brightly upon the web. Whoever made them for you, they're clever people.'

'They're tapestry-makers working in my country,' explained Clémence, 'but I must admit that they come from yours, the master craftsmen at least.[21] Besides, they're people who travel a great deal. My grandmother, who sent me these pictorial tapestries to replace my wedding presents lost at sea, also sent me some weavers. I have set them up near here, for a time at least, where they will continue to weave for me and the Court. And if you would care to employ them, or if Jeanne should, they are most certainly at your disposal. You merely have to order the design you want, and with their hands and their looms they'll produce the picture as you see it.'

'I shall most certainly avail myself of it, Cousin; I accept with gratitude,' declared Mahaut. 'I very much want to decorate my house a little. I'm so bored with it. And since Messire de Conflans controls my tapestry-makers at Arras, the King will forgive me for making some use of your Neapolitans.'

Clémence accepted the point as it had been uttered, with a half-smile. Between herself and the Countess of Artois for one moment was that understanding which marks a taste in common for the luxurious and works of art by human hands.

While the Queen continued to show Jeanne the tapestries upon the walls, Mahaut went towards those which enclosed the royal bed, beside which she had seen a bowl full of sweets.

'Has the King also surrounded himself with pictorial tapestries?' she asked Clémence.

'No, Louis has not much in the way of hangings in his room. I must say that he doesn't sleep there very much.'

She stopped, blushing slightly at her involuntary admission.

'That goes to show how much he likes your company, Cousin,' replied Mahaut in a jolly voice. 'Besides, what man would not appreciate someone as beautiful as you!'

'I had feared,' continued Clémence, with the calm shamelessness peculiar to the pure, 'that Louis would sleep apart when I became pregnant. But not at all! Oh, we sleep as Christian people should!'

'I'm delighted, really delighted,' said Mahaut. 'So he continues to sleep with you, does he; what a worthy fellow! Mine, God keep him, never did as much. What a good husband you have in him!'

She had reached the bedside table.

'May I, Cousin?' she asked, indicating the bowl. 'Do you know that you have given me a taste for sweets?'

Heroically, and in spite of the toothache from which she was still suffering, she took a sweet and chewed it with the sound side of her mouth.

'Oh, this one seems to have been made out of bitter almond,' she said, 'I'll take another.'

Turning her back upon the Queen and Jeanne of Poitiers, who were only some five paces away, she took out of her purse a home-made sweet and slipped it into the bowl.

'Nothing is so much like one sweet as another,' she said to herself, 'and if he finds this one rather bitter to the taste, he'll think that it's the natural bitterness of the almond.' She went over to the other two women.

'Well, Jeanne,' she went on, 'tell Madam your Sister-in-law what you have on your mind, that which you so much desired to tell her.'

'Indeed, Sister,' said Jeanne rather hesitatingly, 'I wanted to tell you what worries me.'

'Now we're coming to the point,' thought Clémence; 'they're going to tell me why they have come.'

'My husband is very far away,' Jeanne continued, 'and his absence distresses me. Could you not persuade the King to let Philippe come back for my lying-in? It's a time when one likes to have one's husband close to one. It may be a weakness, but one feels a certain sense of protection and fears the pains of childbirth less if one knows that the child's father is close at hand. You'll soon know the truth of this, Sister.'

Mahaut had taken pains not to let Jeanne know of her plot, but she used her daughter in every step of her plan. 'If it comes off,' she had thought, 'it will be desirable for Philippe to be in Paris as soon as possible so as to take over the powers of Regency.'

Jeanne's request was of a kind that was well calculated to move Clémence. She had feared that they would speak to her of Artois, and now felt almost relieved at their merely making an appeal to her kindness. She would do everything possible to see that Jeanne's wish was realized.

Jeanne kissed her hands, and Mahaut did the same, crying, 'Oh, how kind you are! I told Jeanne that there was no hope except in appeal to you!'

They then took their leave. Mahaut did not seem to wish to stay any longer.

As she left Vincennes to return to Conflans, she said to herself, 'There, it is done. Now I have nothing to do but wait. I wonder which day he'll eat it? Unless of course Clémence . . . but she does not care for sweetmeats; always provided that she doesn't go and eat that particular one from one of those cravings of pregnancy! Anyway, it would be hitting at Louis just the same by removing at one stroke both his wife and his child. And in any case he would be accused of killing his second wife; one only lends money to the rich.'

'You're very silent, Mother,' Jeanne said in astonishment. 'The interview went off very well. Was there anything which displeased you?'

'Nothing, Daughter, nothing,' replied Mahaut. 'I feel sure we've adopted the right course.'

8

The Monk is Dead

A SIMILAR EVENT TO THAT which, at the Court of France, made the Queen and the Countess of Poitiers so happy, was to sow drama and disaster in a little Manor thirty miles from Paris.

For several weeks Marie de Cressay's face had been ravaged with pain and grief. She hardly answered questions addressed to her. Her dark blue eyes seemed to have grown larger from the purple shadows about them; a little vein showed in the transparency of her forehead. There was a certain aberration in her manner.

'Do you think she's going to develop a wasting disease as she did last year?' asked her brother Pierre.

'No, she's growing no thinner,' replied Dame Eliabel. 'She needs a lover, that's all there is to it; and I think that her thoughts dwell rather too much upon that Guccio. It's high time she was married.'

But the cousin of Saint-Venant, approached by the

Cressays, had replied that he was, for the moment, too busy making war in Artois with his neighbours, but he would think about it as soon as peace was restored.

'He must have heard about the state of our affairs,' said Pierre de Cressay. 'You'll see, Mother, you'll see, one of these days we shall regret having sent Guccio away.'

The young Lombard was still received from time to time at the Manor, where they pretended to treat him as a friend as they had done in the past. The debt of three hundred pounds was still in being, while the interest was still accumulating. Moreover, the famine had not come to an end and it was noted that the bank at Neauphle was only provided with food upon those days when Marie visited it. Jean de Cressay, in an access of pride, had asked Guccio for an account of all the food supplied for the last year and more; but, once he had received the bill, he had neglected to pay it. And Dame Eliabel continued to allow her daughter to go to Neauphle once a week, but only in company with her servant and taking strict account of the time she spent on the way.

The meetings of the secretly married couple were therefore rare. But the young servant-girl showed herself responsive to Guccio's generosity and, what was more, she was not altogether indifferent to Ricard, the chief clerk. She dreamt of attaining a middle-class position, and was quite willing to wait among the strong-boxes and the accounts, listening to the agreeable tinkle of money in the scales, while love was being hurriedly made on the first floor.

These minutes, stolen from the watchfulness of the Cressay family and forbidden by the world, had been at first like islands of light in this strange marriage, which had not yet had ten hours of common existence. Guccio and Marie lived upon the memory of these moments for the whole of each week; the splendour of their marriage night had not been belied.

At their last meetings, however, Guccio had remarked a certain difference in Marie's attitude. Like Dame Eliabel, he too had noticed how strange the young girl looked, and the shadows which were marked beneath her eyes, and the little blue vein on her temple which aroused his tenderness and on which he liked to place his lips.

He had attributed this change to impatience on Marie's part with the false position in which they found themselves. Happiness, when distilled drop by drop, and always clothed in lies, soon becomes torture. 'But it is she who wants us to keep silent,' he said to himself. 'She maintains that her family will never recognize the marriage and will have me arrested. And my uncle agrees with that too. So what are we to do?'

'What are you worrying about, darling?' he asked her on that third day of June. 'The last few times I've seen you you've seemed less happy. What are you afraid of? You know I am here to defend you.'

Beyond the window was a cherry-tree in blossom, all amurmur with birds and wasps. Marie turned to him, and there were tears in her eyes.

'Darling,' she said, even you can't defend me against what has happened.'

'What *has* happened?'

'Nothing more than what, by God's will, should happen to me through you,' Marie replied softly with lowered head.

He wanted to make sure that he had understood her.

'A child?' he murmured.

'I was afraid to admit it. I feared that you might love me less.'

For some seconds he stood there unable to say a word, because none came to his lips. Then he took her face in his hands and forced her to look at him.

Like nearly everyone fated to suffer the madness of passion, Marie had one eye slightly smaller than the other; this minute difference, which in no way lessened the beauty of her face, was more noticeable in her present state of anxiety and made her expression all the more moving.

'Marie, doesn't it make you happy?' said Guccio.

'Yes, of course, if it makes you happy too.'

'But, Marie, it's marvellous!' he cried. 'This completes us, and the fact of our marriage will become clear in the light of day. Now your family will have to accept it. A child! A child! It's a miracle.'

And he looked at her from head to foot, overwhelmed with astonishment that so natural a thing should have happened to them, to her and to him. He felt he was a man, he felt strong. It would have taken little to make him lean from the window and cry the news aloud to the whole town.

Whatever happened to him, this young man only saw it to begin with in the best possible light and as an occasion for acquiring merit. He had secretly married the daughter of a knight and now she had made him a father! He never saw the vexations that might result from his actions till the following day.

The servant's voice came up to them from the ground floor, telling them the hour.

'What shall I do? What shall I do?' said Marie. 'I shall never dare tell my mother.'

'All right, I'll come and tell her,' he replied.

'Wait another week.'

He preceded her down the narrow wooden staircase, holding out his hands to help her descend, step by step, as if she had already become extremely fragile and he must sustain her at every step she took.

'But I'm not yet inconvenienced,' she said.

He suddenly realized how comic his attitude was and laughed loudly and happily. Then he took her in his arms and they exchanged so long a kiss that she was breathless.

'I must go,' she said. 'I must go.'

But Guccio's happiness was contagious and she went on her way reassured. The situation had in no way changed, and yet Marie had regained confidence, simply because Guccio shared her secret.

'You'll see, you'll see what a wonderful life we shall have,' he said to her as he led her to the garden door.

The Creator was immensely wise and charitable when He forbade us knowledge of the future, while He has vouchsafed us the delights of memory and the enchantments of hope. Few people would survive the knowledge of what lies in store for them. If this husband and wife, these two lovers, had known that they would only see each other once again in the whole of their lives, and that only after ten years had gone by, they would probably have killed themselves on the spot.

Marie sang all the way home as she passed fields carpeted with golden flowers and trees in blossom. She wished to stop by the bank of the Mauldre to gather irises.

'It's to decorate our chapel,' she said.

'Madam, you must hurry,' the servant said, 'you'll get into trouble when you get home.'

Marie arrived back at the Manor, went straight up to her room and, as she opened the door, felt the ground giving way beneath her feet. Dame Eliabel was standing in the middle of the room and gazing at a surcoat which was unstitched at the seams about the waist, and upon which Marie had been working that morning. All Marie's wardrobe was spread out upon the bed, and each garment had been enlarged in the same fashion.

'Where have you come from that you're so late back?' Dame Eliabel asked dryly.

Marie replied not a word and let the irises she was still holding in her hand fall to the ground.

'You don't have to tell me, I know,' replied Dame Eliabel. 'Undress.'

'Mother!' said Marie in a strangled voice.

'Take your clothes off, I order you!' cried Dame Eliabel.

'Never,' replied Marie.

Her refusal was answered by a loud smack in the face.

'I have not sinned!' replied Marie with equal violence.

'And what's the meaning of this? What does it mean?' asked Dame Eliabel indicating the clothes.

Her anger was increased by being face to face, not with a child submissive to the maternal will, but suddenly with a woman who stood up to her.

'All right, yes, I am to become a mother; yes, and it's Guccio,' cried Marie. 'And I don't have to blush for it, for I have not sinned. Guccio is my husband.'

Dame Eliabel didn't believe a word of the story about the midnight marriage. Even if she had believed it, it would have changed nothing in her eyes. Marie had acted against the paternal wishes, exercised by herself and her eldest son. Besides, this Italian monk might very well not be a monk at all. No, she quite decidedly did not believe in the marriage.

'Even in the face of death, Mother, do you hear, even in the face of death I should confess to nothing else!' Marie repeated.

The storm lasted a whole hour and Dame Eliabel placed her daughter under lock and key.

'To a convent! We'll send you to a convent for fallen women!' she shouted through the door.

And Marie collapsed in tears amid her scattered dresses.

Dame Eliabel had to wait till evening, when her sons had returned from hunting, to give them the news. The family council was brief. Both the boys were furiously angry, and Pierre, feeling himself almost at fault for having until then defended Guccio, now showed himself the most eager for vengeance. Their sister had been dishonoured and they had been abominably betrayed beneath their own roof! A Lombard! A usurer! They would nail him through the stomach to the door of his bank.

They armed themselves with their hunting spears, mounted their horses, which they had just stabled, and galloped off towards Neauphle.

Meanwhile, Guccio, too excited that night to be able to sleep, was walking up and down the garden. The night was ablaze with stars and filled with scents. The springtime of the

Ile-de-France was at its height; the air smelt fresh, laden with sap and dew.

In the silent countryside Guccio listened with delight to his shoes crunching on the gravel, one step heavy, one lighter, and his breast had not room enough to contain his happiness.

'And to think that for six months,' he thought, 'I lay upon that horrible bed in the Hôtel-Dieu. How good it is to be alive!'

He was dreaming. And while his fate was in fact sealed, he was dreaming of his future happiness. He was already seeing numerous children growing up around him, born of a wonderful love, who would have mingled in their veins the free blood of Sienna and the noble blood of France. He would be the great Baglioni, head of a powerful dynasty; turn his name into French, become Baglion of Neauphle. The King would certainly confer a lordship upon him, and the son Marie was carrying, for he never doubted that it was a boy, would one day be dubbed knight.

His thoughts were interrupted by the sound of horses galloping over the cobbles of Neauphle and then coming to a halt before the bank, and the knocker resounding violently at the door.

'Where is the knave, the rogue, the Jew?' cried a voice which Guccio immediately recognized as that of Pierre de Cressay.

And as the door was not opened quickly enough, the two brothers began banging on the oak panels with the shafts of their spears. Guccio put his hand to his belt. He hadn't got his dagger on him. He heard Ricard descending the stairs with a weighty step.

'All right, all right, I'm coming,' said the clerk in the voice of a man who is angry at having been woken up.

Then there was a sound of bolts being drawn, bars being raised and, immediately afterwards, the sound of an angry argument of which Guccio could only catch occasional words.

'Where's your master? We want to see him at once!'

Guccio couldn't hear Ricard's replies, but the voices of the Cressay brothers sounded again more loudly.

He has dishonoured our sister! The dog, the usurer. We won't leave till we've had his hide!'

The discussion ended in a loud cry. Ricard had certainly been hit.

'Bring us a light,' cried Jean de Cressay.

And Guccio then heard Jean's voice shouting again through the house, 'Guccio, where are you hiding? You can only show courage with the girls! I dare you to come out, you stinking coward!'

Shutters had opened at the windows on the Place. The villagers were whispering, but none of them showed himself. At bottom they were not displeased; they'd have something to talk about for a long time. Moreover they rather liked the idea of a trick being played on their little lords, on these two boys who treated them so haughtily and requisitioned them so often for forced labour. If they had to make a choice they preferred the Lombard, but not to the point all the same of risking a flogging for having taken his part.

Guccio was not lacking in courage; but he still had some sense. Without even a dagger at his side, it would not have done him much good to hand himself over to two furious armed men.

While the brothers Cressay were searching the house, and venting their wrath upon the furniture, Guccio ran to the stables. He once again heard the voice of Ricard groaning through the night, 'My books! My books!'

'It can't be helped,' thought Guccio; 'anyway they won't be able to open the strong-boxes.'

The moon was bright enough to enable him hastily to saddle and bridle his horse; he girthed it in the dark, seized hold of the mane to assist him in mounting, and escaped through the garden door. It was thus that he left the bank.

The brothers Cressay, hearing him break into a gallop, rushed to the windows of the house.

'He's running away, the coward, he's running away! He's taking the road to Paris; after him! Hi, you clodhoppers, cut him off!'

Naturally no one made a move.

Then the two brothers rushed out of the bank and set out in pursuit of Guccio.

But the young Lombard's horse was well bred and fresh from the stable. The horses of the Cressays were poor country-bred nags who were already tired from a day's hunting. Near Renne-Moulins one of them went so badly lame that it had to be abandoned; and the two brothers had to get on the same horse which was, moreover, gone in the wind, that is to say it made a noise in its nostrils like a rasp on wood.

Thus Guccio had plenty of time to increase the distance between them. He arrived in the Rue des Lombards at dawn and found his uncle still in bed.

'The monk? Where's the monk?'

'What monk, my boy? What's happened? Do you want to take holy orders now?'

'No, of course not, *zio* Spinello, don't laugh at me. I must find the monk who married me. I'm being followed and I'm in peril of my life!'

He quickly told his story; he had to find the monk in order to prove that he was in fact Marie's husband.

Tolomei listened to him, one eye open, the other closed. He yawned twice, which exasperated Guccio.

'Don't get so excited. Your monk's dead,' said Tolomei at last.

'Dead?' said Guccio.

'Yes, he is! This ridiculous marriage of yours has at least saved you from suffering his fate; for if you had gone, as Robert of Artois wanted you to do, and taken his message, you would doubtless no longer have to worry yourself about the great-nephews you seem prepared to give me without any encouragement from me. Fra Vincento has been killed in the neighbourhood of Saint-Pol by Thierry d'Hirson's people who caught him. He had a hundred pounds of money on him. Oh, Monseigneur Robert of Artois costs me dear!'

*'Questo e un colpo tremendo!'** groaned Guccio.

Tolomei rang for his valet to bring him a basin of warm water and his clothes.

'But what am I to do, *zio* Spinello? How am I to prove that I really am Marie's husband?'

'That's not the most important thing,' said Tolomei. 'Even if your name and that of your girl were properly written in a

* That's a terrible blow!

register, it would change nothing. You would none the less have married a daughter of the nobility without the consent of her family. The gallants who are in pursuit of you may well draw every drop of blood from your body because they are running no risk. They're nobles, and those people can massacre with impunity. At the most they would have to pay the fine appropriate to the life of a Lombard, a few pounds more than for the hide of a Jew and less than for the bones of the least clodhopper, provided he's a French clodhopper. For two pins they'd be complimented.'

'Well, I seem to have got myself into a fine mess.'

'You may well say so,' said Tolomei, plunging his fat face into the water.

He washed himself for a minute, and then dried himself with a towel.

'I don't think I'm going to have time to get myself shaved today. Oh, *per Bacco*! And I have been as foolish as you.'

For the first time he seemed really concerned.

'The first thing you've got to do is to go undercover,' he went on. 'There can be no question of your hiding at a Lombard's. If your pursuers have aroused a village, they'll equally well go and appeal to the Provost if they don't find you here, and send the Watch to search the houses of all our people. You'd be taken within forty-eight hours. Oh, you're making me cut a fine figure before our Company! There are monasteries, of course . . .'

'Oh, no, no more monks!' said Guccio.

'You're quite right, one can never trust them. Let me think . . . What about Boccaccio?'

'Boccaccio?'

'Yes, your good friend Boccaccio, the traveller for the Bardi.'

'But, Uncle, he's a Lombard as much as we are, and besides, he isn't in France at the moment.'

'Yes, but he's having an affair with a woman who is a citizen of Paris and by whom he has had an illegitimate child.'

'I know, he told me.'

'I know she's a nice woman, and she, at least, will understand your problem. You'll go and ask her to hide you. And I'll receive your charming brothers-in-law; I'll take care of them, provided they don't take care of me and you find that by tonight you have no uncle.'

'Oh, no, Uncle, I don't think you need fear them. They're violent, but noble. They'll respect your age.'

'Weak legs are a fine suit of mail!'

'Perhaps they will have grown weary on the road and won't come here at all.'

Tolomei's head appeared out of the robe that he had just put on over his day-shirt.

'That would surprise me exceedingly,' he replied. 'In any case they'll lay an information and begin an action against us. I shall have to consult some highly placed person who is in a position to squash the affair before it causes a scandal. Valois? Valois promises but never keeps his promises. Robert? One might as well go to the City Heralds and get them to announce it with trumpets.'

'Queen Clémence!' said Guccio. 'She grew very fond of me during our journey.'

'I've answered you that one before! The Queen will talk to the King, who'll talk to the Chancellor, who'll set all

Parliament by the ears. We shall have a fine case to make!'

'Why not Bouville?'

'Ah, that's a better idea,' cried Tolomei, 'and the first you've had in six months. Bouville, of course. He's not brilliantly intelligent, but he has a good deal of credit from the fact that he was King Philip's chamberlain. He is not compromised by any faction and is generally considered an honest man.'

'Besides, he's very fond of me,' said Guccio.

'Yes, of course! It appears that the whole world's fond of you! We should get on better with a little less of it! Go along, go and hide yourself with your friend Boccaccio's woman and, for God's sake, don't let her get fond of you too! As for me, I shall go to Vincennes and talk to Bouville. Really, the things you expect me to do! Bouville is probably the only man who owes me nothing, and it's precisely to him I must go to ask a favour.'

9

Mourning Comes to Vincennes

WHEN MESSIRE TOLOMEI, riding his grey mule and followed by his servant, entered the first court of the Manor of Vincennes, he was surprised to find a considerable concourse of people busily rushing to and fro, men-at-arms, servants, equerries, lords, ministers, and citizens; but this coming and going was taking place in complete silence as if men, beasts, and things had all lost their capacity for making sounds.

The ground had been covered with a thick layer of straw to muffle the rolling of coaches and the sound of footsteps. Everyone spoke in whispers.

'The King is dying,' said a lord of his acquaintance to Tolomei when he spoke to him.

Within the castle all security seemed to have lapsed and the archers of the guard let all comers pass. Murderers and thieves could have entered amid the disorder without its occurring to anyone to stop them. One merely heard murmurs such as 'The apothecary, let the apothecary pass.'

The officers of the household, passing through secret doors, carried basins covered with towels, which they went to present to the physicians.

The latter, who were recognizable by their dress, were holding council between two doors; they were wearing brown capes over their serge gowns, and upon their heads little skullcaps resembling those of monks. The surgeons wore stuff gowns with long narrow sleeves and, attached to their round hats, was a sort of white scarf which covered their cheeks, necks, and shoulders.

Tolomei sought information. The King had suffered from a stomach-ache for the last two days, but had not paid any particular attention to it since he was accustomed to indispositions of that nature, and had indeed played tennis on the previous afternoon; he had got very hot and had asked for a drink of water. Shortly afterwards he had been seen suddenly to bend double and vomit, and had had to take to his bed. His condition had grown so much worse during the night that, of his own accord, he had asked for the last sacraments.

The physicians could not agree upon the nature of his illness; some, taking their stand upon the choking-fits to which the King was subject, announced that the cold water he had drunk after his exercise had caused the indisposition; others affirmed that the water could not have corroded his stomach to the point of a haemorrhage.

Perplexed by the mysterious origin of the disease, and also somewhat paralysed, as frequently happens when too many doctors are called to the bedside of an illustrious invalid, they were counselling only the milder remedies, not one of them daring to take the responsibility of recommending strong measures for fear of being later accused of having killed the patient.

The noble courtiers were hinting to each other about the spell that had been cast upon the King, and adopting airs of knowing more than they were prepared to say. And already other problems were being mooted. Who would become Regent? Some regretted that Monseigneur of Poitiers was absent, others were, on the other hand, delighted. Had the King expressed any formal wish in the matter? No one knew. But he had summoned his Chancellor to dictate a codicil to his will.

Making his way through the silent chaos, Tolomei was able to reach the very room in which the Sovereign was dying. There the crowd was being held back by the Chamberlain, who only allowed the members of his family and his most intimate attendants, which already mounted to a considerable number of people, to come close to his bed.

Standing on tiptoe, the Chief of the Lombard banks was able to see, over a wall of shoulders, Louis X, his body supported upon cushions, and his hollow features grown suddenly thin, wearing the stigmata of the end. One hand upon his breast, the other upon his stomach, his teeth clenched, he seemed to be forbidding himself to groan.

Someone came by and whispered, 'The Queen, the Queen. The King demands the Queen's presence.'

Clémence was in the next room, surrounded by her ladies-in-waiting, by the fat Bouville who was managing to contain his tears with difficulty, and Eudeline. The Queen had not slept for twenty-four hours, and indeed had remained upon her feet practically all that time. And now, at this moment, she was still standing, motionless, her eyes staring, like the effigies of saints upon the churches of her country, while Monseigneur of Valois, all dressed in black, as if he had already donned mourning, said to her, 'My dear, dear Niece, you must be prepared for the worst.'

'I am prepared for it,' thought Clémence, 'and have no need of him to know the truth. Ten months of happiness, is that all I have a right to? And yet it may be much, and God is kind to have vouchsafed it, and I have not thanked Him enough. The worst that can befall us is not death, since we shall come face to face again in the life eternal. The worst feature of the case concerns my child who will be born five months hence, whom Louis will never have known, and who will never know his father till he goes to heaven himself. Why does God permit such things?'

'You may count on me, Niece,' said Valois; 'I shall not cease to protect you and this will make no difference to my attitude towards you. You must let me deal with everything, and merely think that you carry all our hopes in your womb. It really must be a son! Of course your condition will not permit you to assume the task of Regent; moreover the French would take it ill to be governed by the hand of a foreign woman. Blanche de Castille, are you suggesting? Of course, of course, but she had been Queen for many years. The French have not yet learnt to know you well enough. I must relieve you of the duties of the throne, which basically, of course, will make no difference to our relationship.'

The Chamberlain, who was coming to tell the Queen that the dying man was asking for her, entered at this moment, but Valois stopped him with a gesture and went on, 'I don't wish to push myself forward, but I am the only person who can usefully act as Regent; I shall know how to associate you with it, since I wish to inspire the French with the love they ought to have for the mother of their next King.'

'Uncle,' cried Clémence sharply, 'Louis is still breathing. It would be better if you were to pray for a miracle to save him and, if that is impossible, at least defer your proposals until after his death. And rather than detain me here, let me take my rightful place at his bedside.'

'Of course, Niece, of course, but there are things to which one must give one's attention when one is Queen. We may not give way to the sorrows of common people. By his last wishes Louis must decide upon the Regent by name.'

'Eudeline, don't leave me,' murmured the Queen.

And to Bouville she said, as she was going towards the King's room, 'Friend Hugues, friend Hugues, I can't believe it, tell me that it isn't true!'

This was too much for kind Bouville, who began to weep.

'When I think, when I only think,' he said, 'that it was I who went to fetch you from Naples!'

Eudeline, since the King had been taken ill, had shown a stranger attitude. She never left the Queen, who relied upon her for everything she needed, to the point where her ladies-in-waiting were beginning to show resentment. Face to face with the dying agonies of this man, of this sovereign whose first mistress she had been, whom she had loved submissively, and then implacably hated, Eudeline felt no emotion at all. She was thinking neither of him nor of herself. It was as if her memories had died before their creator. All her emotions were centred upon the Queen, her friend. And if Eudeline was suffering at this time, it was from the suffering of Clémence.

The Queen crossed the room, leaning on the arms of Eudeline on one side and of Bouville on the other.

Seeing the latter, Tolomei, still standing in the doorway, suddenly remembered what he had come to do.

'It certainly is no time to talk to Bouville,' he thought. 'And doubtless the two Cressay brothers are in my house at this moment. In truth the King's death could not have occurred at a more awkward moment.'

Just then he felt himself jostled by a powerful body; the Countess Mahaut, her sleeves rolled up, was forcing her way through the crowd. In spite of her disgrace, no one was surprised to see her; it became so near a relation, who was also a peer of the Kingdom, to be present in the circumstances.

She had carefully composed her expression to give an appearance of the utmost stupefaction and dismay.

As she entered the room she muttered, but sufficiently distinctly for at least ten people to hear her, 'God, so soon! It's really too much! Poor France!'

Advancing with a sort of soldierly step she made her way towards the family. Charles de la Marche, his arms crossed, his handsome face somewhat drawn, was flanked by his cousins, Philippe of Valois, and Robert of Artois.

Mahaut extended both her hands to Robert with an expression that seemed to say that she was too moved to speak and that upon such a day all dissension was forgotten. Then she went and knelt by the royal bed and said in a broken voice, 'Sire, I beseech you to forgive me for all the trouble I have caused you.'

Louis looked at her; his large pale eyes were surrounded with the dark shadows of death. They were just in process of changing his bedpan in sight of all; in this uncomfortable situation, trying to keep mastery over himself, he assumed for the first time something of true majesty, something royal indeed, which he had lacked all his life.

'I forgive you, Cousin, if you submit to the King's will,' he replied, when they had slipped a new bedpan under him.

'Sire, I swear it!' replied Mahaut.

And more than one person present was sincerely moved to see the terrible countess bend the knee and make submission.

Robert of Artois's eyes narrowed, and he whispered to Philippe of Valois, 'She couldn't be playing her part better if she'd killed him herself.'

It was the first twinge of suspicion.

The Hutin felt a new crisis of pain and placed his hands on his stomach. His lips parted to reveal clenched teeth; the sweat poured from his temples and matted his hair. After a few seconds he seemed to recover and said, 'Is that what suffering is? Is that what it is? May God forgive me for having made others suffer.'

His head moved a little on the pillows and his eyes rested for a long time upon Clémence.

'My dearest, my darling, what agony it is to leave you! I want you to keep this house, since we loved each other here. Etienne! Etienne!' he said, waving his fingers towards Chancellor de Mornay who was sitting at his bedside, paper in hand, in order to take down the King's last wishes. 'Write that I leave to Queen Clémence this Manor of the Forest of Vincennes and that I wish her to be given twenty-five thousand pounds a year.'

'Louis, my dear lord,' said Clémence, 'don't think of me, you have already given me too much. But, I beseech you, think of those whom you have wronged; you promised me . . .'

'Say on, say on, my darling, and what you desire shall be done.'

'Her daughter,' she murmured.

The dying man's eyebrows puckered, as if he were trying to read the already distant horizon of memory.

'So you knew, Clémence?' he said. 'Very well let Eudeline's daughter be an Abbess and of a royal abbey; I will it.'

Eudeline bowed her head.

'May God bless you, Monseigneur Louis,' she said.

'And who else?' he went on. 'Whom have I wronged? Ah, yes, my godson, Louis de Marigny. I wish him to know I am filled with remorse for having persecuted his father.'

And he had it noted down that he left him ten thousand pounds a year.

'It's not everyone who has had the luck to have a father hanged,' said Robert of Artois to his neighbour. 'To have had him killed in battle, as mine was, appears to be less valuable.'

Charles of Valois, who had joined their group, replied, 'It's easy enough to leave money, but how am I going to find enough to pay it all?'

And he signed to Etienne de Mornay that the list was now long enough, and that he must hurry up and get the codicil signed. The Chancellor took the point at once and obeyed. Louis scratched at the sheet with the pen they handed him.

Then he gazed round upon those present, as if obsessed by some anxiety, looking for someone who should have been there.

'Who do you want, Louis?' asked Clémence.

'My father,' he murmured.

And those about him thought that his delirium was beginning. But in fact he was trying to remember how his father had acted on his deathbed eighteen months earlier. He turned to his confessor, a Dominican from Poissy, and said, 'The miracle. My father transmitted the royal miracle to me, to whom can I transmit it?'

Charles of Valois came forward, ready as always to receive any crumb of power which might fall from the throne. How he would have enjoyed curing scrofula by the laying on of hands!

But the Dominican had bent down to Louis X's ear and was reassuring him. Kings might die in silence; the Church remembered. If Louis had a son, the rite of the miracle would be revealed to him in due course.

Then Louis's eyes turned to Clémence's face, sought her throat, then her waist, and rested there for a long time as if, concentrating the last forces of his will, the dying man was seeking to transmit all that he had received from three centuries of royal ascendancy.

This took place upon June 4th, 1316.

10

Tolomei Prays for the King

WHEN TOLOMEI GOT home in the middle of the afternoon, his chief clerk immediately came to announce that there were two men from the country waiting for him in the antechamber to his study.

'They look very angry indeed,' he added. 'They've been there since nones, have had nothing to eat, and say they won't go away till they've seen you.'

'Yes, I know who they are,' Tolomei replied. 'Close the doors and gather the whole household in my study, clerks, footmen, grooms, and housemaids. And hurry up! Send everyone up there.'

Then he went slowly upstairs himself, assuming the gait of an old man overwhelmed with sorrow; he stopped a moment on the landing, listening to the commotion that his orders had caused in the house; he waited till he could see the first of them coming upstairs, and then went into the ante-chamber, his hand pressed to his forehead.

The brothers Cressay rose to their feet, and Jean, coming towards him, cried, 'Messire Tolomei, we are . . .'

Tolomei stopped him with a wave of his hand.

'Yes, I know!' he said in a broken voice. 'I know who you are, and I know too what you have come to say to me. But all that is nothing in face of our affliction.'

As the other wished to pursue the matter, he turned towards the door and said to his people who were beginning to arrive, 'Come in, my friends, come in, all of you; come and hear the appalling news from your master's mouth! Come in, come in, my friends.'

The room was soon filled. If the brothers Cressay had wished to take any action whatever, they would have immediately been disarmed.

'Really, Messire, what's all this about?' Pierre asked impatiently.

'One moment, one moment,' replied Tolomei. 'Everyone must hear the news.'

Somewhat anxious, the Cressay brothers thought that the banker was about to announce their family dishonour in public. It was more than they had bargained for.

'Is everyone here?' Tolomei asked. 'Very well, my friends, listen to what I have to say.'

He could not go on. There was a long silence. Tolomei had hidden his face in his hands, and everyone thought that he was weeping. When he uncovered his face, the single eye that was open was indeed filled with tears.

'My dear, faithful friends,' he said at last, 'the most appalling thing has happened! Our King, our greatly loved King, has just expired.'

His voice seemed to be strangled in his throat; he beat his breast as if he himself had been responsible for the sovereign's death. He took advantage of the surprise the announcement made to say, 'Now, let us kneel, all of us, and pray for his soul.'

He himself sank heavily to the ground, and all his staff followed his example.

'Really, Messeigneurs, on your knees!' he said reproachfully to the two Cressay brothers who, astounded by the news and completely bewildered by the spectacle confronting them, had alone remained standing.

'*In nomine patris . . .*' Tolomei began.

There was a concert of strident lamentation. The servants of the household, who were all Italians, became a weeping choir in accordance with the best traditions of their country.

'*Requiescat . . .*' the men all murmured together.

'Oh, how kind he was! How good he was! How pious he was!' wept the cook.

And all the housemaids and laundrymaids wept aloud, putting their aprons over their heads and hiding their faces.

Tolomei had risen to his feet and was moving among his staff.

'That's right, pray, pray well! Yes, he was good indeed, yes, he was a saint! Sinners, that's what we are, incurable sinners! Pray, young men,' he said, putting his hands on the heads of the Cressay brothers. 'Indeed, death will take you too! Repent, repent!'

This piece of play-acting lasted a good twenty minutes. Then Tolomei said, 'Close the doors, close down the counters. This is a day of mourning; we shall do no business this evening.'

The servants went out, snivelling. As the head clerk passed him, Tolomei whispered, 'Don't make any payments. Gold may have changed its value by tomorrow.'

The women were still howling as they went downstairs, and their sobs continued throughout the evening and during the whole night. They were competing with each other in vocal grief.

'He was the benefactor of his people!' they sobbed. 'Never, never shall we have so good a king again!'

Tolomei let the hangings which covered the entrance of his study fall back into place.

'Thus,' he said, 'thus pass the glories of the world.'

The two Cressays were completely checkmated. Their personal drama was submerged beneath the general misfortune which had fallen upon the Kingdom.

Besides, they were probably somewhat tired. They had spent a day hare-hunting, followed by a night on horseback, and how ill-mounted!

Their arrival in Paris at dawn, both mounted upon the same broken-winded nag, and dressed in their father's old clothes which they used for hunting, had made the passers-by laugh. A crowd of screaming urchins had escorted them. They had naturally lost themselves in the labyrinthine alleys of the Cité. They were appallingly hungry, which is difficult to bear at twenty. Their assurance, if not their resentment, had greatly weakened when they saw the sumptuousness of Tolomei's house. They were impressed by the wealth they saw on every hand, the large staff of servants better dressed than they were themselves, the tapestries, the carved furniture, the enamels, and the ivories of which merely one of the more inferior pieces would have sufficed to rebuild Cressay. 'When it comes to the point,' they each said to themselves without daring to admit it to the other, 'we may very well have been wrong to show ourselves so touchy about the question of blue blood; a fortune such as this is well worth the rank of a noble.'

'Well, my good friends!' said Tolomei, with the familiarity that their having prayed in common seemed to authorize, 'let us discuss this painful affair because, after all, one has to go on living and the world does not cease to turn because of those who have gone. You wish, naturally, to speak to me of my nephew. The rascal! The rogue! To do such a thing to me who have always overwhelmed him with kindness! What a miserable, shameless boy! That I should be exposed to this additional sorrow upon this day of all days. I know everything, everything; he sent me a message this morning. You see before you a much tried man.'

He stood before them, somewhat bent, his eyes upon the ground, in an attitude of utter dejection.

'And a coward too,' he went on. 'A coward! I'm ashamed to have to admit it, Messeigneurs. He did not dare confront my anger. He left straightaway for Sienna. By now he must be far away. Well, my friends, what are we to do?'

He gave the impression of placing himself in their hands, almost of asking their advice. The two brothers looked at each other. Nothing was turning out quite as they had expected.

Tolomei looked at them from beneath his almost closed right eyelid. 'Good,' he said to himself, 'now that I've got them in hand, they're no longer dangerous; I've now merely got to find some way of sending them home without giving them anything.'

He rose decisively to his feet.

'But I disinherit him! Do you hear, I disinherit him! You won't get anything from me, you little wretch!' he cried, waving a hand vaguely in the direction of Sienna. 'Nothing! Ever! I shall leave everything to the poor and to convents! And should he ever again fall into my hands, I shall deliver him to the justice of the King. Alas! Alas!' he began groaning again. 'The King is dead!'

It was almost up to the other two to give him consolation.

Tolomei now judged them sufficiently prepared to make them see reason. He accepted and approved every reproach, every complaint that they had to make; indeed, he forestalled them all. But what was to be done now? What useful purpose would a lawsuit serve, expensive as it was for people who were not rich, when the criminal was out of reach and would have crossed the frontier before six days were out? Would it save their sister? The scandal would do nothing but harm to the Cressays themselves. Tolomei would once more devote himself to finding a solution. He would take every possible step to repair the harm that had been done; he had powerful and exalted contacts; he was a friend of Monseigneur of Valois who, it seemed likely, would become Regent, of Monseigneur of Artois, and of Messire de Bouville. Some place would be found in which Marie could bear her child of sin in the greatest possible secrecy, and her life would be arranged. For a time, perhaps, a nunnery might shelter her repentance. Let them have confidence in Tolomei! Had he not proved to the Cressays themselves that he was a kindly man by carrying forward the debt of three hundred pounds that they owed him?

'Had I so wished, your castle would have been mine two years ago. But did I wish it? No. You see what I mean.'

The two brothers, already much shaken, perfectly understood the threat which underlay the banker's paternal manner.

'Understand me, I'm demanding nothing,' he added.

But if it came to a lawsuit, he would naturally be obliged to state the facts, and the judges might well be prejudiced against them when they heard of all the presents they had received from Guccio.

Well then, they were a couple of sensible young men; they would go off now to a good inn, and he'd pay the bill, where they could have a good dinner and spend the night, and wait until Tolomei had had time to arrange matters for them. He thought that he would be able to give them some good news the following day.

Pierre and Jean de Cressay bowed to his reasoning and indeed, upon taking leave, shook his hand somewhat effusively.

After their departure Tolomei threw himself into a chair. He felt rather tired.

'And now, let's hope to God the King dies!' he said to himself. For when he had left Vincennes, Louis X was still breathing, though no one thought that he had many hours to live.

II

Who is to be Regent?

Louis X, The Hutin, died during the night, a little after midnight.

For the first time in three hundred and twenty-nine years, a King of France had died without leaving a male heir upon whom the crown might traditionally devolve.

Monseigneur Charles of Valois, generally so anxious to organize royal ceremonies, whether of weddings or funerals, showed himself completely disinterested in the last honours due to be rendered to his nephew.

He summoned the first Chamberlain, Mathieu de Trye, and for his only instruction said, 'Do as was done last time!'

He had other anxieties. He hastily summoned a Council during the course of the morning, not at Vincennes, where he would have been compelled to invite Queen Clémence, but in Paris at the Palace of the Cité.

'We'll leave our dear niece to her sorrow,' he said, 'and do nothing that could imperil the life of the precious burden she carries.'

It was arranged that Bouville should represent the Queen. He was known to be manageable, not very quick on the uptake, and they thought they had nothing to fear from him.

The Council assembled by Valois had at once something of both a family and a governmental assembly. Besides Bouville, there were Charles de la Marche, brother of the deceased, Louis de Clermont, Robert of Artois, Philippe of Valois, present upon his father's orders, the Chancellor de Mornay, and the Archbishop of Sens and Paris, Jean de Marigny, because it was thought desirable to have a high ecclesiastical authority and because Jean de Marigny was in alliance with the Valois clan.

They had not been able to avoid summoning the Countess Mahaut, who was, with Charles of Valois, the only peer of the Kingdom present in Paris.

As for Count Louis of Evreux, whom Valois had informed of their nephew's illness as tardily as possible, he had arrived from Normandy that very morning; he looked drawn and frequently passed his hand across his eyes.

He said to Mahaut, 'It's much to be regretted that Philippe is not here.'

Charles of Valois had taken his seat at the top of the table in the royal chair. Though he still managed to compose his features into an expression of sorrow, he appeared to savour his position.

'Brother, Nephew, Madam, Messeigneurs,' he began, 'we are assembled in this time of sudden mourning to take urgent decisions: the appointment of the Curators of the Stomach whose duty it will be to watch over the pregnancy of Queen Clémence, and also the selection of a Regent for the Kingdom, for there can be no interruption in the exercise of the royal power. I ask your counsel.'

He was already using a sovereign's expressions. His attitude much displeased the Count of Evreux.

'Poor Charles will never have any tact or judgement,' he said to himself. 'He still believes even at his age that authority emanates from the crown when it's the head in control that matters.'

He could not forgive him the Muddy Army, nor all the other disastrous ideas with which he had marred Louis's short reign.

As Valois, answering his own questions, was beginning to link the two propositions, and was proposing that the nomination of the Curators should be placed under the control of the Regent, Evreux interrupted him.

'If you have summoned us, Brother, so that we may listen to you carrying on a monologue, we might just as well have remained at home. Let us get a word in too, when we've got something to say! The choice of a Regent is one thing, for which there are precedents and which is under the control of the Council of Peers. The choice of the Curators is another, which we can settle on the spot.'

'Have you any name to put forward?' asked Valois.

Evreux passed his fingers across his eyelids.

'No, Messeigneurs, I have no one to propose. I merely think that we should choose men of irreproachable antecedents, sufficiently mature to allow us to place complete confidence in their discretion, and who have given great proofs of loyalty and of devotion towards our family.'

While he was speaking, all eyes were turning towards Bouville, who was sitting at the lower end of the table.

'I would have suggested someone such as the Seneschal de Joinville,' went on Louis of Evreux, 'if his great age, which is now approaching a hundred, did not render him extremely infirm. But I see all eyes turning towards Messire de Bouville, who was first Chamberlain to the King our brother, and served him always with such loyalty as we cannot do other than applaud. Today he is representing the young Queen Clémence among us. In my view we could make no better choice.'

Fat Bouville had lowered his head in some confusion.

It is one of the advantages of mediocrity that people frequently decide unanimously upon your name. No one feared Bouville; and the function of the Curator, one largely legal in character, held only a secondary importance in Valois's eyes. Louis of Evreux's proposal was received with general assent.

Bouville rose, much moved. This was the apogee of forty years of devotion to the Crown.

'It is a great honour, a great honour, Messeigneurs,' he said. 'I swear to watch over the pregnancy of Madame Clémence, to protect her against every attack or assault, and to defend her with my life. But, since Monseigneur of Evreux has spoken of Messire de Joinville, I would wish that the Seneschal should also be nominated with me, or if he is not able, his son, so that the spirit of Monseigneur Saint Louis should be present in this guardianship in his servant, as the spirit of King Philip, my master, will be present in me, his servant.'

Bouville had never uttered so many words together at a Council before, and what he wished to express was rather too subtle for him. The end of the speech was not altogether clear, but everyone understood his intention, which was approved, and the Count of Evreux thanked him sincerely.

'Now,' said Valois, 'we can approach the matter of the Regency . . .'

He was interrupted once more, but this time by Bouville, who had risen to his feet again.

'First, Monseigneur . . .'

'What's the matter, Bouville?' asked Valois in an indulgent voice.

'First, Monseigneur, I must pray you with great humility to leave your particular seat, for it is the King's, and for the moment there can be no King but in the womb of Madame Clémence.'

In the silence that fell upon those present nothing could be heard but the knell tolled out by the bells of Paris.

Valois gave Bouville a furious look, but he realized that he must obey and even pretend to do so with a good grace. 'My God, what a set of fools,' he said to himself as he changed his place, 'and one's a fool to put any trust in them. They have ideas no one else would think of.'

Bouville walked round the table, pulled up a stool, and went and sat, his arms crossed, in an attitude of faithful guardianship, to the right of the empty seat which was to be the object of so much intrigue.

Valois whispered something into the ear of Robert of

Artois, who rose to put into execution the plan upon which they had already agreed.

Robert said a few words which were far from tactful and which seemed, in short, to signify: 'Enough of this foolishness, let's get on to more serious things!' Then he proposed, as if he were merely expressing a foregone conclusion, that the Regency should be confided to Charles of Valois.

'One should not change horses in midstream,' he said. 'We all know very well that our cousin Charles has held the reins of government throughout the reign of poor Louis. And before that he was always a member of King Philip's Council, from whom he averted more than one mistake and for whom he won many a battle. He is the eldest of the family and has nearly thirty years of experience in the work of kingship.'

There were only two people at the long table who did not appear to approve his suggestion. Louis of Evreux was thinking of France; Mahaut of Artois was thinking of herself.

'If Charles becomes Regent, he will certainly not remove the Marshal of Conflans from my county,' said Mahaut to herself. 'Perhaps I have moved too quickly; I should have awaited the return of my son-in-law. If I speak on his behalf, I may well run the risk of bringing down suspicion upon myself.'

'Charles,' asked Louis of Evreux, 'if our brother, King Philip, had died while your nephew Louis was still an infant, who would have been Regent by right?'

'Who else but me?' replied Valois, thinking that grist was being brought to his mill.

'Because you were the next brother! Therefore, should

it not be, by right, our nephew, the Count of Poitiers, who should assume the Regency?'

There followed a heated argument. Philippe of Valois having replied that the Count of Poitiers could not be in two places at the same time, both in the Conclave and in Paris, Louis of Evreux cried, 'Lyons is not in the country of the Great Khan! One can travel back from there in a few days. We are not the proper quorum to decide so important a matter. Among the dozen people present I can see but two peers of the Kingdom.'

'And what's more, they aren't in agreement,' said Mahaut; 'because I support your reasoning, cousin Louis, and not Charles's.'

'And as for the family,' went on Evreux, 'not only is Philippe lacking, but also our niece Isabella of England, our aunt Agnes of France, and her son the Duke of Burgundy. If seniority is to gain the day, then Agnes, who is Saint Louis's last surviving daughter, should have more to say in the matter than any of us.'

They took up this name to oppose Louis of Evreux; Robert of Artois rushed to the support of the Valois. Agnes of France and her son, Eudes of Burgundy, were exactly the people they feared the most! Clémence's child had still to be born, if one admitted for the moment that it would be, and one could only then know whether it was male or female. Eudes of Burgundy might very well claim the right to be Regent, because of his niece, the young Jeanne of Navarre, Marguerite's daughter. And this must be avoided at all costs because everyone knew that the child was a bastard!

'You know nothing of the sort, Robert!' cried Louis of

Evreux. 'Assumptions are not certainties, and Marguerite has carried her secret to the grave you dug for her.'

Evreux, when he said 'you', intended a general inclusiveness, which comprehended at once the midnight murder, the Valois, and Robert of Artois. But the latter, who had sound reason for believing that the accusation was aimed at himself alone, took it very ill.

For a moment it looked as if the two brothers-in-law (for Louis of Evreux had married a sister of Robert's who was now dead) would challenge each other and come to blows.

Once more the scandal of the Tower of Nesle was dividing the family before partly destroying it, and with it the Kingdom.

They hurled lies and insults in each other's faces. Why had Jeanne of Poitiers been set free and not Blanche de la Marche? Why was Philippe of Valois so implacably opposed to the honour of the family of Burgundy when he had married Marguerite's sister?

The Archbishop and the Chancellor had entered the argument to support Valois with on the one hand the power of the Church and on the other the customs of France.

'Anyway, I see,' cried Charles of Valois, 'that the Council is numerous enough to name the guardians of the Queen's pregnancy but not numerous enough to nominate the regent of the Kingdom. It must therefore be my person that displeases it!'

At that moment Mathieu de Trye entered the room and said that he had an important communication to make to the Council. He was asked to announce it.

'While the King's body was being embalmed,' said Mathieu

de Trye, 'a dog which had entered the room unnoticed licked the bloody cloth which had been used during the extraction of the entrails.'

'What then?' asked Valois.

'Is that your important communication?'

'The fact is, Messeigneurs, that the dog immediately fell down in agony, whimpered and twisted in pain, and was clearly taken with the same sickness as the King; he may even be dead at this moment.'

Once more, and for some seconds, nothing was to be heard in the room but the sound of the knell tolling. The Countess Mahaut had not moved a muscle, but she was a prey to appalling anxiety.

'Am I to be betrayed by the gluttony of a dog?' she said to herself.

'Do you think, Mathieu, that it is a question of poison?' asked Charles de la Marche.

'A careful inquest must be held,' said Robert of Artois, looking at his aunt.

'Most certainly, Nephew, an inquest must be held,' replied Mahaut as if she suspected him.

Bouville who, throughout the discussion, had remained silent beside the royal chair, now rose.

'Messeigneurs, if someone has made an attempt upon the King's life, there is no reason to suppose that they will not do the same thing towards the child who is to be born. I demand a guard of six equerries and bachelors, armed and under my orders, to guard the Queen's door night and day and bar entry to the criminal.'

He was told to act upon his suggestion. And shortly

afterwards the Council separated without having decided anything except that it was going to meet again on the following day. Current business would be dealt with as usual by Charles of Valois and the Chancellor.

'Are you going to send a courier to Philippe?' Mahaut asked the Count of Evreux in a low voice.

'Yes, Cousin. I shall, and to Agnes too,' he replied.

'Very well, I'll leave the matter in your hands, since we're in complete agreement.'

Bouville, as he left the meeting, found Spinello Tolomei waiting for him in the courtyard of the palace. Tolomei asked him for protection for his nephew.

'Oh, the dear boy, dear Guccio!' replied Bouville. 'Listen, Tolomei, he's exactly the sort of lad I want to watch at the Queen's door. He is alert of mind and quick to act. Madame Clémence was very fond of him. It's a pity that he is neither a bachelor nor an equerry. But, after all, there are occasions when personal qualities are more valuable than blue blood.'

'That's exactly what the girl who wanted to marry him thought,' said Tolomei.

'What, you mean to say he's married?'

The banker tried to explain Guccio's adventure as briefly as he could. But Bouville was barely listening. He was in a hurry. He had to return to Vincennes at once and held to his idea of enlisting Guccio in the Queen's Guard. Tolomei wanted a less prominent and more distant post for his nephew. He would have liked him placed under cover with some high ecclesiastical dignitary, a Cardinal perhaps.

'Very well, my friend, let's send him to Monseigneur Duèze! Tell Guccio to come and see me at Vincennes, where

I shall have to remain permanently for some time. He can tell me his story. But wait a moment! He can do me a considerable service. Tell him to hurry; I shall be waiting for him.'

A few hours later three couriers were galloping towards Lyons by three different roads.

The first courier, going 'by the great road' as it was called at that time, that is to say by Essonnes, Montargis, and Nevers, wore upon his jerkin the arms of France. He carried a letter from the Count of Valois to the Count of Poitiers, announcing in the first place the King's death and in the second that he, Valois, had been elected Regent by a vote of the Council.

The second courier, wearing the insignia of the Count of Evreux and taking 'the pleasant road', by Provins and Troyes, was to make a halt at Dijon at the Duke of Burgundy's; his message was not altogether synonymous with the first.

And the third, dressed in the livery of the Comte de Bouville, took 'the short road' by Orléans, Bourges, and Roanne, and he was Guccio Baglioni. Officially he had been dispatched to Cardinal Duèze. But he was to warn the Count of Poitiers orally that there was a suspicion of poison about his brother's death, and that it was necessary to take steps to protect the Queen.

The destinies of France were upon those three roads.

Historical Notes

1. Charles, Count of Anjou and of Maine, son of Louis VIII and seventh brother of Saint Louis, had married in 1246 the Countess Beatrix who brought him, as Dante expressed it, 'the great dowry of Provence'. Chosen by the Holy See as Champion of the Church in Italy, he was crowned King of Sicily at Saint John Lateran in 1255.

   This was the origin of the southern branch of the Capet family, known by the name of Anjou-Sicily, whose power extended over southern France and southern Italy.

   The son of Charles I of Anjou, Charles II, called the Lame, King of Naples, Sicily, and Jerusalem, Duke of Apulia, Prince of Salerno, Capua, and Taranto, married Marie of Hungary, the sister and heiress of Ladislas, King of Hungary. From this union were born:

Charles Martel, titular King of Hungary, who died in 1295.

Saint Louis of Anjou, Bishop of Toulouse, who died in 1298.

Robert, King of Naples.

Philippe, Prince of Taranto.

Raymond Bérenger, Count of Provence, Piedmont, and Andrea.

Jean, who entered Holy Orders.

Pierre, Count of Eboli and Gravinia.

Marie, wife of Sancho of Aragon, King of Majorca.

Beatrix, who married first Azzon, Marquis of Este, then Bertrand de Baux.

Blanche, who married Jaime II of Aragon.

Marguerite, who was the first wife of Charles of Valois, and died in 1299.

Eleanor, wife of Fredric of Aragon.

The eldest, Charles Martel, married to Clémence of Hapsburg, and for whom Queen Marie had claimed the inheritance of the throne of Hungary, died in 1295 (fourteen years before his father) leaving a son, Charobert, who became King of Hungary, and two daughters, Beatrice, who married the heir to Viennois, and Clémence, who became Queen of France and who appears in this book.

The second son of Charles II, Saint Louis of Anjou, born at Nocera in February 1275, renounced all his rights of succession in order to enter the Church. Designated Bishop of Toulouse, he died at the Château of Brignoles, in Provence, on August 19th, 1298, at the age of twenty-three. He was canonized upon the Thursday after Easter

1317 by Pope John XXII, ex-Cardinal Duèze and the candidate of the Anjou, who had been elected in the preceding summer. The canonization therefore must quite certainly have taken place during the year with which we are dealing. The body of Saint Louis of Anjou was exhumed in November 1319 and transferred to the monastery of the Cordeliers of Marseilles, which was an Angevin town.

Upon the death of Charles II in 1309, the crown of Naples passed, not to the senior line, who seemed sufficiently endowed with the throne of Hungary, but to the third son of Charles the Lame, Robert.

The latter was present in Marseilles in November 1319, when the remains of Saint Louis of Anjou were transferred to the monastery of the Cordeliers in that town. King Robert, however, took the head of his brother to Naples as a souvenir. Forty years later Pope Urban V sent an arm to Montpellier and, finally King Alphonso V of Aragon when he took Marseilles in 1433, exported what remained of the bones to Valence.

2. In the Middle Ages, the Mass celebrated on shipboard, at the foot of the mainmast, was a special one, called 'aride' because it lacked both the consecration and communion of a priest. This peculiar liturgical form was probably due to fear of seasickness.
3. 'Marc': a measure of weight equivalent to eight ounces.
4. The organization and interior economy of the hospitals run by the religious orders in the Middle Ages were based upon the statutes of the Hôtel-Dieu in Paris.

   The hospital was ordinarily under the control of one or

two 'Provisors', who were chosen from the canons of the Cathedral of the town. The personnel of the order was recruited from volunteers, after an exacting examination by the Provisors. At the Hôtel-Dieu in Paris the personnel consisted of four priests, four clerks, thirty brothers, and twenty-five sisters. Husbands and wives were not accepted as volunteers. The brothers wore the same tonsure as the Templars; the sisters had their hair cut like nuns.

The rule imposed upon the hospital personnel was severe. Both brothers and sisters had to take a vow of chastity and renounce all their goods. No brother might communicate with a sister without the permission of the 'Master' or the 'Mistress' designated by the Provisors to be in charge of the personnel. The sisters were forbidden to wash either the heads or the feet of the brothers, these services being rendered only to the bedridden patients. Corporal punishment could be administered to the brothers by the Master and to the sisters by the Mistress. No brother could go out alone into the town, nor with a companion who was not designated by the Master; this rule applied equally to the sisters. The personnel of the hospital was not allowed to receive visitors. Both brothers and sisters might partake of only two meals per day, but must offer the patients food whenever they needed it. The brothers must sleep alone, dressed in a woollen tunic and drawers; this equally applied to the sisters. If a brother or a sister, when they came to die, was found to be in possession of no matter what object which had not been shown to the Master or the Mistress while they were alive, no religious service was to be said for them, and they were to be buried as if they had been excommunicated.

Entry into the hospital was forbidden to anyone who had with them either a dog or a bird.

Every sick person coming to the hospital was first examined by the 'Surgeon of the Door' who wrote their names in a register. Then a label was attached to the patient's arm upon which was written his name and the date of his arrival. He then had to receive Communion; after which he was put to bed and treated 'as if he were master of the house'.

The hospital had always to be provided with several furred dressing-gowns and several pairs of shoes, also lined with fur, for the 'warming' of the patients.

There were night and day nurses for serious cases. After recovery, for fear of a relapse, the patient remained seven whole days in hospital.

The physicians, who were called 'mires', wore, as did the surgeons, a distinctive dress.

The hospital received not only people suffering from temporary diseases, but also the infirm.

The Countess Mahaut of Artois, who appears so frequently in our story, founded, at the hospital of Arras, ten beds furnished with mattresses, pillows, sheets, and blankets, for ten poor incurables. In the inventory of the hospital are to be found listed a number of great basins of wood to be used as baths, and pans 'to be placed under the poor people in their beds', numerous bowls, shaving dishes, etc. The Countess of Artois also founded the hospital at Hesdin, and her Chancellor, Thierry d'Hirson, the hospital of Gasnay.

The medicines were prepared in the hospital dispensary according to the instructions of the 'mires' and the surgeons.

5. Jacques Duèze, born in 1244, at Cahors, as was Clement V to whose entourage he belonged, was appointed Bishop of Fréjus in 1299, Bishop of Avignon in 1309 and, finally, Cardinal-Bishop of Porto in 1312; but Clement V kept him at his side in the capacity of Cardinal of the Curia. He played an important part in the Council of Vienne, summoned in 1311 to deal with the case of the Knights Templar. As secretary of the Council, Duèze advised the suppression of the order in his report, and this was the decision Philip the Fair desired; nevertheless, he brought upon himself the enmity of the King by opposing the posthumous condemnation of Pope Boniface VIII as a heretic, and in refusing to be a party to the profanation of his ashes.

At the death of Clement V at Carpentras in April 1314 (a month after the curse was pronounced), Duèze immediately put forward his candidature to the pontifical throne. He was strongly supported by the Court of Naples, but had against him the Italian cardinals and some of the French cardinals.

The Commission headed by Bertrand de Got and Guillaume de Budos, nephews of Pope Clement, and dispatched, about July 1314, by the Court of France with a strong escort of Gascon soldiers to prevent the election of Duèze, could not have turned out more badly: riots, brawls, incendiarism, and pillage, affrays between the Gascon soldiery and the Cardinal's people, indeed siege was laid to the monastery in which the Conclave was meeting; the members of the Sacred College had ultimately to flee through a window and took refuge in the countryside. They dispersed, some to Avignon, some to Orange, some to Vienne, and some to Lyons, forming that strange mobile Conclave which lasted two years before agreeing upon the name of Jacques Duèze.

In the next volume will be related the part that the Count of Poitiers played in this election and the means, somewhat violent indeed, which he used to compel the Cardinals to make a choice.

6. In the first days of July 1315, Louis X issued two Orders in Council concerning the Lombards. The first stipulated that the Italian aliens were to pay a penny (*sou*) in the pound (*livre*) upon their merchandise, with the condition that they should be exempted from service with the army, all courier service and all military taxes. This amounted to an exceptional tax of five per cent.

The second Order in Council, dated July 9th, instituted general rules concerning the residence and business of Italian merchants. Every transaction in gold or silver, whether by cash or bill, every sale, every purchase, every exchange in general trading, was subject to a tax varying between a penny and fourpence in the pound in accordance with the district and whether the transaction were made in the open market or not. The Italians were no longer permitted to have fixed residence except in the towns of Paris, Saint-Omer, Nîmes, and La Rochelle. It appears that this last regulation was never seriously applied, but the taxes must have been substantially profitable, either to the towns or the Treasury. Agents, appointed by the Royal administration, were charged with the supervision of the Lombards' commercial activities.

7. Charles of Valois had married as his third wife Mahaut de Châtillon, a close relation of the Constable of France.
8. A variety of evidence makes one suppose that the Order of the Knights Templar survived in secrecy and dispersion till the eighteenth century. It appears from all available evidence that the Templars, in the years that immediately followed the liquidation of the Order, were seeking for some means of reforming secretly. Jean de Longwy, the nephew of Jacques de Molay, who had sworn to avenge the memory of his uncle upon the lands of the Count of Burgundy (that is to say Philippe of Poitiers), is reasonably considered to have been the head of this organization.
9. The term 'bachelor' was not employed in university circles in the Middle Ages; the word had a military significance and meant a young man of good family who, not yet having acquired either the age or the means of raising his own 'banner', aspired to become a knight. He was a sort of orderly officer, who formed part, with a rank superior to that of a squire, of the staff of a commander of a 'banner'.
10. The legend by which the Capet family were descendants of a rich Paris butcher was spread across France by the troubadour song concerning Hugues Capet, a pamphlet composed at the beginning of the fourteenth century and

quickly forgotten, save for Dante and later François Villon. As a matter of fact, Hugues Capet was descended from the house of the Dukes of France.

Dante accuses Hugues Capet of having deposed the legitimate heir and imprisoned him in a monastery. This is a confusion between the end of the Merovingians and the end of the Carolingians; it was in fact the last king of the first dynasty, Chilperic III, who was shut up in a monastery. The last legitimate descendant of Charlemagne, at the death of Louis V, the Sluggard, was Duke Charles of Lorraine, who wished to claim the throne from Hugues Capet; but it was not in a monastery that the Duke of Lorraine met his end, but in a prison into which he had been thrown by his rival.

When, in the sixteenth century, Francis I had the 'Divine Comedy' read to him upon the advice of his sister, and heard the passage concerning the Capets, he interrupted the reader, crying: 'Oh, the wicked poet who traduces my House!' and refused to listen to any more.

11. Charles of Valois had been sent into Tuscany to 'pacify' Florence, which at that time was torn by the dissensions between the Guelphs and the Ghibellines. In fact, having entered the town on November 1st, 1301, Charles of Valois surrendered it to the vengeance of the partisans of the Pope. Pillage and massacre continued for five days on end. They were followed by the decrees of banishment. Dante, a notorious Ghibelline and the inspirer of the resistance, had been a member, the preceding summer, of the Seigneurial Council; then, having been sent as Ambassador to Rome, he had been held there as

a hostage. He was condemned by a Florentine Tribunal, on January 27, 1302, to two years' exile and five thousand pounds fine, on the false accusation of political deviation in the execution of his duties. On March 10th a new case was brought against him and he was this time condemned to be burnt alive. Luckily for him he was not in Florence nor in Rome from which he had managed to escape; but he was never to see his fatherland again. One can well understand that he preserved towards Charles of Valois and, by extension, all the French princes, a stubborn hostility. Moreover, it may be noted that there was a singular resemblance between the case brought against Dante and that brought against Enguerrand de Marigny on the instigation of Charles of Valois, thirteen years later. In the false accusations concerning financial dealings, two separate prosecutions and convictions for a multiplicity of crimes, the same type of proceedings can be discovered, and in them the hand of Charles of Valois may be recognized.

12. It is to be remembered (*see The Iron King*) that Jeanne of Burgundy, Countess of Poitiers, had not been convicted of adultery, but merely of complicity in the adultery of her cousin Marguerite and of her sister Blanche. While the two last had been imprisoned in Château-Gaillard, Jeanne of Poitiers had been placed in the Château of Dourdan for an indeterminate period and was subjected to far less severe conditions. In modern terms, one might say that she had been shown the consideration of a political prisoner whereas Marguerite and Blanche had been subjected to a criminal's treatment.

13. Born in 1118 in the village of Epinoy, which was then in the Diocese of Tournai, and later in the Diocese of Arras, Saint Druon was born by a Caesarean operation which was performed upon his mother who was already dead. From his earliest years he showed a singular disposition for piety, and the children of his own age used him cruelly by making him a butt and taunting him with being his mother's murderer. Believing himself to blame, he abandoned himself to every possible penitential practice, hoping thereby to expiate his involuntary crime. At seventeen he gave away the considerable possessions he had inherited, and engaged himself as a shepherd to a widow named Elisabeth Lehaire, in the village of Sebourg, in the County of Hainault, eight miles from Valenciennes. He loved animals so much and looked after them so well that all the inhabitants of the village asked him to mind their sheep as well as those of the widow Lehaire. It was at this time that the angels began to look after his flock while he himself was at Mass.

Then he made a pilgrimage to Rome, enjoyed the process, and thereafter made it nine times on foot. But he had to give up travelling since he suffered from 'a rupture of the intestines', an illness which he bore, so it appears, for forty years, firmly refusing all treatment. In spite of the disgusting stench which emanated from him, his virtues attracted a very large number of penitents from the surrounding district. He demanded that a lodging should be built for him against the church of Sebourg in such a position that he might be able to see the tabernacle, and he vowed that he would not issue forth from it till the end of his days. He faithfully carried out this vow, even upon the day that the church caught fire as did his hut; and since the fire spared him it was clear to all that he was indeed a saint.

He died on April 16th, 1189. For many miles around the populace gathered in tears to kiss his feet and carry away some portion of his ragged clothing. His family, the lords of Epinoy, wished to remove his body to his natal village, but the wagon upon which the corpse had been placed came to a standstill upon leaving Sebourg, and all the horses that were brought to add strength to the team were incapable of advancing it by a single yard. The Saint's corpse was therefore necessarily left where he had died, and his relations had to be content with building a chapel at Carvin-Epinoy, where he is still honoured.

He was much revered in Artois, in Cambraisis, and in Hainault, where several sanctuaries were dedicated to him; his celebrity was greatly increased by the cure of the Count of Hainault and Holland, who was suffering horribly from gravel and who, having hardly knelt before the tomb of Saint Druon in order to recite a prayer, ejected three stones each the size of a nut.

Saint Druon, by reason of the circumstances of his life, is particularly invoked for ruptures, hernias, and 'for the happy deliverance of expectant mothers'; he is also frequently invoked to preserve livestock from epidemics.

14. This son of Mahaut's, who was called Robert like his cousin, played only a very secondary role in history, since he died before he reached the age of eighteen, in 1317. First buried at the Cordeliers of Paris, his body was later

transported to Saint-Denis where his tomb is still to be seen. This honour, paid to someone who died so young, and who was not particularly well known, can only have been due to a decision of his brother-in-law, King Philippe V.

15. The exact date of Louis X's second marriage is controversial. Some historians have maintained that it was August 3rd, others the 13th, or even the 19th. The same is true of the date of the coronation, which varies in different authorities between the 19th, 21st, and August 24th. The collection of the Orders in Council of the Kings of France, which was not printed till the eighteenth century, and in which the chronology is far from certain, would tend to establish the fact that the King was at Rheims on August 3rd, at Soissons on the 6th and 7th, and at Arras on the 18th. However, given that Louis X received the Oriflamme at Saint-Denis on July 24th, it would appear impossible, however short his expedition in Flanders, that he should have had time to return from the Muddy Army and reach the district of Champagne before August 10th.

The chronicals of the period, however, assert that the marriage was celebrated at Saint-Lye, a little village some five miles to the north of Troyes, where a tower of the old castle still stands. The marriage took place in the greatest haste and in the greatest simplicity, because the Treasury was empty and the King was in a hurry to go to Rheims to be crowned. Here we have used the date of August 13th, given by Father Anselm, as the most likely, for, the Coronation having always to take place either on a Sunday or on some great religious feast day, we believe that Louis X was crowned either on August 15th or on Sunday 18th; it is also known that the rejoicings lasted several days, which may easily enough explain the discrepancies in the dates given.

16. There still exist a great number of inventories dating from the beginning of the fourteenth century. The one Mahaut of Artois had made, with the most minute description of her possessions and their value, after the sacking of her castle of Hesdin, for which she demanded compensation, is still preserved.

17. Clémence of Hungary's fortune, in land and in jewels, consisting largely of the gifts of Louis X, was enormous. During their marriage, whose short duration will become evident, Clémence of Hungary received no less than forty castles, among which were numbered some of the most important of the royal residences.

When Clémence of Hungary died, in 1328, that is to say at the beginning of the reign of Philippe VI of Valois, her heir, who was her nephew, the Dauphin of Viennois, sold by auction all the jewels and plate, a sale which lasted several days. The catalogue of the sale is something to dream of: three crowns, bearing in all thirty-four rubies, eighty-two emeralds, and a hundred and sixty pearls; fourteen rings, fifty-four brooches and clasps; and this is only a small part of the treasure. Difficult though it is to establish equivalents in money, one may estimate without being far out that the total of the sale reached £500,000 in today's currency.

The biggest buyers were, on the one hand, King Philippe VI himself – who bought, among other things, the great reliquary containing a fragment of the True Cross, and also the fork which is mentioned farther on in this book; and, on the other hand, the Count of Beaumont, that is to say Robert of Artois.

18. The barons of Artois succeeded in this enterprise in the following September, which was the occasion of the sacking mentioned in Note 16.

19. I apologize for the grossness of the remark, but it is to be found textually in the deposition of the ex-Templar Everard, as it was taken down *in extenso*.

20. The unicorn is a legendary animal which has never existed anywhere except in heraldry, but whose single horn nevertheless was considered to be a universal antidote to poison. What was sold under the name of the horn of a unicorn, at an extremely high price, was in fact the horn of the narwhal.

21. All the tapestry manufactories which existed in Europe, and notably in Italy and Hungary, at the end of the Middle Ages, had been founded by tapestry-makers who had come from Flanders or Artois, while the town of Arras is considered to have been the centre of this growing industry at the beginning of the fourteenth century. Moreover, this prosperity is expressly attributed to the initiative of the Countess Mahaut and to the encouragement she gave to the industries which formed the wealth of her province.

When the Paris tapestry-makers began to compete with the Artois manufactories, Mahaut showed no particular preference for one as against the other and she can be found giving orders to Paris. However, upon this period the documents give very few details and only reveal the names of a few tapestry-makers without any description of their works. The inventory of the possessions of Queen Clémence is one of the first in which one finds mention of woollen tapestries 'worked with parrots and compasses', and again, 'eight tapestries with figures and trees, depicting a hunt'.